Also by

Books

On The Fiddle
How To Be a Tourst

Stories

Duty Calls
A Blow To The Head

Plays

Taking A Liberty
Lao Wai

For Rita, Pat, Colette and Amy

RICE TICKET

Ged Neary

First Published in 2005

PUBLISHED BY
PAUL MOULD PUBLISHING UK

IN ASSOCIATION WITH
EMPIRE PUBLISHING SERVICES, USA

Copyright © Ged Neary

All rights reserved. No part of this publication may be reproduced, stored in a retrieval system or transmitted in any form by any means, electronic, mechanical, photocopying, recording or otherwise without the prior permission of the publisher and copyright holder.

ISBN 1-904959-25-3

Printed in Great Britain by
BAYBASH-RYAN

Part One

Chapter One

In the dining hall of the Double Rainbow hotel, in the north-east suburbs of Beijing, Christopher Chinley felt all eyes upon him as he attempted to prise a button mushroom between his chopsticks. He managed to lift it out of its dish, but before reaching his bowl it fell on to the tablecloth, staining the white linen with a patch of yellow cooking oil. He then tried to retrieve it with a porcelain soup spoon, but succeeded only in pushing it further away, down a trail of glistening grease. Mr Wang, who was co-hosting the banquet with his boss and family friend Mr Deng, scissored the mushroom and dropped it on to Chinley's bowl, saying: "So what exactly are you an expert *in*, Professor?"

Chinley hesitated. Back in England, no-one would in all seriousness have called him 'Professor'. Wang's query had triggered off some muted chuckles amongst the other five guests at the circular table, three men and two women, and Chinley searched the smiling Chinese eyes for any trace of malice, but none was visible. One by one they averted their gaze as he stared back at them: all except Wang's wife, who kept her eyes on his and did not even blink. In contrast to the stern woman in the murky grey suit beside her, who hardly spoke to anyone and who seemed to be concerned mainly with keeping her spectacles high on the bridge of her nose, Wang's wife invited attention. Her face was animated and cheerful, with broad pale cheeks set off against long shiny straight black hair. She had the smile of a playful and inquisitive jester. She spoke softly, with a slight lisp, and gave Chinley the impression that she would much rather not have the wide expanse of the table between them as they talked. But there was something odd about her eyes, her classical Chinese teardrop-shaped eyes: every so often their vitality gave way to a look of longing, a dreaminess, a blankness. It was as though a light inside her head was being switched on and off. No mockery there though, Chinley was sure. No malice. Her husband however seemed to be having such a good time that Chinley suspected *him* of foreigner-baiting: his creviced middle-aged face was bursting with merriment, and while chomping loudly on his food, he managed to sustain a wide sloping grin, showing enormous tea-and-nicotine stained teeth. He had too much hair for a man of his age, decided Chinley. It could all have been a wig, of course, or the result of a transplant gone awry: dark fuzzy tufts sprouted randomly across his scalp like marshland tussocks. But all the diners now had their eyes once again on the Englishman, waiting for his answer to Wang's question.

"Water," said Chinley, eventually, standing up and raising an empty beer glass. "Anything connected with water. Dams, hydro-electric power, drainage, irrigation, desalination, and even - brewing."

He held his glass with both hands at chest level, in imitation of Wang, and bowed to the company, pleased to note, from the huddle of heads and the lapse into whispered Mandarin, that his reply had caused some consternation. Wang now also rose to his feet, belched faintly, and unscrewed the top of a bottle of clear spirit, which he referred to as wine.

"Beer is a cooling drink," he said, "and wine is a warming drink. In the golden season, therefore, between summer and winter, you should have a bit of both."

"And in the spring too I suppose," suggested Chinley, causing another round of mirth, except from the older female guest. He took her to be only in her early fifties: he assumed that the clothes she wore, shapeless blanket wraps, and the sour expression on her face, made her look older than she was.

"Sit down, Professor," said Wang. Despite protestations at each chair, he moved around the table filling thimble-sized cups for all the guests, omitting only his wife. Over Chinley's shoulder, he said: "Do you like Chinese wine, Professor?"

"Oh yes," said Chinley, thinking to himself that the bouquet which now reached his nostrils reminded him of the stacks of cow manure at his brother's farm in Cheshire. Their eyes watering, and their faces blotched brick-red by the alcohol, the two men to either side of him stood up, said something in Chinese, bowed to two empty chairs, then held out their cups for yet another toast.

"Mr Wu and Mr Hu," said Wang. "Our Party Secretaries. They are welcoming you to China. They say they are very pleased to meet you, and Mr and Mrs Fox when they arrive, and they offer you any help which you may need."

Chinley, on his feet once again, tossed the cupful of spirit as far to the rear of his taste buds as he could manage, gulped it down, and bowed to his neighbours. Wang immediately moved in again, with his bottle, leaving the Englishman no chance to refuse a refill. Chinley looked at Wang's wife for sympathy, and she sparkled back at him.

* * *

The woman at the Air China check-in desk at Heathrow airport was Scottish, and she had a challenging line for each of the passengers in the queue. When it was Chinley's turn she looked at the bulges in his well-travelled bags, and said: "What have you got in there, *bricks?*"

"Books," said Chinley. "And medicine."

"Med...?" The Scotswoman's hand flew to her face. "Excuse me," she said, patting the neat straw butt of her hair and proceeding with the paperwork. Chinley imagined how her chest would heave if she knew what the medicine was for. "All right," she said, angling her hat. "We'll let you get away with that then. Have we done the visa job on you?"

"Yes."

She handed him his boarding card and he walked on through the Departure Lounge, wondering when he would next meet someone in uniform who behaved as though they had just had several gin and tonics.

There was still time to change his mind. But he could imagine Dorothy's reaction if he went back home now: nose tilted and eyebrows raised in victory; lips lop-sided in contempt. A looming overseer, like the deputy headmistress who disapproved of everything he did at primary school, and the stepmother who warned him in slightly later life that booze and women would be his downfall. In the past on journeys like this Dorothy had always been with him, and they would by now be squabbling over something or other: how much he was spending on tobacco in the duty-free shop, why he had already set his watch for the time zone of their destination; elbowing him awake whenever he dozed off in the waiting-room, to pre-empt any embarrassment caused her by his inevitable snoring. Now there was no-one to squabble with, so he stocked up with a selection of pipe tobacco, set his watch to Beijing time, then went to sleep as well as he could on a highly-sprung chair overlooking the runway, his arms wrapped around his hand-luggage and his face buried in the hay-scented sleeves of the Donegal tweed jacket borrowed on long term loan from his brother. He was woken by the Scotswoman and he winced, expecting a blow, but unlike his wife she did not use her elbow: instead she rested a long-fingered hand on his shoulder, squeezed gently, and pointed at the departures indicator.

"Oh look, they've got their pinnies on," said the woman in the seat next to him on the aeroplane. He had chosen an aisle seat as a safeguard against being hemmed in by such a fellow-passenger. Now it was the man with her who was hemmed in, but he seemed to ignore most of what she said, apparently preferring to stare at the clouds beyond the window. Lunch was served, and Chinley could no longer pretend to be asleep.

"Our with-profits policy matured this year, you see," continued the woman. "So we got our terminal bonus to splash out with. We'd always wanted to come to China. How about you? Are you on holiday? You look more like an academic to me, if you don't mind me saying so. Please don't misunderstand me. I'm not being offensive. People who talk about eggheads are just envious, you know. An intelligent pate is what I call it. My name's Betty, and he's Arnold." *He* was still looking at the darkening clouds. Chinley kept his mouth full, and nodded. "We're spending two or three days in Peking," said Betty, "then we're off to Cheyenne, to see the warriors."

Chinley told himself that it was not up to him to correct her pronunciation.

"And then to Shanghai," she continued. "I've always been a fan of Noel Coward's."

"No," said Chinley. "I wouldn't call myself an academic. I'm off on a mission." Perhaps this would keep her quiet.

"A *mission*?"

"Yes. A *sexual* mission. Or rather, a sexual omission. Abstinence."

"Sorry?"

"No."

Betty chuckled, turned to look at her crumpled husband, then turned back to study Chinley's straight and elongated face.

"Are you going to the Gorges?" he asked.

"What Gorges?"

So she wasn't. And he was going to tell her nothing about them, and nothing about his interest in the new dam they were building there.

She would only have sniggered, like Dorothy had sniggered just two weeks ago, when he first told her of his plans. Betty had now opened her hand-bag.

"Here you are," she said, handing him a name card. "You never know."

Chinley put the card in his pocket. Yes, he was making the right decision, he felt. Running away. Betty had been put there by Providence to strengthen his resolve. No wonder the Australians talk about the whining Poms. His head was ringing with her complaints and anxieties: the headphones were tacky, the luggage rack was wobbling, water was streaming down the windows, and steam was coming out of the air-vents. Six hours later, and partly out of superstition in case he did not survive the descent into China, when one of the stewardesses, now without her pinnie, told him that they had just entered Pakistani air-space, he decided to be more charitable towards Betty. He told her that, if she was interested, beyond her husband's head there might soon be a good view of the Himalayan peaks.

"The Himalayan peaks?" she said. "Good God. I hope we don't get too close to *them*."

Chinley repositioned his pillow, and closed his eyes. He had tried. After a while, he reached down into the seat pocket in front of him, then into his own pocket, and he put Betty's name card into the sick-bag. He felt a boyish grin pulling at the muscles of his cheeks, then he realised that although Betty herself was now dozing, Arnold had for once turned his head and was staring towards the aisle. Chinley's grin became a pursing of the lips, and he moved his mouth closer to the rim of the sick-bag. In the corner of his vision, he saw Arnold's head swivel back towards the blankness beyond the aeroplane window.

* * *

"Professor Chinley," said Mr Deng, from across the banquet table, "Is your wife coming out to join you in China?" Mr Deng looked well-suited to his position of authority. He was magisterial, dressed formally in a dark grey suit, a white shirt, and a broad tie which flashed like a hologram, in two shades of silver; but he had the indoor eyes of a bureaucrat: dull and ponderous. He had a tough jaw, and strange plasticky duck-like lips.

Chinley judged him to be in his late forties, and considerably overweight by Chinese standards, the result perhaps of having been promoted to a central government office responsible for the vetting and well-being of foreign engineers, academics and businessmen, a promotion which meant that several hours of most working days were spent at the banquet table. A man of thoroughness, Chinley was sure, by now no doubt well-acquainted with the details of his new recruit's more obvious domestic circumstances. Chinley wondered exactly what they had said about him before he came into the room. But he knew that no matter how closely they scrutinised his documents, they would find no evidence that just over a month ago his wife had asked him to take himself as far away from her as he could possibly manage.

It was her rejection routine, but this time he had called her bluff. Whatever file they had on him would not reveal that he was here to show that he could manage without her: without any woman at all, in fact.

"My wife?" said Chinley. "Coming out to China? Now there's a thought."

"But your daughter?" said Wang's wife.

Chinley glanced back at Mr Deng, whose uplifted nose seemed to convey the message "Why shouldn't we talk about you behind your back?" Wang's wife also looked briefly at Mr Deng, as though to check that her information was correct, then she said: "Isn't that right, Professor, you're expecting your daughter to join you here?"

"All I expect my daughter to do," said Chinley, "is the unexpected."

Wang's wife and Mr Deng exchanged glances again, then giggled at each other, perhaps, Chinley imagined, in recognition of his powers of evasion. So here was one person at the table, he noted, who could reduce Mr Deng to a giggle.

"Sturdy bowels," said Mr Wang, and the laughter stopped. "Sturdy bowels and a good bladder. That's what you need, to survive in China."

"I've always heard good reports..." said Chinley. "I mean, things are improving rapidly, aren't they?"

"Bollocks they are," continued Wang. "I'm not talking about Bei*jing*. You've got plenty of everything here, even crap western food if you want it. Big Macs and pizzas, if you must. But *we* live in the provinces, Professor. How will you and your daughter if she comes cope, for example, with crowded public bathrooms, and a diet of dumplings, noodles, and catfish? And sick pigs?"

Chinley saw no reason to mention that his daughter was in all likelihood at that very moment sitting, unconcerned, in conditions similar to those described by Wang, on a slow-moving train somewhere to the east of Moscow. But privately, he shuddered to think of who or what she might have picked up *en route*.

"My daughter might not be coming," he said. "And I am built like an ox."

Thinking a physical gesture would help to communicate his message, he swelled out his chest and positioned his hands as if he was expanding a pair of braces. The Party Secretaries, who were said to understand no English at all, now roared with delight and topped up his glass of spirit, as though to put his claim immediately to the test. While he was beaming his prowess Chinley saw Jane from the reception desk passing by the entrance to the banqueting suite.

To his surprise she had agreed to interpret for him, medically, tomorrow afternoon when she was off duty. She stopped to look in. As their eyes met he attempted a rapid deflation of the lungs, which to his dismay produced a loud and aggressive snort. What the hell, he told himself, as she walked away. What she thinks of me matters not at all: she is barely more than a schoolgirl.

Wang's wife left her seat, and walked over to the drinks table. Her husband followed, and stood directly behind her. Her eyes were in the shadows, but if what Chinley saw there was really a flash of anger, as her husband tapped her on the shoulder, when she turned she was ready to twinkle a dinner-party face at him. They went back to their seats, she still without a drink, and as Wang passed by he stooped and whispered in Chinley's ear: "Excuse my wife, Professor. She has... special needs."

Chapter Two

The Double Rainbow hotel backed on to a narrow river, which showed signs of having recently burst its banks. Huge black tricycles with old wooden trailers were embedded in viscous yellow-grey sediment which oozed on to a footpath at the water's edge. As Chinley made his way along the sand and gravel, leaping from dry patch to dry patch, he suspected that the stillness of dawn in this Beijing outskirt would not be long-lived.

As he squelched his way up the slopes of the river bank towards a coppice of young willow trees, a loud yell from out of the twilight brought him to a standstill. Ahead of him, camouflaged by the shadows of the trees, a man in a baggy blue suit and a black bobble-cap was standing on one leg, with his other leg raised in front of him, bent at the knee. His arms were outstretched for balance, giving him the appearance of a scarecrow with adjustable limbs. Chinley continued walking through the gloom, and the man uttered a second cry, then a third. More human figures now became visible, all men, slowly gyrating their bodies and moving into and out of sight behind the branches of the willows: an outdoor ballet scene in the dim light of day, where all the dancers were silent except for the one maverick with the loud voice, who seemed to be doing a penance of some kind. Chinley sat on a damp stone wall and watched the performance.

Then another body appeared, a more elegant figure, pale and luminous, like a silver fish. A woman. She weaved through the men, taking centre stage, and when she turned her face full towards Chinley he saw that it was Mr Wang's wife. She gave no sign that she had noticed him, and as far as he could tell her eyes remained firmly closed. He now felt that he was trespassing, that he should leave, that he was in a world which had nothing to do with his own, but he could not resist watching for a while longer: the woman seemed water-borne, weightless, her arms slowly rising and falling as though lifted by unseen waves. He shifted his position on the wall and sat with his back to her, taking quick glances over his shoulder.

While retracing his steps slowly towards the hotel Chinley was overtaken by a young Chinese man in brown overalls, who was walking backwards. Their eyes met briefly: Chinley half-expected to be confronted by the manic challenging stare of a psychopath, but all he saw was an expression of mild good humour and an apparent unconcern as to what others might think of this behaviour. As he continued on his way, Chinley was surprised to feel a brief longing for the sight of his wife's raised eyebrows. He blinked her out of his consciousness.

"There they are. Over there, Mr Chinley," said one of the reception girls, as he was crossing the foyer. "Mr and Mrs Fox." She pointed towards an elderly couple who were standing by an assembly of bell-boys, waiting for the lift. "They've just booked in, and they were asking for you. I can catch them if you want."

"No, no, don't worry," said Chinley, hoping that the lift would arrive before they turned and saw him. "They'll be exhausted, I'm sure."

Mrs Fox didn't look like a librarian. More like the coach of a women's rugby team, thought Chinley. She was too restless, dancing first on one foot then on the other. And too noisy. He could hear her voice quite clearly from where he stood: a full-bodied factory supervisor's voice, cutting through the general hubbub around her. And there was her husband. A bit of this, a bit of that, Mr Deng had said Mr Fox would be doing. Right now he looked ready to do nothing at all, except keel over. Whatever, at this time of the day Chinley had no desire to be drawn into another round of polite introductions and potted biographies, and he watched with relief as the doors of the lift closed on the couple, and they disappeared upstairs with two of the bell-boys. He loitered by the reception desk until he saw Jane. *She* would make a good air hostess, he thought. She was tiny. And smart. Dark blue jacket, dark blue skirt. She came over, fingering her white plastic name badge, which was upside down, and suggested he went down town instead of hanging around the hotel, and met her at the Tiananmen Square entrance to Beihai Park, from where she could take him into the back streets where she lived, and where she knew some of the medical practitioners.

As he climbed into the shuttle bus he saw to his satisfaction that no-one from last night's banquet was on board. No-one to ask him where he was going. No-one to follow him. He hoped they were all having a lie-in, and he willed the bus to leave on time in case they were not. But it remained parked in the hotel forecourt. He stared at his knees, to avoid the gaze of the pedestrians passing by. Their growing numbers and their curiosity made him itch. It would not be long, he thought, thus reminded that he was in a foreign land, before ants and whatever began crawling and buzzing around his legs. His attention shifted to his ankles. There was no movement there: nothing stirred or tingled in his socks, and nothing crept over the floor for him to crush underfoot. But what surprised him most of all was that there were no flies.

He half stood up, intending to suggest that they all got a move on, but as he did so the driver turned the ignition key. The bus was dawdling towards the main road when a shout from the rear brought it once more to a standstill. Running awkwardly to catch up, the woman yelling as though in great pain, were Mr and Mrs Fox. Chinley twisted his neck so they would see only the back of his head as they mounted the steps, but a waft of soapy western perfume reached his nostrils, and his own seat rose as Mrs Fox eased herself with a sigh into the adjacent upholstery. Still he kept his head stubbornly twisted away from her, affecting a profound interest in what was happening beyond the window. Like Arnold.

They drove away from their own hotel complex and into several more down a wide highway with the dense mass of cyclists, all moving hypnotically at the same unhurried pace, channelled off into a lane of their own. A short and limping old man, wearing a flat navy-blue cap and a Mao jacket, stepped out from the kerbside without looking and began to make his way diagonally through the traffic. The shuttle bus veered around him. There was a gasp from Mrs Fox, and the old man trudged on blindly across both carriageways, without once looking right or left. "Lucky old bugger," she said. "*He's* a bit of a throwback, isn't he?"

Chinley half-turned towards her, nodded at the back of the seat in front of him, then looked quickly again out of the window. Encouraged by this near-acknowledgement, she boomed in his ear: *"Hey!* You're not Mr Chinley by any chance, are you? Hey?"

He forced the scowl off his face and eyed the woman directly. Her pumice-stone-coloured hair was arranged in neat folded waves, as though it was still in curlers, waves which softened her otherwise angular appearance. She had a broad masculine chin, a long bulbous nose, and her skin was a pink and yellow mosaic, like the pattern of felspar on a polished block of granite.

"Yes," said Chinley, feigning surprise. "You must be..."

"I'm Gladys. Gladys Fox. And he's Terry. My husband."

Chinley swivelled in his seat to greet another he, but the man's eyelids were closed, and his head was swaying loosely with the motion of the bus. He seemed frail and troubled, even though he was to all appearances asleep. His hair was thin and almost white, and Chinley could see that the colour in his cheeks came not from a healthy radiance, but from a red and blue matrix of haemorrhaged veins.

"Is Mr Fox all right?" he asked, wondering at the same time how he could escape from the two of them once they reached their destination. He did not want them traipsing along with Jane and himself around the Beijing drugstores.

"This is all a bit of an ordeal for him I'm afraid," she said. "But thank you for asking. Where are *you* from?"

"Birmingham. Sort of."

"I'm from Wales myself. Swansea. But he's Irish." She tossed her head back, in the general direction of her husband. They were pulling into a lay-by at the Friendship Store.

"We're getting off here," she continued. Chinley smiled at the prospect of enjoying his own company again. "But we'll be moving on to Beihai Park later," she added. "We have an appointment with that nice young receptionist. Jane is it she calls herself? You know the one I mean. She's drawn us a map."

Chinley's smile disappeared, and he sucked in his lips.

"*You're* meeting Jane?" he said. "This afternoon? Are you sure?"

"Yes of course I'm sure." She looked briefly at her dozing husband. "He needs a tonic of some kind to buck him up. Jane offered to show us the Chinese chemist shops. That will kill him or cure him! *Hey?*"

She let out the cackle of a magpie, which woke her husband and caused the driver to swerve. Mr Fox shook his head and smoothed down his few wisps of hair. His eyes were watery but focused and quite clear: a deep blue colour, and Chinley saw them fill with glee as he laughed along with his wife.

Several limousines drove straight at Chinley then skirted him as though he was a traffic bollard. He was walking down towards the main highway into town, down a paved slope fronting the Mirage Hotel. Ahead however he could see more of a segregation between a traffic lane, a bicycle lane, and a dense mass of pedestrians, who were making their way forward with the deliberation of a crowd converging on an imminent large-scale sporting event. He tagged himself on to a line feeding into the main throng, and was irresistibly drawn into the communal lurch by a human slipstream. He had no idea where he was going but there was now no turning back. He resigned himself to moving with the multitude. After half an hour or so he tried to catch the attention of those who were shuffling alongside him, and feeling as though he was selling something he muttered: "Tiananmen Square? Beihai Park?". Several pairs of eyes peered into his, but their gaze was quickly averted.

Then a tall woman with long fair hair and a large blue rucksack looming over her head tried to edge her way past him, loping as well as she could in the circumstances, with immense athletic strides. He tapped her on the shoulder, and she looked at him briefly. Embarrassed and feeling very stupid, he said: "Forbidden City?" She raised a leader's arm, pointed an index finger at the sky and said: "Follow me". He sidestepped into her wake, and set off in pursuit of the bouncing blonde frizz.

He caught up with her underneath a canopy of taut scarlet banners, where she stopped at a drinks stall, and he sat waiting for her on the stone border of a nearby geranium-bed. She turned and said: "Yoghurt. You must have one." Her manner was so assertive that he suspected she really did mean it the way it sounded. Like an order. He shook his head.

"Danish and Chinese," she said. "This yoghurt is a joint venture. Like me. Except my mother was a Russian. Not Chinese."

Chinley chuckled and studied her face for a clue as to how to take this information, but he found her humourless and even glum. She felt in her breast pocket and handed him a name card: *Astrid Larssen*. It was only now when she came close to him that he realised how young she was. She had large bulging chestnut eyes, and prominent dimples. She sat nearby on a high concrete wall noisily sucking the yoghurt through a straw, and swinging her legs like a schoolgirl. He could not see a waste bin anywhere, so he put the name card in his wallet.

"Sons of *Heaven?*" yelled Astrid. "Sons of *bitches*, more like." They were walking in the shade of the curving liver-red wall enclosing the Forbidden City. Couples merged with the shadows, embracing lightly, or viciously bickering with each other. A volley of what must have been abuse was delivered by a thin Chinese girl to her male companion. Encouraged perhaps by the girl's public tirade, Astrid once more took up her invective against the emperors and their ways. "Concubines and orgies!" she shouted. "Slaves massaging their masters' feet and whatever, and no doubt wiping their bums. Fat, lazy, randy, merciless old men. That's all they were, these so-called divinities. How could you worship someone like that?"

Chinley found himself saying that he completely agreed with her, while at the same time allowing his imagination to serve him with images of the orgies and the concubines. Times gone by, he told himself. For them and for him.

The roots of Astrid's hair had darkened with perspiration, which had trickled down inside her blouse to form an artist's palette-shaped pool at the small of her back. Seeing this, Chinley placed a hand in the middle of his own back, to reassure himself that he was sweating less than she was. His shirt was dry, and he took this as a sign that he was in reasonable health.

Years of outdoor work as a water engineer in harsher climates than this had increased his temperature tolerance range, toughened his stomach, leathered his skin, and burnished his increasingly exposed scalp to the colour of dusty copper. Only half-listening to Astrid's ranting on the injustices of the past, he again reached the same self-diagnosis as always: he had trouble with his sinuses and his joints, and trouble with his temper. All passed down in one way or another no doubt, from his father and grandfather, to Joe and himself. Joe had the farm to off-load his aggression; Chinley had a supply of camomile pills. But they were Dorothy's idea, and taking them made him feel that she still had a hold on him. But help was on its way. Later that afternoon with Jane as his interpreter he would begin his enquiry into the claims of Chinese medicine. He remembered with annoyance that Gladys and Terry would also be there. He hoped that a private consulting room of sorts would be available, in whichever establishment Jane took them to.

"Have you got backache?" said Astrid.

Deep in self-assessment, Chinley had absent-mindedly left his hand monitoring the sweat level on his shirt tail. "No," he said. "No."

"What are you doing here in China, anyway? Are you a Foreign Expert?"

"Yes, I suppose so."

"I might have guessed," said Astrid. "Everyone's a Foreign Expert these days. Even if you're a nanny, like me. I suppose they're calling you a Professor?"

"Yes."

"Yes, they would do, especially at your age. Of course, it's all meaningless. I bet they call your wife a Professor too."

"My wife is in England." He looked at Astrid with growing irritation. It was the reference to his age that bothered him, not the fact that he was not really a Professor. "Where's the entrance to this Beihai Park then?" he asked, standing up.

"No sweat," said Astrid. "Or?"

Polished and groomed far more neatly than Chinley, a street trader was keeping an eye on the tall western couple as they approached his stall. He stood with his thumbs tucked behind the revers of his quality black suit, looking like a well-turned-out and wealthy Yorkshire textile merchant.

"It's a bit early in the year to be selling padded sherpa jackets," said Chinley, regaining some of his equanimity in the uninterrupted autumn sunshine. "October?"

"No," said Astrid, accelerating her pace under the gaze of the trader.

"Very cosy. Very comfortable," he shouted. "Try one."

"Today is your National Day," said Chinley, hoping to unsettle the man with obliqueness. But he was a professional, and without hesitation he said, "Yes. And I'm celebrating my National Day by offering a very special discount on the jackets." Out of respect for the man's market skills Chinley was on the brink of naming a starting price, but changed his mind.

"Not my style," he said. "Candy floss pink."

"What about your wife? She is as tall as you are."

Chinley could see the flush rising to Astrid's cheeks as he caught up with her. He grinned back at the trader, and received a salute in response.

"The golden season is all about us," he said, suddenly feeling younger, as they approached the entrance to the park.

"The *gold* season you mean," said Astrid, with a sneer. "Huh! The gold season lasts all year in Beijing. That's why we've got all the gold-diggers here from the countryside."

"I was talking about the trees," said Chinley. He could hear the squeals of children somewhere, and the rumble and toot of distant traffic. But something was missing: the park was quieter than a park should be. Then he realised why.

"No birds," he said. "No birds. How odd."

"They have been destroyed of course," said Astrid. "They were not allowed to land. Mao Zedong declared that they were pests. So they were shooed off their legs whenever they landed. Up into the air again. Day after day, night after night, until they were exhausted and they dropped out of the sky. Dead."

"Aha," said Chinley. "What about the flies then? There are no flies either. Were they shooed off their legs too?"

"No of course not," said Astrid. "The flies were just squashed. Everybody had a quota, to kill at least ten flies a day. Didn't you know *that*? Thousands of millions of flies a day squashed. *That's* why you don't see any now."

"But that was ages ago," said Chinley. "They've had plenty of time to come back."

"Well what explanation have *you* got? Can you see any? Flies or birds?"

"Well... no," said Chinley.

"There you are then. And this is where you must meet your friend," said Astrid, as they reached the park exit. "Is he Chinese?"

"Yes. And he's a she."

"A *she*? Then watch your back."

"What?"

"Watch your back."

"What on earth are you talking about, watch my back? You know nothing about her."

"I don't need to. She'll be after something. Very quietly, very politely, but *after* something. They always are. And they root for the whole family you know. Not like us."

"Nonsense," said Chinley. "She's a perfect lady."

"It's the Chinese dream."

"What is?"

"And at your age you're easy meat," said Astrid. "I have an instinct. I have a nose." Chinley looked her up and down. This was enough. "An instinct?" he said. "A nose? You mean like a horse?"

She bristled. "Well bollocks to you!" she said, her voice becoming soprano. "What do *you* know? You've only just got here. And don't think I haven't seen your wandering eyes. An ageing married man, in China without your wife? You're a pushover."

Chinley drew himself up to his full height. "You don't imagine..? I can assure *you*..." he began, but the Danish girl twirled her rucksack on to her shoulder, and strode away.

"Hello."

He turned to see Jane, flanked by Mr and Mrs Fox.

"Who was that?" she said. "What was she shouting about?"

"No-one. Nothing."

In a musty and cluttered old drugstore, on a narrow side-street to the north of the Mirage hotel, two Chinese pharmacists were walking around Chinley, inspecting him from all angles, as though he were a sculpture. Every so often they murmured in Mandarin to Jane, who alternately nodded or shrugged. Chinley was losing patience but in deference to Jane he tried not to show it, even though he could see he was becoming the focus of attention for an increasing number of customers and passers-by. He had asked her if there was a consulting room, and she had nodded down at the shop floor: this was it.

Just within his line of vision he could see Gladys and Terry. At first they had kept their distance, perhaps out of respect for the patient's right to privacy even in these circumstances, but eventually they too stood and watched as the two Chinese men continued circling their client and muttering to each other. Gladys found a seat, folded her arms and cocked her head, settling down now openly to watch and listen to the proceedings. One pharmacist snapped his finger, eased Chinley forward in his hard-backed chair and took his pulse and blood pressure, while the other, using a small flashlight, peered into his eyeballs.

"What have my eyes got to do with my sinuses?" he whispered, as Jane came and stood by his side.

"In Chinese medicine," she said, placing a hand on his shoulder, "everything is connected."

One of the practitioners then began talking rapidly to Chinley in Chinese, and gestured for Jane to translate. She was silent for a few moments, then she said:

"Is there a potency problem, he wants to know."

Chinley's first reaction was to laugh, but all the Chinese faces around him remained serious. Then he felt a spreading embarrassment, as he noticed Gladys's jaw drop open, and her head move forward an inch or two, as her interest in the diagnosis was clearly given a boost: "Not at all," he said, forcing a chuckle. Then he lowered his voice to a deeper register, and added: "What a ridiculous idea. Quite the opposite in fact, I would say."

Jane's expression remained clinically correct, but as she translated, Chinley suspected that he saw a crinkle of mischief at her lips. "There's nothing abnormal about you," she said, translating further. "But at your age, they say, changes will occur." One of the men murmured in her ear, and she said: "I'm sorry. Do you have a young wife, he wants to know."

"No of course not," said Chinley, hoping that the emphasis of his denial would not be misinterpreted. Gladys's mouth now opened so wide that he could see the gaps between her teeth. Terry was hunched over a page of large-character Chinese script: Chinley took this as a token of the man's decorum.

"But you do have a wife?" said Jane, this time with no prompting.

"What's that got to do with anything?" said Chinley, in a loud whisper.

Chapter Three

Jane shrugged at the older pharmacist, and said something in Chinese. He raised his eyebrows, rubbed his hands, and walked back around the counter, where he wrote out a prescription, and Jane then took Chinley over to the dispensary, where she left him to wait for the medicine. He watched with disapproval as Gladys put her hands on her husband's collar-bone, and pressed him down into a sitting position on the inspection chair. But he seemed acquiescent to the pressure and, still wearing a light cloth sun-cap, he looked relaxed and cheerful. Jane passed him a cup of tea, which he drained in one draught. But when the two pharmacists approached, and began circling and studying him, he stood up, tipped his cap, and walked out of the shop. Just outside the front door he turned and addressed everyone in Chinese. The pharmacists eyed him as he walked off down the street, then they stared at Jane. At this moment Chinley's arm was pushed from behind, and a sullen female assistant gave him a crumpled brown bag. The contents felt like a mixture of dried fruit and nuts, which was what he expected, but when he looked inside the bag he saw what was clearly identifiable as a sticky mass of several hundred insect carcasses.

Leaving Gladys and Jane talking together and pointing at various boxes and bottles on the shelves, he left the drugstore, intending to catch up with Terry. His attention was held by the sound of tinny musical notes, and looking down the street he saw the old Irishman standing by a large wooden wheelbarrow, holding a harmonica to his lips and gently tapping the pavement with his right foot. A crowd of spectators was forming, but as Terry saw Chinley walking towards him he stopped playing and wiped the instrument on his trouser-leg.

"Drop in for a chat with a Chinese chemist," he said. "That's one way to get a cup of tea when you need one. They have all the time in the world. As things are at the moment."

"I think your wife's got a tonic in mind for you," said Chinley. "She's surveying the shelves. With Jane."

"I got all the tonic I need from the Friendship Store," said Terry, and he patted a large bulge in his jacket. "Would you care to come in here with me for a browse?" He indicated a grimy little shop front rather like that of a semi-derelict army and navy surplus store back home, in which there was a display of antique swords, daggers, knives, muskets and handguns, of all shapes and sizes. "The ladies will be some time yet, I imagine," he added.

* * *

"I wonder how Jane feels, about trailing around with three old fogies?" said Gladys. "She should be off with a young man somewhere at her age, pretty little thing." Gladys was sitting between Chinley and Terry, on a concrete bench outside the Mirage hotel. Chinley had just been thinking how closely they resembled a trio of pensioners idling away the afternoon at an English coastal resort, sitting together in silence and staring out at the sea. He had been staring out at the swarm of straight-backed cyclists, admiring their collision-avoiding skill as they criss-crossed each other's path like converging flocks of migrant birds. A common enough scene for the locals though, he reflected: Jane had excused herself, saying she had some urgent business to attend to. He looked inside the brown paper bag again, wondering whether something in there was still alive. But there was no movement. Jane had explained that he should use the preparation simply as a tea mixture: boil it up and drink the broth. The objective, apparently, was to improve the circulation of the body fluids and to clear the passages.

Alarmed by the convincing imitation of *rigor mortis* from Terry and Gladys on the stone bench, and hoping for their sake that it was just an effect of jet lag, he jumped to his feet with a grunt.

"Don't mind me," he said. "I get cramp."

He went off towards the hotel. In the lobby he ordered a teapot and some hot water, and when no-one was looking he pulled a wedge off the stiffening block from the drugstore, and suffused it for several minutes. Nothing seemed to come to life in the resulting black wash, so he drank it all in one long slurp, finding it strong and bitter, like a mulled herbal beer. Through the window he could see Gladys and Terry still motionless on the bench. No Jane yet. He topped up the brew and took a few more sips. Then, in the centre of the lobby, he saw a notice-board which read: *'Institute of Research into Chinese Folk Medicine. Penthouse.'* He checked his watch. If Jane came back now and had to wait, it was her own fault for not coming back sooner. He took a lift to the top floor, located the Penthouse suite and knocked on the door, rapidly inventing an explanation for his presence there.

The door was opened by a heavily made-up woman in a long loose white overall. Her hair was tied back, which drew attention to her large business-sensitive eyes, and gave an extra lift to the cheekbones. She was wearing a glossy deep-red lipstick.

"Yes?" she said. "Do you have an appointment, sir?"

She was barring Chinley's entry by keeping the door half-closed, but over her shoulder he could see a young man in an ivory-coloured silk dressing-gown, lying face-down on a surgical-style exploration slab. Chinley could also see a pair of hands, with long painted fingernails, gently massaging the base of the man's neck.

"I wondered if you could suggest something for my sinuses?" he said, tapping the arch of his nose. "I get headaches and things, and there's a constant irritating dryness in my nostrils." He showed the woman in the overall the brown bag and its contents. "All I've been given so far is this stuff, from a couple of cowboys in a back-street drugstore. Dinosaurs. It might do me more harm than good, don't you think? Treatment in the west I've had doesn't help much either. So I wondered..."

The man in the dressing-gown raised his head off the pillow and looked at Chinley with a blank expression on his handsome face. The hands which had been massaging his neck moved out of sight, and the woman at the door also glared at Chinley in silence, her shining lips tight and thin. Then she said:

"If you have something wrong with your nose, then go to a nose hospital."

"Isn't this a clinic?" said Chinley.

"We only do acupuncture and massage here. Thank you." She attempted to close the door on him, but he blocked it with his knee.

"Acupuncture and massage?" he said, looking at his watch again. "Well, why not? I'll try anything once."

He pushed the door wide open. Standing by a sink, wiping her hands on a flannel, was Jane.

"Mr Chinley," she said. "Are you...?"

"I'm sorry," said Chinley, backing out into the corridor. "I didn't... so sorry."

He nodded at both women, bowed at their supine client, and the door was closed on him.

* * *

"It's something I learnt from my father," said Jane in the taxi on the way back to the Double Rainbow hotel.

"I hope you don't think I was following you," said Chinley. "And please don't think I'm ungrateful about the drugstore men. No particular friends of yours, I hope? I just thought they were a bit prehistoric, that's all."

"Yes. But please don't mention the clinic to anyone. I'm supposed to devote myself to the reception desk."

"Well," said Chinley. "You can't make much in the way of tips, can you, standing behind a reception desk all day? And there are so many of you."

"Make much from what?"

"Tips."

"Tips? What's that?"

He looked at the Chinese girl, wondering if this was her way of saying that her share of the gratuities was negligible, but he could see by the puzzled expression on her face that she really did not know what he was talking about. He tried to explain, but she showed no interest. No gold digger there, as Astrid would have it. Jane was just an innocent moonlighter. And who wasn't? Chinley was disturbed from these thoughts by a hard poke on the shoulder, from behind him.

"That's the Hanging Bridge over there. Did you know that?"

Terry leaned forward, and pointed at a commonplace wooden Chinese bridge, spanning a busy intersection and ascending, in what seemed at first glance the wrong direction, in broad steps and platforms. The blue and yellow pastel paintwork was peeling and smutty, and Chinley tried to equate all this with what Terry had just said, which made it sound like a lesser-known wonder of the oriental world.

"It's hardly up to willow-pattern standards, is it?" he said. "Hanging. Am I missing something? Hanging in the early morning mist? Hanging above the clouds of pollution?"

"No," said Terry. "*Hanging.*" With both hands gripping his own throat, he thrust his head over Chinley's shoulder. "Strung up. Lynched. What a way to go."

Jane looked at him in some alarm, then at Gladys, who was sitting with her large freckled forearms folded over the shopping, her thoughts clearly elsewhere.

"Is your husband feeling sick, Mrs Fox?" said Jane. "Does he need to leave the taxi?"

"No, he's fine," said Gladys, with her eyes closed.

"This is where one of the soldiers was strung up in the troubles of eighty-nine," said Terry. Chinley looked back at the dusty bridge.

"How do you know that?" he said.

"I've seen the photographs. Unmistakable. Barbaric. A good clean swish of the sword or the axe, that's a more gentlemanly way of dealing with such matters. As long as you know what you're doing. More dignified than to leave you dangling in the air like that." He reached down and patted the long thin wooden packing-case which lay at his feet on the floor of the taxi.

"What do you think about this then?" he said.

"Don't ask me," said Chinley. "I'm a layman." He was not impressed by the purchase. To him it had no more appeal than the discarded blade of a rusty old lawn-mower.

"She's no beauty I know," said Terry. "But a compulsion is a compulsion."

* * *

Hearing the piano, Chinley crossed the foyer to the lounge and settled down on the plush green leather sofa towards which he was becoming proprietorial. He ordered an Irish coffee to help diminish the bitter medical taste in his mouth, though he approved of the discomfort the drugstore mixture was now causing him. At least there *was* a taste. That was more than could be said for the camomile pills. He picked up a copy of the *China Daily*, but was distracted by the pumping bare right leg of the pianist. She was wearing a long green silk dress split at the side. Her hair was piled high over a flat aristocratic forehead, and fashioned into a mass of spiralling black curls. She looked over, parted her lips, and gave a brief bow. He could do without this, he told himself, holding the *China Daily* up high enough to block the view.

His view was soon further blocked off by Jane, now in uniform and holding out a small chrome-plated tray on which there was an envelope containing, she said, a note from Mr Deng. *'Professor Chinley,'* it read. *'You will all leave Beijing for Wuhan tomorrow. You must tell the Professors Fox. Final meeting tonight at my place. I will collect you. Please be in. Deng Siyou.'*

Jane stood with her hands clasped in front of her, waiting for Chinley's reaction. "Wuhan," he said. "I'm not even sure where it is."

"You're going to Wuhan?"

"Yes."

"My father lives in Wuhan. I was born there."

Chinley looked up from the message.

"Your father lives in Wuhan?" he said. "You won't see much of him then."

"We don't have many free days here you know. But we're going to see him next week."

"We?"

"Yes. Me and my sister."

"And what does your sister do?"

Jane laughed, and nodded towards the pianist.

"That's my sister. Well, one of them. Alison. The other one still lives with my father. She's a bit younger than us, but people say she's the clever one in the family. And the one with the looks."

"And what does your father do?"

"He's a bean curd salesman. He used to be a professor of Physical Training and Martial Arts, but he's more or less retired from that. He teaches more gently now, *t'ai chi* and things like that. You know?"

Chinley remembered the ghostly figures in the early morning by the river bank. Yes, that was a gentle touch. The silent men. And Wang's wife.

"Sort of," he said.

"In Wuhan we can be your guide. Me and my sisters. You are welcome to my home.

He suspected that this formula was Jane's way of conveniently rounding off the conversation. But she stayed where she was, still apparently eager to be at his service, fiddling with her hair and fidgeting from one foot to the other.

"Do you have a map of China in your room?" she said.

He nodded.

"If it's no trouble," she continued, "I can show you where you're going."

He nodded again, and she led the way to the lift-shaft, past several saluting bellboys. Chinley gave them a second look, while he was waiting for the lift to arrive, because he had a feeling that one or two of them were trying hard not to grin at him.

The bed took up so much space in the room that Jane could not help but stand by it. She was still giving Chinley her complete attention. He spread out the map on the king-size duvet and knelt down, embarrassed by a creaking in his joints. She got on her knees beside him, unbuttoning her jacket as the collar hitched up her neck. She wore no make-up, and no perfume that he could detect; he was aware only of a soapy freshness. She seemed short-sighted, peering at the print from a distance of a few inches as she traced the route of the railway line running south from Beijing to the Yangtse River. Her hip pressed close, and again the thought occurred to Chinley that he could do without this sort of nonsense. Jane, however, seemed to be concentrating only on the lie of the land on the map.

"There it is," she said, stabbing at the paper. "Right on the river."

She stood up and wandered around the room, fiddling with the curtains, the pillow-cases, and the towels. She laid a footmat beside the bed, went into the bathroom, turned on all the taps for a while, then turned them off again and came and waited by the wardrobe, smiling. Chinley looked at the scarlet fingernails, recollecting the unhurried way she had been kneading the neck muscles of the young man in the silk dressing-gown, and he found himself wondering. It was all right to wonder, he told himself. Perhaps there was a *bathroom* service here. Why was she testing the taps? He had heard about what goes on in the bathrooms in China. Or was it in Japan?

"Can I go now?" she said.

"Go? Yes," said Chinley. "Yes of course. Thank you."

"I see you've started the medicine." She sniffed, and pointed at the teapot and the open brown bag on the desk. "Just put hot water on it, like tea. Five times a day."

"Right."

"You're very kind," she said, as she turned the door-handle. "Very gentle. Just like my grandfather."

Kind and gentle, repeated Chinley once he was alone again. Like her *grandfather* for Christ's sake. Not even her father. And he was retired, wasn't he? He opened the top drawer of the dressing-table, went into the bathroom, and flushed away the entire supply of the camomile pills packed for him by Dorothy.

* * *

The muted assembly at Mr Deng's apartment was brought to life by the entrance of Wang and his wife; Gladys having been so far highly noticeable but causing no fuss, like a huge tortoise with its head retracted. Chinley and Terry were on high stools in front of a makeshift bar at one end of what Mr Deng referred to as his 'parlour'. The walls were panelled with pale lacquered oak, and the rice-paper shades on the dimmed alcove lights gave the room an antique brown and yellow appearance. Chinley did not at first recognise Wang's wife: the chirpy clownishness of last night had gone; so too had the vigour of the outdoor gymnast; all replaced by a sleepy-eyed sophistication. She looked much taller tonight, in a black satin shoulderless evening dress and high heels, and, as though posed in a sepia photograph, she was framed by the smoke from the cigarettes of Mr Hu and Mr Wu, who stood one to each side of her, like bodyguards.

Gladys had now reclined to an almost horizontal position in her low armchair. The severe lady official who was at the banquet last night was there, still in the same checked grey suit. Chinley had forgotten her name. As far as he remembered he had not been told what her job was, though he could imagine her in some monitoring or surveillance role.

Several foreign diplomats were there, from the British and American embassies, and whenever one of them slipped him a calling card, if there was enough empty space on it he crossed out the original details and wrote his own contact address, ready to pass one on later to Jane, so she could find him in Wuhan, if she really wanted to. Those cards which were too cluttered with print went straight into the bin. Mr Deng came by with a bottle of vintage Rioja, and Chinley automatically held out his half-empty glass for a refill.

"That's the way, Professor," said Mr Deng. "Make the most of it while you can. It's genuine in case you're wondering. I'm afraid you'll be saying goodbye to the good life tomorrow."

"I don't agree with that at all," said Wang's wife, moving in. "Not at all. Not these days. Not with all the foreigners all over the place now, and all the new joint ventures. Joint wine ventures, for example. Sino-French. Sino-Italian."

Her husband came and stood between her and Chinley, and she walked away.

"So Wuhan is still... developing?" suggested Chinley.

"So polite. So cautious," said Mr Deng. "Our Professor."

Hypocritical more like, thought Chinley. Other words: backward, under-developed, emerging, poor, primitive, and traditional had also been in his mind. But Mr Deng was his host, and for all Chinley knew Wuhan might have been *his* home town, as well as Jane's.

"Where do you come from yourself, Mr Deng?" he asked.

"Shaoshan. In Hunan province."

There was a pause, during which Mr Deng raised his thick brushstroke eyebrows, as though anticipating a response.

"Aha," said Chinley, checking an impulse to say that he had never heard of the place. "Shao*shan*. Right."

"Yes indeed," said Mr Deng. "Mao Zedong's birthplace, no less."

"That's right," said Chinley. Off-hand he could think of nothing to say about the man, but he felt an onus to continue in some relevant way. Remembering Astrid's claim, he said:

"Flies."

"What?" said Mr Deng.

"Flies, in China."

"What does?"

"No." Chinley was using his arms to imitate rapidly flapping wings. A silence fell around him, and he pretended to be brushing down his jacket. "Is it true, Mr Deng," he continued, lowering his voice, "that during the time of Chairman Mao there was a campaign to eliminate flies?"

Mr Deng's mouth was rounding, but no sound came out. Terry's eyes lit up. There were a few diplomatic coughs at Chinley's rear, and the conversation in the room reverted to its previous buzz. Wang's wife returned to the now speechless circle of men, and fingered a complicated bracelet. She leaned back against the bar, elbows propped behind her, and asked Mr Deng for an orange juice. While it was being prepared Wang started waving his hands about and weaving his head from side to side, like a snake.

"The invisible man!" he shouted at Chinley. "You have not been in your hotel all day, Professor. And what's this? Western wine?"

"Yes."

Wang peered into Chinley's glass, then into his wife's glass of orange juice, then flapped away. Chinley caught Terry's eye and was delighted to see him wink. He went close to the Irishman and whispered.

"You can't imagine, or maybe you can, the kind of drinks that man's been forcing down my throat."

"But are they any worse," said Terry, "than some of the drinks young Jane's been organising for *you?*"

"What?"

"Your prescription. Your infusion."

"Oh that. Revolting stuff. But so it should be. For my sinuses, you know."

"I doubt that it will do your sinuses much good. Do you know what they were calling it in the drugstore? How good's your Chinese?"

"Almost non-existent."

"Old man-young wife mixture, is what they've given you. Isn't that what you wanted? A kind of Chinese Viagra?"

"Good God no," said Chinley, with a quick look to either side of him. No-one appeared to be listening in. "The last thing I need here is an aphrodisiac."

"Well that's what they've given you. But I wouldn't worry. They have fancy names for everything, the Chinese. One of those guys in the drugstore, by the way, the older one, is Jane's uncle. Her father's brother. A dutiful niece, don't you think? Looking after the family business. And we thought she was taking us there simply out of the goodness of her heart."

"Well, why not both?" said Chinley. "I bet they're all much of a muchness these places, anyway."

"Perhaps. But she told them an awful lot about *you.* Your wife not being here. Your daughter who may or may not be coming. You going to Wuhan tomorrow. She must have known that before you did."

In answer to Chinley's frown, Terry said: "*Guanxi.* You can find out whatever you like, if you know people in high places."

Mr Deng's boardroom voice rose above the leisurely Chinese dance music coming from the speakers. "Sorry you missed the banquet last night Professor Fox," he said, looking down at Gladys. "And no-one there to meet you off the plane. I'm afraid Beijing does not have the best airport in the world, not quite, not yet. What do *you* think?"

Slouching low to the floor in her vast armchair, Gladys stared at him for a while, from behind a large glass of what looked like whisky, then she said: "Quite honestly, I think it looks and smells like nothing more than an enormous toilet. Something should be done about it."

Hearing Gladys echoing Betty, whom he had almost forgotten, Chinley felt an odd sensation in his stomach, as though someone were strapping him into a harness. Terry winked again and said: "She speaks her mind does Gladys, when she's relaxed."

Trying to show his teeth through lips which could not have been more puckered if Gladys had slapped him across the face, Mr Deng went behind the bar and said: "Have a cocktail or something, Professor Chinley. While you still have the chance."

Mr Wu and Mr Hu had moved in closer now, and they nodded their encouragement: though, Chinley assumed, they would not know exactly what was on offer. In the hoarse voice of a man whose vocal cords have for a long period been lacerated by strong liquor, one of them, Chinley was not sure which, at last recognisably pronounced the words: "Jack Daniels. Have a Jack Daniels. Professor."

"No," Wang's wife called out. She was hidden by the broad shoulders of Mr Wu and Mr Hu, and she had to stand on tiptoe to make herself visible to Chinley. "Have a Silk Stocking, Professor. Have a Silk Stocking."

Everyone around the bar chuckled at this, but over by the wall-panelling Chinley saw just one cheerless grey face and cheerless grey figure, blurred by the thickening smoke. Mr Deng handed him a Jack Daniels.

"Now please Professor," said Wang, returning from his flurry around the room. "Now please have a dance with my wife. After you finish your drink."

"Did Jane get you what you wanted?" said Wang's wife, reinserting her head into the group of men. Her husband unfurled his raw-liver lips, bowed, and moved away. What *didn't* they know about me, thought Chinley.

"What I wanted?"

"Yes."

"Well... So you've met Jane then?"

"Mr Deng and I got Jane and her sister their jobs here," said Wang's wife. "And I buy my bean curd from their father. He's an ex-Professor, you know, at our place, so it's the least we can do for him. Help his daughters, I mean."

"There's another one, isn't there?" said Chinley.

"Another what?"

"Another daughter."

"Yes. A beautiful girl. Or woman, I should say. She won't take a job here with her sisters though. Or in any other hotel, I would say. Why don't you finish your drink, Professor? And we'll have that dance my husband promised you."

She danced lightly and expertly along to the slow Chinese music, her slender body responding easily and imaginatively to Chinley's self-conscious and clumsy steps. He remembered her amongst the willows that morning. She probably knew that he was there, but he said nothing about it and neither did she. Surveillance here was enough in evidence already: no-one would want to be reminded of it. Even now he could sense that many eyes were watching them. She was eager to talk as she danced, and he felt her lips close to his ear, and her hair brushing his face.

"So you've all been successfully vetted," she said. "You and the Fox's."

"It seems so."

"Don't worry about Mr Deng. What he says about Wuhan. He thinks you have to be in the capital to enjoy the good life. He's not alone in that. It's surprising the length some people will go to, to get themselves here."

"So I've heard," said Chinley.

"On the campus in Wuhan I enjoy the world of the spirit *and* the world of the flesh. The more so since I've known Professor Ward."

"Professor Ward?"

"My good friend the American. He's in your block. You'll all be together in the foreigners' block. Cosy. He looks like a bear you know, but he dances well, and he tutors me in what he calls the ways of the west."

"The ways of the west? Good God. What ways of the west?"

"You know. The way you are with each other. Men and women.

People. Don't tell me you don't know what I'm talking about. But maybe you're a Buddhist? A lot of you come over here for that. Meditation. Diet. Exercise. Control."

"No, no," said Chinley. "No. I'm not one of those. Maybe I should be."

The slow music stopped, and gave way to a rumba. Wang's wife raised her palms, and locked her fingers with Chinley's.

"Don't stand so far away from me," she said, pulling him towards her. "I have to keep chasing you. And by the way, my name is Belinda."

He coughed, stiffened his neck and elbows, and looked over her shoulder at the cumulus of smoke near the ceiling, aware of the unfading smile, and the dilated staring eyes, which gave him the impression that she was not really thinking much about what she was saying. Then he saw two small red spots of light chasing each other. Mr Wu and Mr Hu were waving their cigarettes at him, from a darkened corner of the room.

Part Two

Chapter Four

Five farm labourers marched in step, in single file, down the country lane dividing their rice furrows. A chain gang without the chain. Their bundles were balanced at either end of bamboo shoulder-poles, and their eyes were shielded from the low autumn sun by wide-brimmed conical straw hats. Despite the overtones of an open prison it would have been a peaceful rustic scene but for the fumes and the horn-blaring of the trucks and buses cannonballing their way downhill towards the city of Wuhan.

Chinley sat on a roadside log sipping from a flask of his medicinal brew, his newly-acquired bicycle propped in the shade of an aspen tree. The labourers passed him by, with a communal but uncommunicative stare. He raised his plastic cup in greeting, but was not surprised to see no reaction other than a slight widening of the eyeballs. No, they were not like Joe's men at all. Their faces remained expressionless and dour, and in the shoddy work clothes at close quarters they looked increasingly like convicts on hard graft. Chinley himself had just escaped from a kind of imprisonment, from the relentless company of Wang and his comrades.

He had been in Wuhan a week now and although the Dong Hu university campus where he lived was well-forested and shrubbed, and the apartment which he had been allocated was spacious, though dark and dank, he had not until today been able to get away from *people*. He ventured outside the university grounds now and then, on foot, but found that this brought him only to an uncongenially noisy and overcrowded suburban sprawl of concrete.

The Foreign Experts' building, where he had his rooms, was at the summit of a modest rise in the land: more of a mound than a hill. But from this vantage point, when he awoke to see his first dawn there, he had the impression of being at the centre of extensive parkland. Even from his pillow he could see yellowing sycamore trees, full of extremely fat and squawking sparrows silhouetted against a pale marble sky. Beyond the sycamore trees was a lawn, criss-crossed by narrow paths giving access to washing-lines. The lawn was bordered by a wall of blue masson pines facing, incongruously, a line of stubby-bowled palm-trees, like large pineapples.

Downhill from the Foreign Experts' building was a dense copse of bamboo saplings, with black rings and luminous olive-green trunks. But a brief post-breakfast inspection of his environment soon revealed the narrow limits of these private gardens, and to reach anything resembling a wide open space he certainly needed the second-hand bicycle, a reciprocal present from Wang. On his own home ground, Chinley noticed, Wang was a different person: normal and butlerish now, compared to the goofy show-off he had been in Beijing. It was as though he had been performing there, for the benefit of his boss, Mr Deng, who seemed to be everyone's boss or sponsor. Both the protector and the penaliser, depending on how he saw you, as Terry put it.

Chinley saw Wang's wife now and again from a distance, on his early morning walks, sometimes glinting like a futuristic beacon in her metallic body stocking, amongst the *t'ai chi* enthusiasts; sometimes on her own halfway up a hill, leaning against a tree, blending with the landscape in a floral green and white jacket. At Huban she taught Voice, in a building at the other side of the campus from Chinley's Ecology Department. She was an Associate Professor, whatever that meant, but Chinley wondered if she had once taught in the local primary school and had a reputation for being fierce: if so, that might explain why children invariably gave her a wide berth.

With uniformed guards at the campus gates and young women in stiff white jackets monitoring the comings and goings of visitors to his building, Chinley had for the past week felt like a patient on a day ward at a psychiatric hospital. Even now, as he sat sipping his brew on the roadside log, he wondered whether reports on his movements and his behaviour were being relayed back to the institution which was housing him, and from there perhaps to the lady in grey in Beijing. She said no more to him than was absolutely necessary during their two so-called social gatherings in the capital, and he had the impression that she had only just looked away each time he checked to see if she was watching him. The feeling of being under observation was reinforced by the ubiquitous presence of Mr Hu and Mr Wu, who almost frog-marched him through the human barrier of would-be passengers at Beijing railway station, past the wooden signs which were held up like hymn-boards to indicate the numbers of the trains, and on to the platform, guarding him like a suspect under escort. Wang's wife was closeted away somewhere with her husband for the journey; Terry offered Chinley some of the half-bottle of rum which he kept in his inside pocket, then the Irishman and his wife passed half a day lying on their backs, in their bunks.

Chinley and the Party Secretaries had spent so much time together, making mutually incomprehensible noises at each other, he assumed they would now be as tired of his company as he was of theirs. Yet on his first morning at work, while he was in the staff canteen, he looked up from his bowl of soya milk porridge to see both Mr Wu and Mr Hu watching him from a corner again, waving their cigarettes and grinning whenever their eyes met. He was now able to distinguish between the two men, though they were similar in many respects: they looked in their late-forties, were roughly the same height, and had the same boyish pudding-bowl haircut and quiff across the forehead. But there was something of the itinerant about them: in urban England they could have mirrored each other at either end of a park bench, lifting a bottle to the lips at fixed intervals and in unison, like clockwork figures in a Victorian museum. They no longer wore their blue Beijing suits, but both men now had dowdy brown comrade-tailored jackets; and they both had black bicycles.

Before leaving the breakfast canteen Chinley went to the gents' toilet, and was startled to discover that Mr Wu was trailing him. The Chinese man put on a spurt and overtook him as they reached the entrance to the gents', clearly eager to be the first through the door. Chinley rationalised this as Mr Wu's effort to look after him, in this case by making sure that all the facilities he may need were in good working order. But as he relieved himself he was aware of a shadowy presence, which remained behind him, muttering something in Russian. It was this ultimate intrusion on his privacy, which spurred him into immediate and vigorous use of the bicycle from Wang.

An odd message from Wang's wife arrived the day after the bicycle was delivered. It was a Welcome card, saying she believed her doctors when they told her that physical exercise was essential for both the body and the mind, and she added that she hoped Professor Chinley did not hate cycling as much as her friend Professor Ward did. *Doctors,* noted Chinley. Even *he* only had one doctor.

A small purplish lizard, dusty and shrivelled like a dry twig, splayed itself in the sun on a boulder between the log and the bicycle. It was the only sign of wild life he had seen apart from the branchful of fat sparrows outside his bedroom window each morning. Otherwise there were only the farm animals: strangely docile water buffalo with rhinoceros hides, separated from him by a roadside ditch, tamely and lifelessly pulling their ploughs. There were no goats and no sheep, but some soil-coloured hump-backed cows, and a few cocks and hens running in and out of tumbledown allotment sheds.

It was a warm afternoon and Chinley, once again grateful for the absence of flies, would have dozed off but for the siren blare as every bus and truck warned him of its approach. But through the fumes and the haze, from these foothills he could at least now see for some distance. Most of the journey from Beijing had been in the dark, and when the train slowed down to cross the Yangtse bridge at Wuhan he had the feeling that he was coming in to land by aeroplane: he was suspended in a void, with a vast expanse of dark yellowish water far below and, not so far above, a cardboard-grey dome of cloud and mist. Now at last the urban sprawl of the city was in small perspective, on the skyline: slag heaps, factories, cranes, goods yards, warehouses, and a nightmarish labyrinth of residential blocks, stark and functional, like colossal pigeon-coops.

But even here, by the woods and the ponds, and the yellow clumps of rice-stalks, there was a constant trickle of passers-by: countryfolk in their inverted-wok shaped woven sun hats, with carrying poles straddling their shoulders.

A young woman scraped by in high heels. She was wearing western clothes: tight denim jeans and a lime-green blouse, and she gave Chinley a long look, but did not seem over-surprised by his presence. He watched her make her way awkwardly down the lane, stopping every now and then to extract a stone chipping from the sole of her shoe. She didn't look like a farmgirl.

But a more unexpected sight was a trio appearing suddenly from out of a hole in the privets, while Chinley was pumping up his tyres in preparation for the return journey. A short stocky old man, flanked by two young girls who could have been his grand-daughters, descended into the ditch, then re-appeared at the roadside. With his forked silver-grey beard, his bright anthracite eyes and polished-pine complexion, the old man looked like a rare and precious mandarin doll, even more so as the girls seemed to be almost carrying him: they moved along at their own brisk pace, with the old man's feet hardly touching the ground. Chinley was mesmerised, and when they looked in his direction he bowed, as he was learning to.

They floated on, like three characters from a Beijing opera, the girls displaying the Chinese trick of making good headway while apparently barely moving their feet. Chinley wondered if Jane and her sisters transported their father around the fields like this, but from Jane's account her father, though retired, was still active enough to teach martial arts, and to go off each morning on his tricycle peddling bean curd. No doubt the youngest daughter, the one who was still at home, was content for the moment to see to his domestic needs, reflected Chinley as he followed the trio's mad carousel down a footpath and into another field. Jane had also mentioned a grandfather, he remembered with discomfort, though she had not said whether he was alive or not.

He wanted to be off the road by nightfall. No cyclist here used lights, and in the darkness they flitted out of nowhere, like bats, miraculously avoiding each other's metalwork. He finished off the remains of the brew, and began the largely freewheeling descent back into town. When he arrived at his room he found a note from a Mr Feng slipped under the door, informing him that on the following morning he would be requested to present himself at the local hospital for a medical inspection.

* * *

"You are very calm, Professor," said Mr Feng. Feng worked at the Foreign Affairs Office on the Huban campus. He had just told Chinley that although he was only thirty years old, he had already been in the job for almost ten years, ever since graduating from the same university. Chinley guessed that this was Feng's way of saying that he knew what he was doing. He looked efficient enough, having a permanent street-wise expression superimposed on otherwise delicate choirboy features: a small nose and button-eyes; and a puckish sneer of confidence. His careful and fashionable grooming was marred only by a stray tuft of coarse black hair apparently permanently scuffed up at the nape of his neck, like a peewit's crest. He also told Chinley he wanted conversation practice to improve his command of English. Chinley grinned back when he heard this, and made a mental note to avoid the man whenever possible.

They were now in a Foreign Affairs Office car on their way to the hospital, and Chinley was not quite as calm as he looked. He preferred visits to such places to be his own choice, not someone else's. They might find something wrong with him that he did not know about. Still, he told himself, he could always refuse to co-operate, if necessary.

"Doesn't being an Expert," he said, half-jokingly, "exempt me from this sort of thing?"

Feng grinned and shook his head, and said again: "You look *very* calm."

"I *am* calm," said Chinley. "Why shouldn't I be?"

"No, you should be."

"One of the reasons I am calm," continued Chinley, "is that quite recently I was given a thorough medical examination by my own general practitioner, at home. And I was told that for my age I was reasonably fit."

"Good," said Feng.

The closer they came to the hospital the more Chinley was inclined to talk, and Feng must have taken this as a sign that he was, after all, apprehensive.

"All foreigners must see the doctor within two weeks of arriving in China, if you want to work here," said Feng, which sounded to Chinley as though being a foreigner, as far as the Chinese authorities were concerned, meant that there was probably something wrong with you, physically or otherwise.

"It is quite normal," continued Feng. "This is the first hurdle you have to leap over. There is nothing to worry about."

He explained that without a clean bill of health Chinley could not be issued with his green card, nor his orange card, nor his red card. Inquiring as to the use of each of these, Chinley was told that, together, they would enable him to prove to whoever was interested that he was not as foreign as some of the other foreigners here, and he would therefore be entitled to certain privileges. Chinley wanted to ask why all three cards could not be combined into one, but he refrained from doing so because he had begun to identify Feng's talent for supplying answers which were plausible but pure on-the-spot invention.

"Aliens or foreigners?" said Feng, wriggling a hand into the inside pocket of his starched black jacket.

"What?"

"What's better? Aliens or foreigners?"

"What do you mean, better?"

"It doesn't matter, I suppose." Feng returned his hand to his knee. "Sometimes," he continued, "it is an advantage for an alien in China to be Chinese."

Chinley raised both hands and massaged his forehead with hot sweaty fingers. He stared at the floor, at his dull canvas moccasins, at the sheen on the shoes of the man beside him, and he stifled a yell.

The guard at the hospital gate bent low to look at Feng and his passenger through the car window, then he waved them on across a sandy yard to the main building, a soulless, Soviet-style monolith. As he and Feng walked across the chilly reception area, he felt once again bound by invisible handcuffs, a suspect on his way to be interrogated on charges which were yet to be specified.

"The doctor wants you to take off your jacket and roll up your sleeve." Feng was translating, in a room which looked more like an out-dated accountant's office than a surgery, for a man who was wearing an open-necked shirt, an old pullover, and trainers with the laces undone.

"Which doctor?" asked Chinley.

"This one."

"He's a *doctor*?"

"Of course."

"Why? I mean, why roll my sleeve up?"

"We would like to take some of your blood."

Why, Chinley wondered, was Feng saying 'we', rather than 'he'? Would they attempt to stick the needle in by force, if necessary?

"What does he think he might find, this doctor?" asked Chinley.

"Oh, perhaps... you know... sexual disorders?"

Chinley was prepared for this. He took his own doctor's signed and stamped certificate out of his wallet and handed it over to Feng. "There you are," he said. "Everything in order."

Both Feng and the doctor seemed to be even more short-sighted than Jane: they inspected the certificate from a distance of an inch or two, occasionally looking at each other, looking at Chinley, and muttering in Chinese. At last, Feng leaned back in his chair, and smiled.

"We would still like to have some of your blood," he said.

"You mean you don't accept my results from England?"

"Yes. Of course we accept. But there are one or two hidden gems. And there is a smell."

Chinley paused for a moment, then said: "What on earth..."

"I'm sorry," said Feng. "I mean missing links."

"Missing links? What the fuck..."

"Missing details."

"Such as what?" Chinley pulled the paper towards him. "Look. Here, and here, and here. Normal, normal, normal. No abnormalities, it says. And here. I know what you're after. HIV negative."

"Yes. But there are other sexual diseases," said Feng, his smile widening. "And the form does not say that you do not have them."

"For example?"

"For example... what is it... saphallus?"

"Can't you tell by looking at me," said Chinley, "that I don't have syphilis? What sort of life do you think I lead?"

"Syphilis. That's it."

Feng reached again inside his jacket. He produced a note-book, and held it out to Chinley, with a pen. "Spell it. I need this word. Write it down."

Chinley took the note-book and pen, and wrote down 'saphallus'. They were not going to have everything their own way. He knew he had lost his argument, but there were precautions to insist on before he let them have his blood.

"Can I have a look at the needle?" he said. Feng translated. The doctor pointed to an ante-room, where Chinley could see medical staff in white coats and what looked to him like bakers' hats.

"Please come with me first," said Feng. "I would also like to ask you some questions, about the smell. Is it from you, or is it external? I recognised it from your room, I think."

The following morning, Feng telephoned Chinley to tell him that the blood test result was satisfactory, so the Professor could now be issued with all his cards. It was like a reward for good behaviour. He also said that if the smell was what he thought it was, and if the Professor really felt the need for this enhancer, as he called it, then he should balance its effect with periods of serenity and meditation.

Although Feng was calling from less than half a mile away, the internal campus line was crackly and the two men could hear each other only intermittently, so Chinley was forced to repeat loudly more or less everything he heard, to determine its accuracy. His efforts were interrupted by a powerful voice yelling down at him from the darkness of the upstairs landing.

"Can't you keep your damn *voice* down?"

The tones were those of a petulant academic, and the accent was American. The overhead light was switched on, and Chinley saw a wide mop-head of reddish-brown hair, and a beard of a darker brown, so full that it seemed false, ready for use with a theatrical costume. The man's eyes were charcoal hollows in puff-pastry swellings of pale grey flesh. Chinley assumed he was looking at Professor Ward, as mentioned by Wang's wife a couple of times, and he waited to see if the man was going to introduce himself. But instead he pounded his ears a few times with his fists, then switched off the light and went back into the upstairs apartment.

"Are you still there, Professor?" said Feng.

"Yes. I've just been having a chat with a neighbour. The man upstairs. He didn't look too well."

"Ah yes, that would be Professor Ward. The American. So you've met him at last then?"

"No, I wouldn't say that. He just seems somehow bothered by me being on the telephone."

"Ah yes," said Feng. "That's Professor Ward for you. He is disturbed by voices."

"Has *he* had his hospital visit yet?" asked Chinley.

"Oh yes. Some time ago. Every foreigner must leap over this first hurdle. Even Mr and Mrs Fox."

Yes, thought Chinley. In their own way, Feng and the man upstairs could be as mad as each other. "Is he an Expert?" he asked.

"Professor Ward?"

"Yes."

"Of course."

"What in?"

"Erm... I think he's an economist."

"Good God." said Chinley. "An excitable economist. Sounds a dangerous combination to me."

"Yes," said Feng. "*What?*"

"Nothing."

"Combination? You mean collocation?"

"Nothing."

Chinley could sense Feng ready to fumble for his notebook. He wanted to carry on talking now for the sake of talking, just to see if he could provoke the upstairs neighbour once more out of his lair, and have another look at him. Make it clear that he was not intimidated. He could hear some heavy footfalls and creaking floorboards overhead, behind a closed door. But he did not want to talk to Feng any more. He reached inside his jacket pocket, and took a scrap of crumpled hotel notepaper out of his wallet.

"Mr Feng, can I telephone Beijing from here?" he asked.

"Of course. Just dial a zero, then zero one."

Jane was on duty. She sounded genuinely pleased to hear from Chinley, and told him that she and her sister would definitely be coming to Wuhan by train that weekend. She said she hoped he would be free to join them for dinner at their father's house, or maybe at a place not far from there, in the village, which might be more appropriate, as she put it. Although Chinley could hear her quite well, she was shouting at the top of her voice, perhaps because the line at her end was not so clear. So he took the chance to shout back, and cocked an ear towards the upstairs landing. The arrangements for dinner made, he replaced the receiver.

He had not heard Jeffrey Ward come out of his apartment. But now the man stood in silence at the top of the stairs, the naked bulb in the ceiling once more illuminating his hairy features. His hands were set on his hips, and his belly loomed like a wind direction indicator. He was unkempt, with sagging light-grey trousers, a threadbare dark blue pullover, and black boots the size of coal-shuttles, with thick leather tongues dangling out, like razor straps.

His whiskers were glistening with sweat, and seemed to be stirred into motion by air currents rising from an over-heated body. But this time he said nothing, and the two men eyed each other in silence, like boxers waiting for the bell. Chinley turned away first, and went into his apartment reflecting that although he was a hefty man himself, with a long-established temper, he had never actually been a fighter, and probably never could be. Whereas the man at the top of the stairs looked quite ready to inflict much more than just a few cuffs on the ear.

* * *

"So you only have a daughter?" Chinley automatically mumbled a reply to Wang's question without reflecting on its implications, because his attention was focused in astonishment on the man's wife. She had transformed her appearance yet again: her face was now daubed with pale powdery make-up, around a slash of scarlet lips, and her previously heavy eyebrows had become thin black arcs, like brush-strokes of Chinese ink.

She was wearing impossibly narrow high-heel scarlet shoes, and had given herself additional height by back-combing her hair into a beehive. A shiny obsidian beehive. She had also given herself extra width at the shoulders, with a broad red jacket spangled all over with small gold buttons. Chinley readjusted his initial guess at her age, and saw her now as at least ten years younger than her husband, and therefore in her early forties.

"No sons yet then?" continued Wang.

"*What?* No."

Chinley remembered Astrid's observation in the park that most of the children passing them by were boys, but he made no comment on this to the Wangs, who as far as he knew were childless. Astrid was anyway not to be taken seriously. She had made a fool of him over the flies, and she had been wrong about Jane. Well, mostly wrong.

Chinley and the Wangs had met by chance on the main campus boulevard and were now walking slowly in the general direction of the Foreign Experts' guest house, which was still some distance away.

"Where is *Mrs* Chinley these days, Professor? Your wife? In England, I suppose?" asked Wang's wife.

"Yes, she's in England." Don't pretend you don't know, Chinley said to himself.

"And you say he will not be coming out here?" asked Wang.

"What?"

"Is he coming out here or not?"

"Who?"

"Your wife. Is he coming out here. To China."

"*He?*"

"Yes."

Chinley said nothing, wondering if Wang was doing this on purpose, for some reason, to irritate him. Perhaps there was something in his file about his temper. Anyway, he did not want to lecture the man on the correct use of English pronouns; he had done enough lecturing for the day. So instead, he decided to prolong the absurdity.

"He may or may not be coming. Probably not."

"He?" said Wang.

Chinley looked sideways at the wide spread of the equine teeth, but in the man's eyes he saw only an expression of innocence. His wife giggled, and said: "I don't know if you've noticed, Professor, but this is not the way to your guest-house. Are you lost?"

Chinley looked from one side of the road to the other, and realised that he had no idea where he was.

"You're not thinking of going up the pagoda at this time of night, surely?" Wang's wife laughed again. "It's tricky enough even by day."

"No," said Chinley. "Which pagoda?"

She lifted her chin, nodded at the silhouette of a line of trees, and said: "Do you see that ring of lights high in the sky beyond the trees? Well, that's the top of our pagoda."

"It's just a crumbling old ruin," said Wang.

"A wonderful magnificent old ruin," said his wife. "And a good landmark for you to find us by, Mr Chinley. We live in that block over there, on the other side of the road. Top floor."

"And now, I suppose," said Wang, "my wife will escort you home. Excuse me, I have to prepare for tomorrow."

"No, really," said Chinley. He turned and scanned the darkness around him for a clue as to his whereabouts.

"No matter," said Wang. "She likes walking. It keeps her quiet. I'll see you in the morning, Professor. Goodnight."

He bowed his farewell and left Chinley and his wife standing in the road together. She pointed at a small path leading into a wood, told Chinley it was a short cut to where he lived, and beckoned him to follow her.

He made slow progress through the sodden undergrowth and the fallen leaves, every so often catching his shoe in a rib-cage of pine tree roots. She, despite her inappropriate footwear, skipped ahead until all he could see of her was the reflection of the nearly full moon on her hair. He soon lost sight of her completely, but saw no reason to hurry, and stopped to sniff at the tangy pinewood odour rising from the branches which swept down as low as his knees. He could no longer tell which way she had gone, and there was no further splintering of twigs to guide him. But as he stopped to listen he heard a woman's voice, singing, and heading towards the sound he saw her pale face looking up at him, like an owl, from below an embankment which led down towards an open road.

"It should be me seeing *you* home," he said, sitting next to her on a brick wall.

"Why?"

"Well..."

"I hardly think so. You're new here. You don't know your way."

"What did your husband mean just now, when he said he *supposed* you would escort me home?"

"Did he say that?"

"Yes."

"I've no idea. How was your first morning in public?"

"A good audience," said Chinley. "Very welcoming. And they all seem to have English names, which makes life easier. For me."

"Some have had English names since they were at primary school."

"So you worked in a primary school before, then?"

"No. What makes you think that?"

"Nothing. But you got Belinda from primary school?"

"No. I got it when I was an undergraduate."

"Belinda. Hmm. Why Belinda?"

"There was a teacher who came here once, an Englishman. He gave it to me. He was the first person to tell me anything about life outside China. It was some years ago, when I was as young as the Li sisters. He said Belinda means 'very beautiful'."

"I see," said Chinley. "Well..."

"Listen!"

"What?"

"Jeffrey Ward's boots. Let's go before he gets here."

"Why?"

"He'll... he'll be thinking. He goes out at night, thinking. It's best not to disturb him."

The boots echoed and scraped.

"It's okay, he's going the other way," she said. She stood up and pointed into the darkness beyond the brick wall.

"Not much further now. Just up through the bamboo and we'll be at your gate."

From where he was sitting Chinley now recognised the curve of the road, and he was aware enough of his surroundings to know that a diversion into the bamboo would be no short cut at all. But Wang's wife was already amongst the trees, so he followed her.

Chapter Five

"There are times to admire the moon, Professor," said Wang, "and times *not* to admire the moon."

Wang and Terry were in Chinley's apartment. His left leg was bandaged from knee to ankle and propped on a cane stool. The accident happened just as he was emerging from the bamboo plantation. He found Wang's wife waiting for him at the edge of the wood and he drew her attention to the night sky. After a few moments silence she asked if she could see the inside of his apartment, and as he moved towards the building, preoccupied with thoughts on how to diplomatically send her packing, back off to her husband, he stepped into a deep trench hidden in the shadows. Then, with her arm around his waist he limped up to his room on the first floor, where she washed away the blood and bandaged the cuts.

"In a way, you were lucky," said Wang.

Chinley looked at him, wondering if this was a reference to the attention he had received from the man's wife. Wang unscrewed the cap of a bottle of the liquid which he insisted on calling wine, and tilted it into Chinley's half-empty glass.

"Drink it," he said. "Finish it. Then have some more."

Terry intervened. "That stuff would be put to better use," he said, "as surgical spirit."

"Yes, lucky," continued Wang, pointing at the bandages. "Your hole was empty. But Professor Ward, for example, fell into an open sewer. Pride, you see. Have you met him yet? He would not accept my bicycle, you see. He would walk everywhere. It's not so easy to get into the sewer with a bicycle."

"You mean him upstairs with the beard and the boots?" said Terry.

"Yes. Professor Ward," said Wang. "But he follows only his own advice, I think."

As though to remind Chinley of yesterday's confrontation on the stairs, the telephone rang on the landing. He tried to struggle to his feet, thinking it might be a message from Jane, but Wang insisted on answering it for him. Once he was out of the room Terry said: "Toss it down the sink for God's sake. Pass it over. I'll get you some decent stuff." He took hold of the glass, and Chinley made no attempt to stop him. "All these Professors," continued the Irishman. "Jesus."

"You've met the one upstairs, then?" said Chinley.

"I've *seen* him. All hair and boots. Walking along with that fellow's wife."

"What, Wang's wife?"

"Aye."

Terry went off to the kitchen to pour the Chinese spirit down the sink, and Wang returned from the landing. "It's the security men at the main gate, Professor," he said. "There's a foreign woman there, asking for *you*. She says she's your daughter." Terry went downstairs for the rum, then he and Wang went off to the campus gate. Half an hour later they returned, with Lisa Chinley.

She was red-eyed and bedraggled, her blonde hair darkened and matted, as though she had been swimming in a muddy stream and was still sporting the flotsam. Her face and her fingers were as black as a chimney-sweep's, shiny with streaks of oil and soot, and she was trussed out like a poor Chinese toddler, in multi-coloured layers of shoddy wool.

This is what she sleeps in, thought her father. This is what she has been sleeping in for God knows how long. He was used to seeing her in such a condition, and she was used to presenting herself in this way, but now, as he struggled to his feet to embrace her, she held him firmly at arm's length. Looking over her shoulder she saw that Wang and Terry were out of earshot, at the other end of the sitting room inspecting a bottle, and she whispered to her father: "Don't come too close."

"What?"

"Don't come too close. *Lice. Everywhere.*"

Terry caught Chinley's eye, and said: "Right. We'll leave you to it, then." He put his arm around Wang's shoulder, and led him away.

* * *

The following morning, with the aid of an old-fashioned crutch supplied by the Foreign Affairs Office, Chinley made his way downstairs and over to the stone wall outside the Foreign Experts' guest house, where he sat smoking his pipe and looking at the trench which he had fallen into and which looked so harmless in the daylight. Lisa was still asleep, in the spare room. Last night he ran her a steaming bath, then helped her wash her hair in water as hot as she could bear. She didn't seem too bothered by her condition. She was yawning and scratching herself all over, and he said nothing when he saw she had brought the rum in from the sitting room and placed it on the bathroom floor beside the tub. He had looked into her room once or twice this morning, but as yet there was no sign of her stirring. It was unlikely she would have any snippets from Dorothy to pass on: she had no mobile phone, she wouldn't have the cash to call home, and reversing the charges would, he knew, in her eyes be a weakness. Close but not clinging, that was how they were as a family. Or how they used to be.

There was a powerful exhalation of air behind him, and Chinley turned to see Gladys standing there, her sausage fingers splayed on her bulky hips. She reminded him of a matronly District Nurse in a period play, and for a moment he considered asking her if she knew anything about lice; but he decided that a woman like her, left to her own devices with his daughter, may resort to the penal use of shears and a scouring pad. Forcing Lisa's mucky head under the hot water tap to teach her a lesson. He hardly knew her. She might not keep a confidence. And if word got back to Feng and the scruffy doctor, for example, Chinley could imagine he and his daughter forced into quarantine.

"Something should be done about that hole in the ground over there," said Gladys. "They should put a fence around it. But *you're* a silly bugger, aren't you? Wandering about in the woods in the middle of the night like that? On your own, was it?"

"On my own was it," said Chinley, recognising that Terry, at least, was not a gossiper, otherwise Gladys would know the full circumstances by now. "By the way Mrs Fox," he continued. "My daughter's here, came last night. Didn't Terry mention it? She's dead to the world at the moment, but I'm sure she'll come down and present herself when she's... presentable."

"Your *daughter*? No. Terry said nothing about that. He's busy with his weapons, you know. Is she a dancer, your daughter? How old is she?"

"Twenty-three. A dancer?"

"Yes. I like a bit of life, after being stuck in the library all day. I give the youngsters here country dancing lessons, maybe you know that, and your daughter could help me out."

"Well, she's always out at discos and things," said Chinley, "but I wouldn't call her a dancer, not in the sense of dancing. So I don't think she'd be much use to you. What kind of...?"

"Entertainment can be a bit thin out here don't forget. So Terry tells me. He was out here on his own you know, before we got married. But he must have told you all about that."

"No, he hasn't said a word. So that's where he picked up his Chinese? He must have a good memory then. It must have been some time ago, if it was before you were married. And he's remembered it?"

"Mr Chinley. Terry and I are newly-weds. It's only two years since he was last out here."

"Just two years? I must talk to him about that," said Chinley.

"Nothing much to say, really. We were both widowed. We met at the club over the Co-op in Swansea. I taught Welsh dancing and he played the mouth-organ."

"No, I meant..." began Chinley, then stopped himself.

"He's ten years older than I am," said Gladys. "But we think the world of each other. And it's him who keeps me youthful-looking."

"Yes. Yes. What did he do here? Before?"

"Same as now. He's always been into the weapons. He's got a fair stretch ahead of him here now, with me the breadwinner, plenty of spare time, so he's hoping to pick up something *special*. There's an awful lot of crap around in the shops if you're not careful, he tells me. It might be his last chance to get out here for a while. He's got an old mother in Limerick who needs looking after. And what about you? Why are *you* here? Apart from the obvious."

"What obvious?"

"Earning a living."

"Right. Well, you know," said Chinley. "I want to see how China's changing."

Gladys raised her nose and shifted her jaw-bone.

"Have a look at the new dams on the Yangtse river, for example," he added.

"Without your wife?"

"What?"

"Aren't you married?"

"Yes."
"Without your wife then?"
"Yes."
"I see."

Two young Chinese women were walking arm in arm along the road towards the guest house. Chinley wondered if they were from the audience who had responded so warmly to him yesterday. These two were wearing printed floral jackets and black slacks. They kept their heads bent towards the ground, but when they looked up he saw the familiar smiles of Jane and Alison. He hobbled towards them, pointed at the roadside trench to half-explain his injury, and suggested they all went upstairs to his rooms.

"No. You can't disturb your daughter," said Gladys, taking charge. "Let her rest in peace, as it were. Come in to me."

With her lead-grey hair now folded into an austere bun, her matriarchal profile reminded Chinley of Queen Victoria as seen on very old pennies. Her father would have been very much the head of the household, he imagined, a Welsh chapel minister perhaps, an energetic man dressed in black indoors and out. Too abstemious for anyone's good. Just as well Terry met her in later life: with a father like that looking on, it would not have been easy to get Gladys on the whisky. So she would get on fine with the modest Chinese girls and with Lisa too, for different reasons: the Chinese girls here seemed to drink nothing but water or tea, which might remind Gladys of her past.

Pressing the two sisters to accept her invitation, Gladys jerked a thumb in Chinley's direction, and said: "That will save our crippled friend from tackling the stairs. At his time of life you have to be careful." The girls looked ready to lift him off the ground, if necessary. Chinley forced a loud laugh and walked on ahead of them as fast as he could.

Terry was busy with a long-bladed felling-axe, a huge cleaver, chopping through the protective steel tape on a batch of wooden delivery crates. He prised one crate open, and slid the corrugated cardboard wrapping off the contents: a rusty and tarnished old sword.

"Disappointing," he said, to Alison and Jane, who nodded. "Neglected. But see *this*." He held out the axe towards the two girls. "That's Qing, too. But a much better buy. I got it off your man here Mr Feng, one of our minders." He put the axe back in its box, and took up the sword, swinging it low to the ground, in the manner of a golf club.

"No, no," said Alison. "Not that way. You must never swing it behind you like that. My father or my young sister can show you how to use it safely, if you want. We have many swords. All different."

"Do you now?" said Terry. "What, old ones?"

"Some. But the best one is with our grandfather, in Sichuan."

"What do you mean, they can show him how to *use* it?" said Gladys. "Use it for *what*? I prefer to see them left hanging on the wall. Sharpened up and polished maybe, but hanging on the wall."

"So your grandfather's in Sichuan?" said Terry. "That's only a boat ride away."

"Certainly," said Jane. "A long boat ride though. Mr Fox, we've come to invite Mr Chinley over to eat with us this afternoon. Why don't you and your wife come along too? Meet my father. And Silvia."

"Silvia?" said Terry.

"The young one," said Jane.

"My husband has a long day ahead of him," said Gladys. "He's got his boxes to sort out."

"Well come any time," said Alison. "After we've gone back to Beijing, also fine, Silvia can be your interpreter."

"But Mr Fox can speak excellent Chinese," said Jane. "I've heard him."

"Mr Fox can argue the toss in Chinese, if necessary," said Terry. The young women looked at him. "I can negotiate," he explained, tapping his nose and winking, "in the market place. My own arms deals, you might say. And on the subject of the market economy Jane, how's your uncle's drugstore business these days?"

"Fine," said Jane, with no hint of embarrassment.

But Chinley felt a momentary panic. This turn to the conversation was unwelcome. Terry looked at him with gleeful eyes, and said:

"Well girls, your uncle's done this man a great favour. I suppose. Helping to keep his pecker up."

Jane and Alison looked at each other, and Chinley sent Terry a silent plea.

"Girls," Terry continued, "do either of you drink rum?"

He pulled open the doors of a worm-ravaged sideboard, and held up another half bottle of his stocks from the Friendship Store.

"Is it wine?" asked Jane.

"In a way."

The girls giggled, with their hands over their mouths, and told him that they didn't drink wine. He half-filled two glasses and passed one over to Chinley.

"You don't mind if we do then?" he said, and the girls giggled again. "Watch this man," continued Terry, nodding towards Chinley. "In ten minutes he'll be able to climb upstairs. Without his crutch. Report *that* to your uncle in Beijing."

* * *

When Chinley left the Foreign Experts' guest house that afternoon to meet Jane at Pagoda Hill, which she said was half-way to her father's house, Lisa was out of bed but in no condition, even by her own standards, to undergo public scrutiny. The idea of what lay hidden and crawling in her knotted hair, and no doubt in her knotted pullovers too, brought an itchiness to her father's scalp, and he agreed that it was wiser for the moment to come into contact with as few people as possible. Perhaps it was the rum, perhaps it was the insect brew, or both, but Chinley found he could now use his crutch like a vaulting pole, pivoting and thrusting himself forward like an athlete determined to conquer a few knocks. Exhilarated, he left the tarmac and took the woodland route. Jane said she would wait for him at the junction of the main boulevard with the cycle path leading to the Wangs' apartment block. In the daylight Chinley now saw the hill rising beyond the line of poplars, and the buckled old ruin at the summit, black-ringed like an enormous fossilised bamboo, the lights at the top still switched on. When he saw Jane he steadied himself on one leg and waved his crutch in greeting.

"What took you into the forest?" she said.

"A short cut I was shown."

"By who? That's no short cut. And you've missed Silvia now. She's gone up looking for you on the main road."

"Oh. Sorry about that. Missed her then."

"Let's go. It's just across the fields there. Can I help you?"

"No, no. That's all right."

* * *

From a distance Chinley was not sure whether Jane's father was wearing a large hat, or holding an umbrella over his head. He was standing near a huge wooden wheelbarrow. Chinley gathered from Jane that her father's fortunes had fluctuated along with the fortunes of the whole country, for the past forty years or so. He had taught Botany and Physical Education in Yi Chang, a town on the Yangtse river some three hundred miles upstream from Wuhan. Then, for nine years during the Cultural Revolution he had been sent with his wife and the one daughter they had at the time, Jane's older sister Alison, out into the tea and rice plantation south of the river, to a place called Xianning County. Twice in the following years there had been hope for a son, as Jane put it, but she and Silvia had come along instead. Their mother died from pneumonia, a year after Silvia was born. Their father was unable to return to his previous job as he no longer had the necessary contacts; and there was too much competition from those who did, and from younger and fitter men, so he became a kind of educated peasant. And now here he was after all that, a widower in semi-retirement, and a bean-curd salesman.

Chinley was able to see now that it was indeed a hat: a buff-coloured woven fibre cone, of immense proportions, which to western eyes looked impressive but at the same time somewhat ridiculous. It seemed uncomfortably bulky, but when he scanned the surrounding fields he saw that the neighbours were without exception similarly attired. The hat was unquestionably practical, acting not only as a shelter from the rain but also as a shade, and a shield against any imaginable angle of sunlight. Chinley shifted his concentration to the ground below him, to hobble around a series of puddles leading towards the track where the wheelbarrow was at rest, loaded high with its pale slabs of bean curd.

"What should I call your father, Jane?"

"His name is Li Yang. But maybe you can call him Mr Li."

Jane's father was still unaware of their approach: his shoulders were bent towards the ground and he seemed to be trying to light a cigarette, demonstrating that his headgear could if necessary also function as a draught excluder.

"It's a pity Lisa can't join us," said Jane.

"Yes," said Chinley. "It's not like her to miss out on a social event."

"Do you think she'll answer the door if she hears somebody knocking?" said Jane. "Silvia would be so disappointed to find nobody in. When we were out walking together sometimes, before I went to Beijing, Silvia would stand and stare at the guest house from a long way off, for minutes on end, wishing she could go and knock on some foreigner's door there."

"Well, now she can. And don't worry, Lisa will certainly show herself, whatever condition she's in."

"What's she doing here? Hasn't she got a job? Or is she a journalist?"

"No, no job."

"How long will she be staying?"

"I never ask her what her plans are," said Chinley. "But after making such an effort to get here I don't suppose she'll be leaving in too much of a hurry."

"Well," said Jane, "in that case she might be just the sort of person Silvia needs to get to know."

Mr Li's hat now at last cocked upwards, at the sound of their voices, to reveal a face as worn and crumpled as an old money-pouch. He looked at his second oldest daughter through a veil of thin blue smoke, then he nodded at her foreign visitor, took off his hat, and said: "Where's Zhao Di?"

"Gone to look at the foreigner's house," said Jane, like her father enunciating standard Mandarin for Chinley's benefit.

The three of them made their unsteady way down a muddy track, Chinley increasingly bothered by an aching and swollen calf, as the effect of his tonic wore off; Jane's father was also limping a little as he hauled the goods, and Jane was trying to prevent her high-heeled shoes from slipping off her feet into the soft clay.

She explained that Zhao Di was Silvia's Chinese name, and she had chosen the English name Silvia because she thought it made her sound like a woman of wealth. They walked past a pile of charred red building bricks, which reminded Chinley of those in his home town in the English Midlands, and on towards a row of sheds put together simply out of planks of wood and sheets of iron and tin. They greeted an old woman sitting on the kerb by a small cardboard box full of satsumas. She was crooning and cradling a baby, its face just visible through a flap in a huge ball of brown and yellow wool.

"The parents have gone abroad," said Jane. "Aren't they lucky?"

"Lucky?"

"Yes. And to have this one as well. A son."

Her father rested his barrow and led the way into one of the sheds. With just two tables, and eight stools, it was nevertheless managing to operate as a restaurant. He shouted at the waitress and gestured towards his daughter and her guest. The waitress in turn yelled in the direction of a black space in the corner of the shack, which Chinley assumed was the entrance to the kitchen. The old man tapped his cigarette ash on to the floor, peppering the greasy grey layer of customer droppings. Chinley took out his pipe.

Using his daughter as an occasional translator Li Yang tried to find out what he could about Chinley, and it was not long before his questions became increasingly personal. Why was he in China? Where was he from? How old was he? What did he earn? Where were his wife and children? Judging by her father's unblinking study of the grimy concrete floor, and his neglect of his cigarette, Chinley could see that Jane was having difficulty explaining his family circumstances.

"He wants to know why your daughter's here," she said, "and why she's on her own."

Chinley did not want to say that Lisa had turned up half-unexpectedly, as that made her sound fickle and disorganised, as though she had a take-it-or-leave-it attitude towards China. Neither, in case his words were reported back to her, did he want to suggest she was eager to visit her father.

"She usually travels alone," he said. "She keeps telling me that she considers herself a free spirit, or is it a free agent? So I suppose she's happy with her own company, and personally I admire her for that."

As he suspected, this took some time for Jane to translate, so he worked on his pipe, to give the impression that he was relaxed.

"And are *you* a free spirit?" asked Jane eventually. "My father wants to know."

"I'm a married man," said Chinley, with a chuckle.

The waitress was a wild-looking country girl, with a surprisingly small head, which with its close-cropped curly hair, reminded Chinley of a blackberry. She yelled out in a strong local dialect each time she banged down a dish on their rotting timber table. Aubergine, chicken and peanuts, soya milk, crisp fried eggs, and a tray of dumplings, hot and steaming in a nest of shredded bamboo. Chinley watched her wiping her hands on a greasy pinafore, then clump back into the dark recess out of which the food had appeared. Lisa's mother, he reflected, would never stay long in a place like this; Lisa herself on the other hand would have sought it out. He felt a sudden satisfaction that she was now here with him, even if she *was* spreading lice around his apartment. Both Jane and her father ignored the food in front of them, and as Li Yang made no attempt to extinguish his cigarette Chinley continued puffing on his pipe.

"As you know from life in China," he said to Jane, "it is often necessary, for economic reasons, for a family to be separated by long distances, for long periods of time. Like you and your father. Like that baby out there and its parents."

"But very often," she replied, "if it's a man and wife who are separated, they never see each other, ever again."

Chinley looked at her in silence for a moment, then said: "Well, going back to why Lisa's here, she's been learning some Mandarin you know. She wants to improve on that. And she's interested in Chinese culture, generally."

There was now a brief exchange between Li Yang and his daughter, after which she said: "And what about you, Mr Chinley, my father wants to know. Are *you* interested in Chinese culture generally?"

"Oh yes," he said, feeling patronising, and a little foolish under the unsmiling gaze of Li Yang.

"Well," said Jane. "As you're interested in Chinese culture generally, would you be interested in *t'ai chi* or something like that, specifically? My father wants to know." She began to pick at the food.

Chinley looked across at Li Yang, who lifted his bowl of soya milk to his dry and grizzled lips and vacuum-sucked the liquid into his mouth. The effect resembled the sound of bath-water rushing down an overflow conduit. Chinley laid down his pipe and stabbed at the doughy balls in the dish, hoping to speed up the eating process by impaling a dumpling with just one of his chopsticks, in order to transfer it securely to his open jaw. As it dangled in the air by his teeth, Jane lowered her bowl to the table and shouted

"*No!*"

But it was too late. He snapped at the ball and ruptured it. It was full of hot gravy, which spurted vigorously in several directions, leaving a brown pattern on the table-top which resembled an incomplete charting of the points of the compass.

"Sorry about that," he said. "*Dui bu qi*, Mr Li."

Li Yang dipped his head bird-like several times, but Chinley was not sure whether this was an acknowledgement of his apology, or whether he was myopically checking to see if his bowl was empty.

Jane then said something quickly to her father, something, Chinley suspected, along the lines of 'what else can you expect from an ignorant foreigner?' But the old man was smiling when he replied.

"He says he thinks you may be a jumpy person. But *t'ai chi* will help you to lose your tension. Generally. It will improve your blood circulation, and other things. Without medicine."

"Yes, *t'ai chi*," said Chinley, wondering if the reference to 'other things' meant that Jane had told her father about their trip to her uncle's drugstore in Beijing, to his brother's place according to Terry, and if so, how much of her uncle's diagnosis she had revealed.

"My father has taught *t'ai chi* for many years. And he's also a master swordsman, and a master of self-defence."

"Have you told him about Terry? About Mr Fox?"

"No. But I will. Of course, not all his activities are military."

Chinley blinked away his irritation at the words 'of course'. "So he has plenty of hobbies, your father?"

"Yes. He plays the *erhu*, for example."

"The what?"

"A Chinese fiddle. Yes, many hobbies. He says if you're interested he can teach you."

"Teach me what?"

"*T'ai chi*. For example."

"Hmm..." mumbled Chinley. He thought again of the early morning shadow-boxing amongst the willow trees on the river bank in Beijing; and the man shouting out Chinese numbers as he stood on one leg. He could not imagine himself at ease in such company. But if he could do it all privately, and if it really was beneficial for the blood circulation, as it should be, it might be worth considering. "Please tell your father," he continued, "that we could come to some agreement. Some arrangement."

Whatever interpretation Jane put on this Chinley had no way of telling, but after she passed on the message Li Yang's eyes brightened, and some of the wrinkles disappeared from under his eyes. But before the two men could negotiate further, they were distracted by female shouts from the doorway, and the scratching of two pairs of high heels on the stone threshold.

"Here she comes," said Jane. "My little sister."

Chapter Six

Silvia Li was thinner and slightly taller than her two sisters, with less of the complexion of a country girl, and a colder brightness in her eyes. The sort of youngster, Chinley felt, who might be chosen as a trainee manageress by the woman who ran the massage and acupuncture clinic at the Mirage hotel in Beijing. Though Wang's wife had already suggested that Silvia was not inclined to work in any hotel. Alison stood behind her, like a servant.

There was a solemn sulky look on Silvia's face, and her perfect skin was as taut as a mask. She wore an immaculate high-necked white pullover, over a rust-coloured maxi-skirt, and her thick glossy hair was pulled back tightly through a steel clasp, forming a long ponytail. Chinley was reminded of somebody from the past, somewhere in England, but he could not recall the name. He took her hand. It was cool and limp, and the contact was brief, not a Chinese handshake at all. Her cheeks glowed pale pink. Her fingernails were the same deep red as Jane's, and matched them in length. She was less loose-limbed than her sisters, standing as straight and still as a statue, and Chinley noticed that she seemed unable to move her head without also moving her shoulders in the same direction, as though she was suffering from a stiff neck.

Samantha. The name which Chinley had been searching for came back to him. More than thirty years ago, in the streets of his Birmingham suburb, Samantha was referred to as 'the girl with the legs and the Chinese mother'. She made an impression on him at a Chinese theme party, as the only person there with any claim to authenticity.

"She looks like a scholar, doesn't she?" said Alison. "Nobody believes that's our younger sister."

"I knocked on your door at the guest house," said Silvia, with the shallowest of bows. "So I met your daughter. She's quite friendly. But is she all right? Not ill in some way?"

From her sharp and matter-of-fact tone of voice Chinley sensed that she was no more concerned for his daughter's health than a rent-collector would be.

"Exhausted after a long journey," he said. "As you'd expect."

And hung-over probably too, he thought. Apart from the rum which she took to the bathroom, Lisa had also been drawn towards the bottle of 'fine old Chinese brandy' in the study, claiming that it would help her to wind down. The rum was not quite finished yet but this morning it was still on the floor by the bath-tub.

"I'm sorry if your time was wasted, Silvia," added Chinley. "I went through the woods."

"Through the woods? In that case I think *your* time was wasted. *My* time was well spent actually. I met your friend as I was leaving."

"My friend?" said Chinley. "Mr Fox downstairs?"

"No. I don't know about him. I mean the man up above you. The American professor, I forget his name. He said that any friend of yours was a friend of his."

"Did he?" said Chinley, indignation bubbling in his throat. "Well as far as I'm aware the opposite is the case. *No* friend of mine is a friend of his." He again found himself the focus of a ring of eyes. "Not yet," he added, more gently.

"Mr Chinley's taking up *t'ai chi*," said Jane. She addressed Silvia, as though she was seeking her younger sister's approval. "Father's going to teach him."

"He's very skilful our father." said Alison. "And maybe he needs a man in the house now and again. He treats us all a bit like sons, but all we can do is calligraphy. Except Silvia. She can do more. Or she could. She was just like a boy once. Before she grew up she could handle a sword as well as any boy. But now as you see she's a woman, so that's that. And the sword was packed off to her grandfather's."

"Ah, *that* sword. That's hers then, is it?" said Chinley.

"Yes. But she still helps our father, with his performances."

"Performances?"

"He gets bookings now and again, in clubs and things. And she's not afraid, she's never been afraid. It's all a matter of trust. And it's good money."

"That's enough, Alison," said Silvia. She snapped her fingers and shouted for service. The curly-haired waitress screeched an acknowledgement across the room, and all three sisters screeched back at her. Alison straddled a stool and thumped a dislodged table-leg back into position. Silvia sat next to her father on the bench, adjusted her maxi-skirt, and patted down the creases in her polo-neck sweater.

***

Jeffrey Ward was pacing up and down outside the guest house porch, scrunching the gravel on the driveway, when Chinley arrived home from his evening with the Li family. Chinley nodded a greeting, and Ward said: "Where's the doormat?"

"What?" said Chinley, bristling at the man's headmasterly tone.

"The doormat has disappeared. Again."

"Really? The doormat."

"Yes. Typical."

"I wasn't aware there was one," said Chinley, struggling to be breezy. As he made his way indoors he noticed that the American was glaring at him again, in the same way he had glared at him on the stairs, over a raised beard; as though Chinley were either questioning his sanity or calling him a liar. No, he was not prepared to be drawn into an argument about doormats. He swallowed, to ease the tightening in his throat, and said: "Well, Jeff is it? I'll let you know if I see one on my travels. Maybe it's a flying carpet."

He turned and walked away, and was halfway up to his apartment when he heard a voice behind him, the voice of an offended academic, bellowing up the stairs: "Just a moment! The name is Jeffrey. Not Jeff." Chinley raised an arm, but did not bother to turn his head.

Lisa heard her father fumbling with his key in the lock, and she opened the door for him. She had a towel wrapped like a turban around her hair. He walked past her, threw his arms in the air, and said: "The man's bonkers. Off his trolley. *Doormats?* Jeff, Jeffrey, What the hell? I thought Americans prefer their names to be shortened."

Seeing his daughter shake her hair free, other considerations now took over, and the re-surfacing memory of her lice infestation once more brought an itchiness to his own scalp, and with it a sensation that minute organisms were nibbling away at his follicles. He had no idea what a louse looked like, nor did he know how it followed its parasitical pursuits; so on his internal retina his brain blew up a highly magnified image of a spindly black creature, with thorny tentacles and a disproportionately wide mouth, opening on to layered rows of needle-teeth. Or, he wondered, was his brain dealing with a Dorothy-Betty-Gladys monster? He propped himself up by resting the crutch on his stomach, he raised his fingers to scalp-level and wiggled them in exasperation as he resisted the urge to scratch; then he sat down in his Foreign Expert's armchair, lowered his head, and let out a long sigh. He looked out of the window and, to the evening return of sparrows on the sycamore branches, he said:

"I should have just gone for a long limp off on my own somewhere. A long limp up and down the rice paddies."

Then he became aware of a smell with which he had recently become familiar, and he panned the air with his nostrils, sniffing.

"I see you've been at the *baijiu* bottle, as well as the brandy and the rum," he said.

"*Baijiu*? What's that?" said Lisa.

"That Chinese spirit stuff."

She grinned.

"Be warned," continued her father. "It's powerful."

"That's what I was hoping," she said.

"Good God," said Chinley. "I don't know where you get it from. Why are you such a dipso? I thought daughters were supposed to take after their mothers in things like that. Your mother hardly touches a drop. In fact, she goes too far the other way."

"She's been drinking a lot more since you left home. A hell of a lot more, in fact."

"So you *have* been calling home, then. That's not like you."

"No. Uncle Joe's. Reverse charges. His idea. A sort of going away present. It's no use talking to mum herself, she'd just say everything was fine. You know that. *He* told me it wasn't."

Chinley caught himself giving his daughter a belligerent stare, mimicking the American, and he immediately softened his expression.

"At the speed Joe talks," he said, "it must have cost him a fortune. It's just as well telephones are not normally voice-activated, otherwise you'd never find out what he wants to tell you."

"He can afford it," said Lisa. "Anyway, what I meant was, I was hoping this Chinese spirit stuff would get rid of the lice. I've been washing my hair in it."

"Jesus. And are there signs of it working?"

"It was painful. My whole head has gone numb."

"Sounds promising," said Chinley.

"By the way," said Lisa, leaning back on a pillow which she had used to enhance the cushioning on one of the armchairs. "What were you chuntering about just now when you came in? Something about Jeff or Jeffrey being off his trolley. Who's Jeffrey?"

"Jeffrey is our neighbour, whom we are supposed to love. The man upstairs."

"What, that was him yelling just now?"

"He does not like people using the telephone, if he can hear them. How about that? He worries about missing doormats. *And*... and, he's desperate to be called Jeffrey, not Jeff. In other words, he's off his trolley. You only need to look at him to see he's unbalanced."

Chinley was reluctant to prolong his criticism of the man, as he was well aware of his daughter's tendency to spring to the defence of anyone attacked by either of her parents. But it was too late: the seeds for the counter-attack had already been sown.

"Where's he from?" said Lisa.

"America."

"Good. Makes a change. And is he a Professor, too? In the Chinese sense, I mean. Ascribed status, earned on the basis of being a foreigner over a certain age."

"Yes," said Chinley, aware of what was coming next. "But that's got nothing to do with it."

"So what do you expect?" interrupted Lisa. "Englishmen don't have the monopoly on eccentricity. And if he's American, he probably really *is* a professor. Not like the English, who can mostly only pretend to be professors when they're abroad. Like you."

"It's the Chinese, as you say," said Chinley. "They call me Professor. I don't... I've never..."

"Oh, come off it!" persisted Lisa. "You wish you really *were* a Professor, like this chap upstairs, don't you? Instead of being a pretend one. Admit it!"

"I admit nothing," said Chinley. He wrinkled his nose and said: "By the way. I suppose you realise you smell as if you've spent a week in your uncle's cowshed?"

"Well I did, didn't I? More than a week. And when it comes to offensive odours," said Lisa, "what's that you've got in the saucepan in the kitchen?

"That's for me."

"It looks like something from a witch doctor. What's it for?"

"It's for me. Never you mind."

"The American would say it's *you* that's peculiar."

Chinley said nothing, but shook his head at the sudden recollection that this was the man Belinda kept referring to as her 'very good friend'.

"Well, whether your neighbour is crazy or not," continued Lisa, "he had a charming visitor this afternoon. A beautiful young Chinese girl. Just a bit stiff-jointed, that's all. But otherwise quite beautiful, lovely satin skin. Lovely *face*."

"No he didn't," said Chinley.

"What do you mean, he didn't? I spoke to her myself. She was looking for a professor, so I sent her upstairs."

"She was looking for *me*. She's the daughter of the family I've just had dinner with."

Lisa fell silent. In desperation at the tingling in his scalp, Chinley now at last raked his fingers back and forth through his hair, whooping with relief as he did so; then he inspected a small solid ball which he extracted from the roots.

"Dry skin," said Lisa. "Nothing to worry about."

* * *

Two days later Chinley walked over to Mr Li's house for his first *t'ai chi* lesson. He asked Terry to go with him, so the Irishman could have a look at the weaponry, but when Terry discovered the main purpose behind Chinley's visit he declined the offer, saying that even watching aerobics left him short of breath. He preferred to relax with a bottle of rum and a few tunes on the harmonica. Gladys had a private word with Chinley, as he was leaving. She said it was the right decision for Terry not to go, because, knowing him, he would want to join in with whatever horseplay was going on, and any unusual exercise, as she put it, might be bad for his heart.

Mr Li's tricycle was parked inside the house, harnessed to a small wooden cart laden with various types of bean curd: hot, cold, soft, hard, plain, spicy, smoked. After standing for a while in concrete corridors of sour and rancid air, Chinley was relieved to be taken outdoors for his lesson, into a yard cluttered with heavy old allotment tools and bundles of bleached grey wooden chippings. None of the girls were at home, so he found it easier to concentrate on the instruction and demonstration of his teacher. Mr Li took him through a few basic steps: he felt a complete fool and was glad that, as far as he could tell, nobody was watching him. But Mr Li clearly took the whole thing very seriously, and whenever he positioned himself for a sequence of movements, the smile left his face and his eyes lost their focus. For minutes on end he was in a world of his own.

Watching his tutor with growing admiration, Chinley felt that it would perhaps be worthwhile making a spectacle of himself, just to achieve this condition of apparent oblivion to the rest of the human race. He could then at will, for example, forget his differences with his wife, strengthen his resolve to remain immune to the opposite sex, to the pert young faces in the audience at his lectures, to the wide inquisitive eyes of the female passengers floating by like ballerinas, as they perched side-saddle at the rear end of a bicycle. Even if the drugstore brew did have aphrodisiac side-effects, which he doubted, all would be under control. He looked at his teacher and saw mind in action over matter. The brew was for nothing more than to help keep the body fluids moving as they should, to clear the sinuses, clear the head, and tame the temper.

After an hour of swaying his hips, balancing on one leg, and waving his arms around, Chinley tried out some of the elementary Chinese which Terry had taught him, suggesting that they had a break and went off to see the noisy waitresses down the street, for a bottle of beer. Mr Li had some difficulty in following the drift, so Chinley resorted to sign language again, using what he hoped were international gestures for opening a bottle and drinking its contents. He pointed towards the row of shacks in the distance, where they had been together for dinner earlier that week. Then he linked arms with his teacher and started marching on the spot. Mr Li cackled with approval, put on his threadbare Mao jacket, angled his blue cotton cap, and waited for his pupil to lead the way. There is a lot to be said for the company of men, thought Chinley, as they walked in silence down the slope towards the makeshift restaurant.

* * *

"One of your lady friends called by while you were out," said Lisa, when her father arrived home. Several names occurred to him, but to demonstrate his indifference he walked straight past his daughter and into the kitchen, to make a cup of insect tea.

"She left a note for you, on your desk. She looks fun."

"Aha. Why did you leave the top off this thermos flask? The water's nearly cold."

"Well, aren't you going to read it? The note."

"Who did you say it was from?"

"I didn't. She said you would know her. She seemed the theatrical type to me. She was singing to herself when she left. Out loud. I mean, really loud."

"They all do that. All the Chinese. I put it down to the absence of private bathrooms. How's the lice?"

"You know, I believe that paint-stripper stuff has killed them off. A multi-purpose liquid. Gets rid of parasites, wounds, and melancholy. Removes stubborn stains. Covers up the whiff of more offensive odours. And if you're really desperate, you can drink it."

"I'm glad to see you still have good taste in some things," said Chinley, opening a copy of the *China Daily* newspaper. "You still draw the line somewhere, then. There's hope for you yet."

"You needn't pretend you're not interested in the note," said Lisa. "I think a woman like that would be good company for you, out here. And anyway, *I'd* like to see her again. There's something about her. She looks... actressy. And she's up front. She admitted you were an afterthought. She was actually here to see the man upstairs, but he wasn't in. So she knocked on our door instead."

Chinley stayed in his armchair, sipping his brew and delicately spitting away the floating carcass flakes. He looked at his watch and switched on a short-wave radio, for the hourly news bulletin. To a background noise of what sounded like fat sizzling in a frying-pan, he heard the words 'This is London', followed by a distorted musical jingle. The headlines were inaudible so he tried to locate the *Voice of America* instead, but found only another hissing noise, at a slightly different pitch. *Radio Moscow* was coming through loud and clear, but he found himself unable to concentrate on the content, as he was distracted by the English Midlands accent of the presenter.

"Listen to that, Lisa," he said. "Sounds like your uncle Joe."

Lisa walked over to the radio and switched it off.

"This is not entertainment," she said. "What you need is *company.*

Human contact. I'm sure mum would understand, if that's the problem. I'm not here as a spy. Go on, read your note. Should I read it for you?"

"I can entertain myself with a radio for hours," said Chinley. "Scanning through the short wave bands. A radio broadens your outlook on the world. You can't always get that from *company.* Listen."

He switched the radio back on, and keyed in numbers until he found a signal, which was free from atmospheric distortion.

'This is the *Voice of America,*' it said. 'From Washington. Signing off.'

"Very satisfying, I'm sure," said Lisa. "Have you been along to Building Ten yet?"

"Building Ten?"

"That's where the woman downstairs gives her dancing classes. I called in on the old couple while you were out, and she asked me if I was a dancer."

"Not your style though, is it?"

"Why not? I think she and the old man deserve our support, whatever they're planning. I'll do whatever she wants me to."

"*Your* support," said Chinley. "Don't drag *me* into it."

He sank deeper into the armchair and busied himself with his pipe, wondering if his daughter's concern for his well-being was as straightforward as it seemed to be. Or was she really on the watch for her mother? She is just like her mother in some ways, he thought. Neither of them can sit still. Neither of them can leave well alone. They have to go around organising people, changing things. But his daughter and *Gladys* joining forces? That would need watching. Lisa went to look out at the view from the window.

"Beautiful colours," she said. "Look at the leaves this time of day. Platinum, copper, gold, silver. You're very lucky, you know, to have these surroundings. It's like living in the middle of a wood."

"They call this the golden season," said Chinley, and Wang came to mind. It was probably his wife who had left the note. "In a good year," he added, "it can last until the end of December. So they say. The golden season."

Lisa had raised herself on tip-toe, to look at the sycamore trees, and she was chuckling.

"What's that?" said Chinley.

"Christ," said Lisa. "I'd say the man upstairs is not *completely* off his trolley."

"What?"

"At *his* age. Well, his golden season's getting a boost. Come and have a look at this. He's making what looks to me like the Chinese equivalent of a daisy chain. You seen the size of his boots? They make him look like a fork-lift truck."

Chinley remained immobile for a while, then he slowly eased himself out of the armchair, re-lit his pipe, and joined his daughter at the window-sill. Directly below them, sitting cross-legged on the lawn and chortling like a pair of country lovers, were Jeffrey Ward, and Silvia Li.

Chapter Seven

"Glad you were free," said Belinda, as Chinley opened his door to the quiet Chinese knock. "We can go by bicycle, if you like."

Her hair was now hanging loose again, but straighter and shorter, now framing her face sphinx-like to just below the chin. This shorn appearance made her eyes seem larger, and her mouth wider, and gave an added lift to the high cheekbones. She stood for a while in silence in the doorway, her tongue protruding slightly between neat faultless teeth. She was breathless, and glowing. Chinley invited her in, wondering how long it would be before his daughter came home.

"Yes," she continued. "I can smell that there's a woman about the house now." He took a quick sniff at the air, but could identify only a stale mixture of the Chinese spirit and the insect brew. Belinda looked at Lisa's scattered belongings in the sitting-room and said:

"Yes, a typical young woman. Chinese, English, whatever. They're all the same, aren't they? But you must tell her to be careful when she's out in the neighbourhood. Blonde girls cause many accidents here, in the streets. Everyone looks at them, and at nothing else, so it could be expensive for you. The compensation money, I mean. If somebody makes a claim on you."

She moved a tangled heap of clothes to clear a sitting place on an armchair. According to her note of the day before the plan was to visit the East Lake, which up until now Chinley knew only as a large light-blue blotch on his map of the outskirts of Wuhan. Now, over a cupful of hot water, she explained that there were for her too many people along most of the East Lake shoreline, but she knew a little-used jetty off the main causeway, which would provide them with a secluded spot. Chinley was half-lookng at the map, and half-eyeing his guest, when he heard a key turn in the lock of his front door, and Lisa came in. Belinda asked her if she would like to join them.

"Yes," said her father. "You must come with us."

"I'm about to collapse," said Lisa. "Cycling around a few blocks here, and up and down a few hills, is enough for me. Anyway, that would make three of us, and we only have two bicycles. But apart from that I don't want to cramp my father's style. As we say in England, two's company."

Belinda looked at Chinley.

"What Lisa means," he said, floundering, "is that two people can be company. Company enough."

"Of course," said Belinda. She nodded, and licked her teeth.

Lisa tapped her father's arm as he was about to leave the apartment. Belinda was already downstairs. "Don't worry," she whispered. "Chinese body language is not the same as ours. It's not how it looks. Trust your daughter's judgement for a change."

The first part of the journey around the shores of the East Lake was not an easy ride. Wheel-rutted mud-banks at the water's edge impeded the progress of those on bicycles as much as those on foot, so for a slow half an hour Chinley and Belinda were jolted and thrust up and down in their saddles, juddering to a halt every so often and dismounting to negotiate the craters and the mud stacks. Others on the move seemed unaware of anything around them, unless they spotted Chinley, in which case they gave him their full attention, occasionally shifting their gaze to the woman whom he was trailing. Pedestrians wandered wherever their whims took them, and back on the tarmac motorists forced a passage down the centre of the bumpy highway, fingers pressed on horns, sending the day-dreaming strollers scattering in all directions at the loud blare, like cattle in a field panicking at the scream of a low-flying jet. Belinda bounced ahead acrobatically, and waited for Chinley by a pothole-free stretch of road, beckoning him over to a row of old stone-built cottages.

They sat opposite each other with their knees pressed tightly together. There was no choice: the café was minute, the table was small, they were sealed in by the other customers, and by Chinese standards Chinley's legs were anyway excessively long. A man very like Mr Li was collecting the cash, and an elderly woman with a patient smile and caring watchful eyes hovered nearby to check that all was satisfactory.

"China's changing," said Belinda. She accepted the woman's acknowledgement, then turned back to Chinley. "Some years ago I couldn't have come in here with you like this, without having a lot of explaining to do. But you see this woman now? She approves of you."

He looked at the alert old lady, who clasped her hands in front of her and bowed her head when she caught his eye, as though condoning something. The warmth of her welcome unsettled him: he had the sensation that England was receding too quickly, as though he was viewing its blur through the wrong end of a telescope.

Re-energised, they wheeled their bicycles along a parched pastel-yellow pathway, between a line of silver birch trees with branches still full of crisp reddish-brown leaves which looked ready to fall at the slightest wind. But the air was still, and hazy. The lake was murky though placid, and in the middle distance it merged into a thickening mist, through which the blue-grey smudge of land formed a vague horizon. They reached the causeway, which veered off apparently aimlessly into a flat low-lying cloud, out of which poked the broad bell-shaped summit of a well-forested hill.

"There it is," said Belinda. "Mo Shan. Our destination. But first there's a statue I want you to see."

He followed her on to the narrow pebbled pathway of a priveted rock-garden, in the middle of which, on an inscribed cream-coloured plinth, was the weather-beaten life-size marble figure of a man in traditional Chinese costume.

"Qu Yuan," said Belinda. "A poet and philosopher. He lived here sometimes, by the lake, hundreds of years ago. He drowned himself."

"Do we know why?" asked Chinley.

"He was disillusioned."

"What? Lovesick or something?"

"No no, nothing like that. Society. He was disillusioned with the State. So he drowned himself. In the water."

Chinley looked again at the unworldly but besmirched face, the beechnut-shaped head, the unobtrusive nose, the half-closed mournful eyes, and the wispy mandarin beard.

"They've made him look as though nothing could ever ruffle him," he said.

"That's the Chinese way," said Belinda. "Be like a mountain. Don't show your feelings. A public display is for the stage and the screen. We hope."

"Good God yes," said Chinley, moving closer to the statue, "a couple of weeks ago I saw somebody just like him. Older, shorter, fatter. But otherwise... Yes, remarkable."

"Where?"

"Out in the country, somewhere near the South Lake. He was just like a big wooden doll, all polished up. Two young girls with him were pulling him through a hedge, almost carrying him, as though they'd found him lying in a field out there."

"Perhaps they had."

"Yes. *What?*"

"This was out in the countryside, then?"

"Yes."

"Yes it would be. Did he have a walking stick?"

"Yes. But he didn't look like a farmer. More like a scholar, I suppose you'd call it."

"How does a farmer look?"

"Rougher. Like my brother. He's a farmer. Built like a carthorse. But this man's face was a young boy's face, just like on that statue. No wrinkles even. And it's the exposed bits that go first, isn't it? I bet his whole body was like that. Unblemished."

Belinda stood between Chinley and Qu Yuan's statue, and held out both her hands. They were chapped and calloused, and somewhat mis-shapen, with swollen knuckles.

"Not like me," she said. "That's what comes of having to grow up in the rice fields. Ten years I was out there. From when I was fifteen till when I was more than twenty-five. So I started to feel and look like a real peasant. If you were a healthy young woman then, you were given all the mucky jobs. It's almost as though you were being punished for not being a boy."

He took hold of the offered hands then looked up at her smooth forehead, and remembered the sheen on the flesh above her black evening dress, and the electric touch of the skin when he placed a hand on her shoulder while they were dancing together in Beijing.

"No, you're a very beautiful woman, Belinda," he said.

She laughed and shook her head, then pulled her hands away from his and looked towards the causeway. They cycled off again, and left behind the oarsmen calling for business from their canopied rowing-boats, passed the occasional modern couple strolling in fine clothes by the water's edge, and found themselves alone on the causeway. The road was gentler here and there was no sound except for the creaking of saddles, pedals, chains and brakes. In the silence and empty space Chinley felt as though he was ski-ing effortlessly across a snowfield. Belinda swerved off the causeway down a narrow trail, and he followed her.

No-one was in sight. A three-storey mansion with eaves tilting upwards like the toes of clogs lay ahead of them, the centrepiece of a tangled garden. The house seemed deserted: no lights, no people. Belinda walked her bicycle around the house to a lawn, which reached down to the water's edge. Then she sat down and began to unpack her rucksack. Chinley was thinking about the years she had spent in the fields and the muck, which must have been from about twenty-five years ago to fifteen years ago. That would mean she was now at least in her early forties, closer than he had at first imagined to her husband's age.

Wang suddenly became conspicuous by his absence. She could have a drink now if she wanted one. And no Mr Wu or Mr Hu. She must be relieved to shrug them all off. The power of the bicycle. She would go mad here surely, thought Chinley, without a bicycle.

He looked up at the dark windows of the mansion. There was still no sign that it was occupied. It occurred to him that this was the first time in nearly a month that he had been alone for so long with any woman apart from his daughter. The two bottles of Xin Jiang wine which he had brought along would be unpleasantly sweet, he knew, but they might at least serve the purpose of keeping him calm, and undisturbed by Belinda's habit of constantly caressing her teeth with the tip of her tongue. He poured out two generous measures of the beetroot-red liquid.

"Is one of those meant for me?" she said.

"Well, yes."

"I don't. I'm sorry. I can't."

"No?"

"No. I thought you knew. It's not allowed for me. And apart from that, my face goes blotchy, and I feel sick."

"I see," said Chinley. "Well, we don't want that."

Not *allowed*? Not allowed by whom, and why? Those doctors, he supposed. An allergy, no doubt. But surely, just a little... He felt at once like a concerned grandfather, a sugar daddy, and a nervous teenager unsure of what to do next. Dorothy would love to be proxy to this. "Yes, I remember now," he said. "In Beijing, you were drinking orange juice."

"And I wanted *you* to have a Silk Stocking. Remember?"

"Did you?"

In one gulp he emptied the contents of one of the glasses. Drinking both bottles in quick succession now seemed to him the appropriate move, so that if necessary he could lay the blame for any foolish act on the alcohol. He drank the wine from the second glass, then checked the mansion windows once more. No inquisitive face had appeared there. As his hand moved paternally towards Belinda's knee, he looked over her shoulder. Sitting in a rowing boat moored by the jetty - there was no way of knowing how long she had been there - was a denim-clad oarswoman, staring at them from below a peaked cap, her dull grey hair fringing her ears in stiff ringlets, like dirty meat hooks. Her face seemed coated with a grimy yellow dust. She called out and Belinda turned to look at her.

"Let's give the old lady some business," she said.

On the lake the mist thickened until Chinley could see nothing solid apart from the blue ridge of Mo Shan, rising from the far shore like a plume of smoke. The water, the mist, and the sky all mingled together now to resemble the pale parchment background of a Chinese scroll painting. Then his view was blocked completely by Belinda, who for some reason decided to stand, in the space between him and the oarswoman. He was startled to see that an archness had altered her features: her lips became hard and thin, and she was looking down her wrinkled nose at him with furious eyes.

"Are you all right?" he said.

She made no reply, but turned the upper half of her body slightly, showing him her profile, and keeping her neck and shoulders stiff, just like Silvia. She held this pose for a while, and he reached for some more wine straight from the bottle. She looked at him over her shoulder, stretched out an arm, and said:

"Go on then. Give me a sip."

He handed her the bottle, and suggested she sat down. She ignored him, and took several lengthy swigs of wine. She started humming the tune she sang the night she took him through the bamboo plantation, and she reinserted the cork. The jester's grin was back on her face now, but she once again stiffened her body, as if guarding herself against becoming too relaxed, standing erect, and holding her arms straight by her side as though at attention.

"Poor old Qu Yuan," she said. "When he walked into the water, no-one was there to save him. So we're told."

She was now gently rocking the boat and softly singing. The oarswoman cackled. Chinley looked at the uninviting waves: a smear of litter, dented beer cans and the soggy remains of western-brand cigarette packets floated by in a brown soup. She can't be mad enough to jump in, he thought.

"Are you worried by water?" she said.

"No. Have a seat?"

She remained on her feet, uncorked the bottle, and helped herself to a further generous draught of wine. The old woman stopped rowing, and as they were slowing to a standstill Belinda started dancing, pumping an even rhythm into the swaying timbers. Then she swivelled her hips, and grabbed an oar from its rowlock. The old woman cackled again and made no attempt to stop her. With the uncorked bottle in one hand, and the oar in the other, Belinda tried to steady herself, and dropped the bottle, which rolled down towards Chinley's end of the boat. He reached out to help her, and she whacked him hard across the arm with the wooden paddle. He looked up at her, his mouth wide open, and he saw that tears were trickling down her face. She sat down, and he left her alone, just watching her as she dipped and lifted the one oar abstractedly in and out of the water. The old woman was silent now. After turning in gradually increasing circles, with no landmark to assist his orientation, Chinley felt giddy, and deprived of several of his senses. He rubbed his arm and closed his eyes. When he opened them again, in response to a sudden surge through the waves, he saw that the old woman was once more striking out, with both oars now in her grip. Belinda sat with her chin resting on her knees, and they were making some headway towards land. Back at the jetty Chinley stumbled over the boards to pay the oarswoman the agreed amount of money, and finding his face close to hers he fancied he saw an anxious expression in her eyes. It was like catching a fortune-teller off-guard, revealing something, which she would prefer him not to know.

He and Belinda hindered rather than helped each other as they climbed back on to the tiled edging of the mansion lawn, and they packed the remains of their picnic away in silence. But now, as he cycled along the causeway, the reeling sensation in his head began to clear, as recognisable objects came into view. Ahead he could see a gleaming hump-backed marble bridge. Reflected in the water of the lake, it seemed to him, in his present condition, like a huge set of dentures, and he laughed out loud. Belinda looked back at him and wobbled on. He laughed again, to himself this time. He could hear the chipping noise of chisels from a gang working on fresh white marble slabs by the roadside; but as he passed by, for once not one of them turned to stare. At the far end of the causeway they dismounted and pushed their bicycles up the lower slopes of Mo Shan, through tiers of blue-green pine trees, and onwards between banks of red earth, which crumbled like sawdust at their feet. A winding flight of warped and worn stone steps took them up into the clouds and eventually to the Mo Shan summit, where they found a deserted pavilion. Belinda invited Chinley to join her, near the pavilion, on a flat-topped moss-covered boulder.

At this height there was a chilly buffeting wind, and it was beginning to drizzle. Chinley indicated the shelter close at hand, but Belinda shook her head and patted the moss. He sat down beside her on the slippery green surface, and felt a dampness rising and spreading in the seat of his trousers. He thought it wiser not to mention the discomfort.

"That was a welcome change," he said.

"What was?"

"Those men down there chipping away at the bridge. That's the first time all day we've not been stared at."

"That's because they're prisoners," said Belinda. "They didn't look at *us* because they don't want us to look at *them*. They've been humiliated, and nothing worse can happen to a Chinese than humiliation. Do you know that?"

"Sort of."

She edged closer, and said: "You don't look too comfortable there, you keep shifting your bottom. You must be overheated, after all the exercise. Should I loosen your robes?"

"My *robes*?"

"Sitting like that you look just like the Buddha you gave my husband. Remember?" She unbuttoned his jacket, and slipped a hand inside, resting it against his chest. He had deserved the smack on the arm, he decided. There were reasons, obviously, why it was better for her not to drink. She massaged his stomach and said: "Do you know that in China we say that a fat man need fear nothing?"

"No."

"Jeffrey Ward's fat. Fatter than you."

"Maybe it's muscle."

"No. it's fat. Believe me."

"You know him quite well then?"

"Yes. I told you, he's a good friend. He said he's going to help me."

"Help you what?"

"It's easier for him. Maybe."

"What is? Easier than for who?"

But she closed her eyes to the world, hiccupped, and rested her head on the lapel of Chinley's jacket.

Chapter Eight

On the landing opposite the entrance to Chinley's apartment was a large bay window fitted with the thin green protective gauze of a mosquito screen. Below was a well-mown treeless lawn, where several experienced *t'ai chi* practitioners, all men, had assembled to go through their late afternoon routine communally. Although the window was open not a sound could be heard: not a voice, not a clearing of the throat, not a footfall; and the intervening shade of the mosquito screen made the men on the lawn look like a ghostly dancing troupe from another world. But their movements were fluid and controlled, and Chinley wondered how long it would be before he had the nerve or the skill to join them out there. He felt his own body relax in sympathy with the experts, but his concentration was disturbed by the heavy thud of boots coming up the stairs. Jeffrey Ward stopped at the landing, and looked over Chinley's shoulder at the scene below.

"Buncha fairies," he said, and tramped on up to his room on the higher floor.

But Chinley could see what he meant: one of the men, wearing what looked like an astronaut suit of shining jasmine-yellow silk, was waving his hands loosely in the air as though conducting a slow movement played by an invisible and inaudible orchestra; another one, standing with his legs wide apart, appeared to be blowing kisses to no-one in particular. Chinley had by now mastered a dozen or so basic moves, and he imagined that he was beginning to feel the benefit. His body was changing for the better, he decided: the stomach was not so spongy, neglected muscles were once more making their presence felt. The trip to the East Lake with Belinda had further loosened his limbs, and on his return, after a tepid shower and a change into the light canvas footwear recommended by Mr Li he had sensed his body fluids pulsing in his veins, cruising along as they should.

Lisa was down in the Fox's apartment, and Chinley called by to collect her and Terry and Gladys to cycle over to Li Yang's house for the evening, as Jane and Alison were returning to Beijing tomorrow. They left through the south exit of the Dong Hu campus and free-wheeled down towards Pagoda Hill. Chinley glanced at the bleak old tower, then across to the other side of the road, where Wang and Belinda lived. He looked along the full length of the residential block, wondering which windows were theirs. As he swerved around a curve, down the slope leading to the South Lake, he almost collided with Mr Wu and Mr Hu, who were standing in the gutter smoking a cigarette. They grinned, nodded, and waved, exactly as they had done earlier that afternoon at the campus security porch, when they saw Chinley and Belinda returning from their day out together.

Jane and Alison were low-spirited at the prospect of leaving their father and sister yet again and going back to work; Silvia seemed preoccupied and had little to say. After a brief interval in the company of her father's guests she excused herself, explaining that she had something important to get on with, and she went off to the room which had become exclusively hers since her sisters' move to the capital.

Mr Li was now in the habit of talking quite rapidly to Chinley in Chinese, either unaware or not caring that his *t'ai chi* pupil understood little of what he said. But Chinley was becoming used to listening to him and by watching the expression on his face he could usually guess at the general drift. Soon after Silvia left them to be alone, Li Yang jerked his head in the direction of her room and spoke with what seemed to Chinley a combination of admiration and alarm. Chinley looked at Jane and Alison, and raised his eyebrows.

"Father says that she's certainly brainy," said Alison. "But she's brought too many books home. Foreign books. With maps and pictures and things. But we can't afford to send her to college, if that's what she's got in mind."

"Did you ask her?" said Chinley.

"Yes," said Alison. "And she says, quite fairly, that all she wants to do is keep her options open."

Li Yang stood up, unscrewed a bottle, and filled eight egg-cup size glasses with clear spirit. Chinley looked at the label and recognised it as the same brand of *baijiu* which Lisa had used to get rid of her lice. The aroma was unmistakable. But he took a glass and without waiting to toast anyone he drank the liquid in one gulp, to Li Yang's obvious satisfaction. Jane took one in to Silvia, and returned immediately with it empty.

"Varnishing her fingernails," she said.

Lisa glanced at her father. He was grinning, and she warned him with a stare not to say anything.

Li Yang clamped his hoary fingers on Terry's elbow and led him over to a corner table where he had laid out an assortment of blunt and dusty swords and daggers, and one or two mis-shapen long-barrelled shotguns. Terry picked up a sword and ran a knuckle along its pitted blade.

"Could do with a bit of *sharpening*," said Gladys, and the men ignored her. Terry's eyes were bright with approval, but Li Yang shook his head and mumbled incoherently.

"My father's embarrassed by the poor condition of his collection," said Jane. "He's sorry you can't see the one our grandfather's keeping for Silvia. Or rather, nowadays, for her *son*. It's in far better condition. You can still see the carving."

"Is it for sale?" said Terry, in Chinese. "The one in Sichuan?"

Li Yang nodded at the wall behind which Silvia was busy with her fingernails, and said: "It's up to her."

"*Silvia's* got a *son?*" yelled Gladys.

"No of course not," said Jane. "Not yet. She's not married."

"How old is your grandfather?" continued Gladys.

"Ninety something."

Chinley looked at Jane. *Ninety?* This was the man she had once compared him to. Unless... Failing to catch her eye, he said: "And do you have another grandfather, Jane? On your mother's side?"

"What?" she said. "No. He's gone."

"Your father must be getting on himself then," said Gladys. "But he seems quite fit to me. Apart from his limp."

"He's seventy-one," said Jane. "But he does *t'ai chi* every day, and exercises with the sword. He has his performances too, in the clubs, with Silvia. That's the only time she picks up a sword herself these days. And he goes dancing with her sometimes, though she's not so keen on that any more either. So you see, he's active enough. He rides his tricycle round the village, pulling the bean curd, and now and again he's chosen to play along with our local Beijing Opera group."

"Play what?" asked Terry.

"A Chinese fiddle, would you believe?" said Chinley.

"The *erhu*," said Alison. "That one on the wall."

She pointed to a small stringed instrument, which looked to Chinley like another weapon, an archer's tackle: a cross-bow, which had somehow become entangled with its own arrow sheath. Mr Li took the instrument off its hook on the wall. Then with Alison standing motionless at his side he positioned himself on a straight-backed chair, ready to play. The result was somewhat scratchy to Chinley's ears but in a way heart-rending. He was startled to see the old man's eyes become moist. At one point Li Yang faltered, stared at the wall between himself and Silvia. He started playing again, accelerating the tempo. Then to Chinley's dismay, Alison joined in with a high-pitched wailing screech. He turned to his daughter and whispered: "She sounds like a goose being strangled."

"She's *supposed* to sound like that," said Lisa. "In *pain*. She's acting the part of an old woman who *is* in pain."

"Very convincing," said Chinley, leaning back in his chair. He caught Terry's eye. The Irishman winked at him then concentrated on tapping his foot to the rhythm, on Mr Li's bare and grimy concrete floor. Gladys folded her arms to support her large bosom, and her head lolled forward as though she was being sent to sleep by the persistent moaning of a patient she was visiting in hospital.

The song lasted for half an hour. When it was over Alison walked over to Chinley, took his hand, and said: "Now it's your turn."

"That's impossible," he said. "My daughter will tell you. I have no voice."

"My father has no voice," said Lisa.

"No," explained Alison. "*My* father wants his pupil to demonstrate what he has learnt from his lessons."

At least this is better than being forced to sing, thought Chinley, as he took up a conventional stance opposite his teacher: legs apart, knees bent, feet flush to the concrete. He went smoothly through the sequence of movements which he had now mastered. Even Lisa was impressed. Then under instruction from his teacher he took on the role of the assailant, so that Mr Li could demonstrate how the same techniques could be used in self-defence. He always felt humbled at this point, even when no-one was watching, because despite his height and weight, or perhaps as a consequence of it, the old Chinese teacher, twenty years his senior, was adept enough to effortlessly send him staggering off balance no matter how he varied his attack. And with his sparring partner being cheered relentlessly on by the women, Chinley felt even more ridiculous.

"It's a sensible occupation for middle-aged men," said Jane. "It keeps you from stiffening up too much."

"Quite the opposite," said Chinley. "Especially in combination with your uncle's brew. Middle-aged men or not."

He felt a smirk take control of his lips, as several puzzled female faces turned towards him. Only Terry had a glint in his eye. Lisa looked as though she could not believe that her father had meant to say what he had just said.

When it was time for everyone to leave Silvia reappeared, and kept her distance, like a tired waitress willing the customers to go home. Chinley attempted to catch her eye, but failed.

Outside in the dark lane he unlocked his bicycle. As he was adjusting his trouser-clips Jane ran towards him, laid a hand on his arm, and whispered: "I hope that you and your daughter will become good friends with Silvia. Can you help her?"

* * *

"Adultery," said Mr Wang. He stopped on his way towards the library exit and rested his chin between his thumb and forefinger, as though deep in thought. Chinley gave him a sideways glance, and affected a smile. "Adultery," he continued, "is like truancy. Like having a day off school without permission."

He waited for a response.

"If you say so," said Chinley. "Yes, I see what you mean. Or like... jabbing your fork into somebody else's bowl of rice. Or should I say, your chopsticks." He was not at all sure whether Wang intended this as a subject for genuine analysis, or as an oblique accusation. Or a caution. He remembered that both Mr Wu and Mr Hu had seen him and Belinda returning home from their East Lake trip together, and he wondered if the two Party Secretaries were drawing their own conclusions. True, while his body heat was helping to warm Belinda's hands, thoughts about how he and she could make use of their flat-topped boulder had inevitably run through his mind, but that would be true for most men, wouldn't it? Anyway, the ensuing erotic scenes developed only in his imagination, harmlessly. Still, it seemed as though

Wang might need some reassurance, so he added: "But of course personally, I wouldn't know."

He was now looking for his own reassurance: the sight of Wang's chaotic teeth on cheerful display, but Wang kept his mouth tightly closed: an effort, which made him look profoundly miserable.

"Robinson," said Wang, solemnly. "Peter Robinson."

"Robinson?"

"Yes. An American I think. This idea about truancy and adultery, it's the opening line in one of his books. I happened across it just now while I was waiting for you in the library."

"Aha," said Chinley, still wary. He was here at the library because a message had come to him via Gladys that Wang wanted to see him there, urgently, in the entrance hall. But as he was now well aware, the timing of explanations in China rarely coincided with the timing back home, so he just stood shoulder-to-shoulder with Belinda's husband and stared at the shingle at the foot of the library steps.

"Of course, there's much more of that sort of thing in the West, isn't there?" asked Wang.

"What sort of thing?"

"You know. Adultery and stuff."

"So they say," said Chinley.

"And do the English behave the same way as the Americans? In this respect?"

"I think it's impossible for me to say," said Chinley, feeling as though he was being manouevred into admitting some sort of guilt, and suspecting that this was Wang's way of indicating his mistrust of at least two of the Professors in the guest house. He must surely know there was some sort of connection between his wife and Ward.

"Our Chinese women," continued Wang. "I would say, generally, they have a high moral standard. Most of them. But of course there are the exceptions. These days more than ever."

"Yes," said Chinley, wondering if Wang was now going to tell him where he could find the exceptions, even if only to keep him away from his wife, if that was where his suspicions lay. But he didn't.

"I heard a song on the television last night," Wang continued. "The message was how wonderful life is in Hong Kong, now that it's part of China again. This young girl, she must still be in her teens, was singing about what to her was the excitement of all-night movies, fast food bars and discos, all those new shops and things. That's the young people here now. They want to be westernised. They want to be *corrupted*."

"They've got a long way to go," said Chinley.

"You mean you're in favour of it? In favour of corruption?"

"I didn't say that," said Chinley, conscious that he might be jeopardising his job, or at least the trust placed in him as a Professor, if he confessed to having mixed feelings about corruption, at least that sort of corruption. Tricky devil this Wang, he thought: a match for Dorothy, even.

Dorothy. It was odd, saying her name to himself like this. It made her sound like someone he didn't know. The two men were now at the foot of the library steps, and walking in silence towards a clearing in the woods. Wang stopped suddenly, turned to face Chinley, and said: "Tell me. Why does a wife burst into tears every night?"

"I... does she?"

"Yes. She's done it before many times, but never so much as this last week or so. I know she's... not right in some ways. But I've never seen her as bad as this, even though she's off the booze now. I hope they don't have to *look* at her again. And I hope I don't have to throw her out of the house."

Careful, Chinley told himself. Don't say a word. Different people. Different ways. Both men fixed their eyes on the sand at their feet, and eventually Wang said: "By the way, I wanted to meet you, to give you an invitation."

"Urgently, so I heard."

"Urgently? Is that what you heard? Never mind. It's just that Mr Deng is coming down from Beijing in a few days. We must all be ready for him. He reports back to the State Education Commission, you know."

"Yes. I can imagine."

"With Hilda."

"Hilda? Oh yes, you mean the other one?"

"Yes. So we would like to invite you to be the guest house leader. Spokesman if you like. To represent the Foreign Experts including, of course, your daughter. To keep everything in order. Everything *harmonious*. And tell them all not to worry if they see any unusual activity in the coming days. We have to be prepared, on our best behaviour. Please be patient until he has gone away, and please explain to your friends at the guest house that the disturbance will be temporary. We have chosen you to pass the message on, Professor Chinley, because, well, Mr Fox is the senior resident I know, but he is perhaps a little *too* senior. On the other hand, your daughter is too junior. Mrs Fox has a strange accent, don't you think? And Professor Ward... well, you seem to be more approachable than he is. More co-operative."

"That's the invitation?" said Chinley, impressed by Wang's ability to stretch the meaning of the word.

Why couldn't he call it a request? Perhaps because that would leave him with a debt to pay. Whereas this way round, by some perverse protocol, the debt would be Chinley's. Tricky buggers all of them so far, definitely.

"Can I get this right?" Chinley continued. "You are inviting me to warn the people at the guest house that Mr Deng is coming?" He wished matters were a little different with Belinda, so he could say: "Leave Mr Deng to your wife. She's the only one here who can soften his centre, I've seen her in action with him, in Beijing."

"Yes. Do you accept?"

"Well, all right. Thank you for thinking of me."

"That's okay. Mr Deng has long fingers, you see. He can help us all, if he feels like it. My age group, we fear inspection. We were not inspected for many years, not at school or college, anyway. My family was an intellectual family, and we suffered greatly during the Agricultural Revolution."

"The Agricultural Revolution?"

"Yes, why not? We had nothing to learn. No real schools, no tests. We're not used to college inspections. College inspections were abolished then, and restored only in the late nineteen seventies, after eleven years of suspense."

As the two men began to retrace their steps back towards the library and the bicycle-shed, Chinley laughed out loud and kicked at a pile of dry leaves. With a surge of affection he put his long bony arm around Wang's shoulders, and saw the reassuring upper teeth appear, large and stained, but gleaming, like grimy stalactites.

* * *

"What are we going to do about the fungus on your father's neck?"

Lisa was talking to Silvia, who had called in on her every day since her sisters' departure for Beijing. They were in the sitting room of Chinley's apartment, and when he heard his daughter's query he took his pipe out of his mouth and looked at her over the rim of his reading spectacles. But it was clear that on this occasion she was serious. She was waiting for an answer, with a concerned look in her eye, and a straight face.

"It recurs," said Silvia. Her chronic stiffness was to Chinley robotic. Whenever she spoke she moved only her lips, and even those almost imperceptibly. There was no back-up message from the eyes; no flick of the pony-tail. Lisa had told her she should loosen up a bit and learn to enjoy her body, as she put it. She had persuaded her to join in the Tuesday night fling, with Gladys and Terry at Building Ten, but Gladys had not helped by being un-Chinese and very obviously losing patience, eventually, and maliciously, according to Lisa, asking Silvia to act as a maypole around which everyone else could try out a new dance.

But there were signs of a growing bond between the two young women. And after Jane's appeal to him in the lane outside her father's house Chinley was content to see Silvia becoming one of the family, not just someone who brushed past him on the stairs on her way up to visit Jeffrey Ward. Lisa for her part had clearly spent enough time at Silvia's house to identify a skin infection on her father's neck.

"Is it from the bean curd?" she asked.

Her father looked up at her again, thinking that she had either developed a latent dramatic talent, or she really was taking Mr Li's fungal complaint to heart.

"We never thought of that," said Silvia.

"Is it seasonal?"

"Maybe. It's worse, I think, when the humidity's high."

"My father..."

"Yes?" said Chinley, wondering how his daughter could possibly involve him in either the diagnosis or the treatment.

"I was only going to say," continued Lisa, "that my father has some cream."

"Cream?" said Silvia, looking at Chinley's bookcase, but not at him.

"Yes," said Lisa. "For athlete's foot or something. He won't buy a sensible shoe, that's why. Why not give it a try?" She added, "We've got plenty of it."

Over the past few weeks Chinley had become increasingly aware of how little privacy there was in China. Whether in sickness or in health. No-one could hide their ailments or their joys, whether physical or mental, quite simply because no-one could hide, not even he and the other Foreign Experts cocooned in their guest house.

Here he was now, for example, under public scrutiny in his own home, one of his more intimate afflictions being discussed in front of him as though he was not there. And for all his attempts to catch Silvia's eye, he might as well really not have been there. But he kept his temper: he was, after all, aligning himself with his daughter's interest in the girl, as he was fond of both her sisters and her father. And another reason for shrugging off this exposure of his athlete's foot was that he knew from experience that any prolonged reference to it could well bring on a further attack. As a calming measure, he reminded himself that compared to his Chinese neighbours in their overpopulated high-rise blocks he had about as much privacy as he could hope for.

Not far from the guest house, for example, and certainly within earshot, a number of music enthusiasts had been herded together in the same building. Amongst them was a novice trumpet player, who despite unrelenting practice had not yet managed to complete an identifiable octave on his instrument. On the other hand, there was a pianist who played nothing but identifiable octaves, up and down the scale, very loudly, over and over again. The owner of a Chinese fiddle was constantly scratching out a rhythmic but to Chinley's ears jarring accompaniment to a woman's uninhibited bursts from what Lisa informed him were local operatic airs: although he considered the outcome to be not so much an air, but more of a tormented miauling.

Yet Chinley had never heard anyone complaining. Everyone's performance was inevitably a public performance. There was no room for shyness, so it was quite common to hear the Chinese singing loudly to themselves, just like Belinda did, even in a crowded street. With a surge of undirected anger, he remembered that he had not seen Belinda nor heard her voice in the stairwell for two weeks now. She had not even called by as an afterthought.

"Can Silvia take a tube of your cream home then?" asked Lisa.

"*What?* A whole tube? Yes, of course she can. Just make sure they understand the instructions. Make sure they know it's for external use only. We don't want her father stirring it in his tea."

Lisa went off to the bathroom, leaving Chinley and Silvia alone together, a few yards apart, her eyes averted from his. He hoped the ensuing silence would at last become awkward enough to trigger a response from her. Yes, it would be unfortunate if her father's fungus was not contained, and spread on to *her* skin. The immaculate complexion. It was a special radiance, an oriental glow, not a western blush, but he doubted that she was capable of a real blush. He found himself wondering if she was still a virgin. Not a word passed between them for half a minute or so, then she stood up, walked over to the bookshelves, and pulled out a bound collection of photographs of ancient Celtic burial sites: a fair indication to Chinley that she was for some reason ill-at-ease in his presence.

"What's your Chinese name again?" he asked.

"Zhao Di."

"Zhao Di. Does it have a meaning?"

"Yes, of course it has a meaning. It's my name."

Silence again.

"So what does it mean, then?" said Chinley.

"It means 'give a boy', or 'bring a boy'."

"Bring a boy? Bring a *boy?*"

"Yes."

"How odd. But... *why?*"

"Why what?"

"Why did they call you that?"

"Because I was girl number three. It's obvious. My parents wanted a boy. But they never got one."

"So they were hoping you'd bring them a grandson? Whenever."

"That's right. Whenever." A deeper yellow flush came to her cheeks, a flush of anger maybe. "It's ridiculous. My grandfather even keeping the old sword ready to hand over when I deliver the goods. We might as well sell it. Mr Fox wants it, doesn't he? There will *be* no grandson. Not through me. Not in my plans. I don't want *any* children, and I don't want to get married."

"Very wise," said Chinley, automatically, as Lisa walked into the room with two large tubes of the fungal cream. But she was in no mood for banter with her father, and she sat down to study the application procedure for the liniment. Silvia seemed to regain her composure now that Lisa was back in the room.

"And anyway," she continued, lowering her voice. "How can I meet a perfect boy in the back streets where *I* live? All the boys I meet round here are common. Country bums. They have no... special abilities. I want to meet somebody with an education. A businessman. But I'm the one left at home to look after my father. Like this." She pointed at the tubes of cream.

Chinley considered telling her that he could introduce her to a large number of businessmen who had no special abilities, as she put it, and, on the other hand, a large number of country bums who did. Like his brother Joe. But both girls were now ignoring him, so he pushed an armchair over to a corner of the sitting room which still caught the sun, and he hid himself from their view.

He loosened the shreds of a new wedge of tobacco and filled his pipe bowl. He sat quietly, admiring the dry golden leaves of the sycamore trees, which scraped now and again on the sitting-room windows in the breeze. He thought about Silvia's home, a kind of damp, dark and dirty cell, and he thought about the apartment, which he now occupied, a relative palace. He guessed that Belinda's rooms would be as stark as the Li's, and wondered if that was why he had not been invited over there yet.

He reached for a bottle of ginseng wine, one of Lisa's finds, and poured himself a generous measure. He put his feet up, and went through some *t'ai chi* motions in his head, throwing his teacher and other random assailants around like rag dolls. Then he picked at the remaining crumbs of the cheese which Jane and Alison had brought him from Beijing. They certainly knew how to please a Westerner. For the next couple of weeks he would also be able to enjoy the coffee which had arrived in the post that morning, freshly ground and sent out from England, by his wife. But addressed to his daughter.

Someone was thumping at the front door. Chinley rose from his armchair, his face livid. He opened the door with a quick jerk, but no-one was there. He stared for a while at the scuffed dark red carpet on the steps leading to the upper landing, then he turned to see Silvia checking her watch and folding her raincoat over her arm.

"That was for me, I suppose," she said, stuffing the tubes into a pocket. "Thanks for the cream."

Lisa joined her father in the doorway, and they both watched her climb up to Ward's room on the upper floor, in her new brown maxi-skirt, wobbling on the stiletto-heel shoes, which her sisters had brought her from the capital city.

Chapter Nine

"Tidy up?" said Chinley. "What, you mean pick up the litter?"

Answering his apartment door this time to a gentler knock, Chinley found Mr Feng standing there, ready to congratulate him on his new position as guest house representative. He had come with some information to pass on, regarding the preparation for Mr Deng's arrival.

"That's one thing," said Feng. "Then there's the leaves to clear away, the mosquito screen to repair, and the windows and the paintwork to wash. And yes, only certain types of clothing will be allowed." Feng's gaze rested on the recumbent figure of Lisa, now stretched out luxuriantly on her back, with her eyes closed, on a large floor cushion in a corner of her father's sitting-room; her *Save the Dolphins* T-shirt awry, and her jeans patched and stained with ink after a calligraphy lesson from Silvia.

"Of course," continued Feng, his thin tenor voice soaring, "foreigners are an exception. To all this. You will just carry on as normal. More or less. Don't worry. Only the students and some of the staff will be bending over, to make us look presentable for the inspection. I mean, for the visit. We do not expect *you* to twist your knickers."

"Right," said Chinley. He heard a muffled noise coming from the floor cushion, into which Lisa now buried her head.

"But... there won't be any dances until the labour days are over," said Feng.

"What dances?" asked Chinley. "Building Ten?"

"Anywhere. It gives the impression of loose living."

"What about Mrs Fox's evening class? That's not really dancing at all, is it? Can't you call it Education?"

As her father said this Lisa, snorting with suppressed laughter, sat up and hugged herself. Feng turned to face her, and let out a high-pitched giggle. "Even Mrs Fox must be silenced," he added. Lisa covered her head with her folded arms.

"What about Mr Wang's wife?" said Chinley, in the hope that Feng would confirm his impression that for some reason Belinda received preferential treatment from the Beijing bureaucrat. "Are you going to stop her singing while she's walking around the campus? Or is she a special case?"

"No-one is a special case," said Feng, his button mouth contracting to its official diameter. "Except the foreigners. It's only a temporary measure. Of course, there's music from other sources. We will re-connect your tannoy speakers for example, out beyond the lawn."

Throughout the entire campus there was a public relay system which operated each day except Sunday from early morning until late afternoon, sending out messages and music. The earliest broadcast, however, was more of a military-style *reveille* call, exhorting the campus lower ranks to conform to a sequence of numbered exercises. But whenever Chinley happened to be in the *reveille* zone at an early hour, as far as he could tell no-one took the slightest notice of the broadcast instructions, and the targeted youngsters could only be seen slouching in cotton slippers or trainers to the dining-hall, clutching their enamel breakfast bowls. Feng now turned to the window and nodded at the trees.

"Your speakers will be re-connected later today," he said.

Lisa groaned. "What?" she said. "You mean we have to put up with all that military nonsense?"

"Yes."

"Can't you just leave things as they are?" said Chinley. "Out the back here at least?"

"No."

"Why were they disconnected in the first place?"

Feng pointed at the ceiling and lowered his voice. "Professor Ward," he said. "Some months ago he took a pair of step ladders out into the garden and snipped through all the wires with a pair of hedge-clippers. He surprised us with his access."

"At least we all have that to thank him for," said Chinley.

"But now that you are the guest house leader," continued Feng, "perhaps you can make sure that he doesn't do it again?"

"I think you're making a mistake," said Chinley. "We'll all get even rattier with each other if we're woken up too early in the morning. Ratty. You know ratty? *Angry*. There's no saying what we might do."

"Cover it up," said Feng. He sniffed the air. "Hmm. Galvanise yourself. Contain it. Sublimate. Be an example."

"I might just do the snipping myself," said Lisa. "Women are better prepared for such things than men. We have the tools."

Feng laughed hollowly, then standing up to leave he said: "You and your daughter, Professor. You have mosquito nets? Not screens. Nets over the bed, I mean. Some mosquitoes have been reported."

"Yes we do, Mr Feng. Lisa uses hers, I think. But I don't bother. I've only ever seen one mosquito since I've been here. Or should I say, I've only ever *heard* one. It comes out when it's dark. In the bedroom."

"How do you know there's only one?" said Feng.

"I don't. But I'm only ever aware of one. And I don't think it's worth covering myself with a net, and reducing my oxygen supply, just for him. Or her. It."

Feng held out his hands and began to grin.

"Actually," continued Chinley, deciding that Feng had stayed there long enough. "There's another reason why I don't use your mosquito net. When it's opened out, it always reminds me of a shroud. A white shroud. And there we have two symbols of death in one bedroom. One from the West, the shroud, and one from the East, the colour white. You are Chinese, Mr Feng. You should understand this. There's nothing shameful in being superstitious. *I'm* superstitious. Aren't *you?*"

Keeping an eye on the Englishman, Feng rounded his lips and moved his head slowly to one side, as though hoping for a clue to whether he should take all this seriously or not, but no clue was offered, so he began to make his exit, for some reason being careful not to turn his back as he inched his way out of the apartment.

"Steady on, Feng," Chinley muttered as the door closed. "I'm only a Professor. Not an Emperor."

But it was not a mosquito which woke Chinley and his daughter and all the other residents of the guest house, long before dawn on the following day. An explosion had inserted itself into Chinley's dreams, and he opened his eyes with relief that he was not really on the steam train, which was blown up as it crossed an antique wooden bridge in the mountains of Sichuan province. In reality the explosion was a loud and rapid spluttering from the engine of a large dumper truck parked in the middle of the lawn below the bedroom window.

The washing and the washing lines were gone. The entire expanse of grass and sycamore trees was now like a battlefield: an army of sweepers arrived with brooms, shovels and sacks, to clear the fallen leaves. The clean-up operation was on a war footing scale. Neither

Feng nor Wang had mentioned that the manoeuvres would begin long before sunrise, at four o'clock in the morning, and with such attack. Like factory workers on a night shift trying to make themselves heard in a production line clattering with machinery, the sweepers yelled at each other over the throbbing engine of their dumper truck for more than two hours. Then the dawn came, thinning their numbers and softening their din.

But now one voice rose above the muted chatter. The voice of Jeffrey Ward, yelling abuse down from his vantage point on the top floor. In the lull which followed Ward's outburst, Chinley heard the tell-tale crackling of the re-wired speakers coming to life, hidden deep within the beige autumn foliage, on the sycamore branches level with his window. Marching music filtered through, soft and slow at first, then increasing in speed and volume.

When he dismounted outside the Ecology Department building later that morning Chinley was still mentally preparing the talk which he was about to give. The night's disturbance prevented him from working on his speech while having breakfast, as planned, as he had overslept. Still only half-awake, he failed to notice that he had chained his bicycle not by the usual birch tree but to the wooden leg of a temporary sign, its announcement written in Chinese characters, with no translation provided. As he was walking towards the Department entrance he saw one of the Party Secretaries, Mr Hu, for once on his own, waving at him. He approached, bowed, and said something in Chinese, in his strong local dialect. Chinley forced a grin, looked at his watch, and tried to move on, but the Party Secretary was clearly agitated and was, it seemed, trying to tell him something about his bicycle. At this point Feng arrived, and placed a hand gently on Chinley's shoulder, ready to interpret.

"What's the matter with Hu?" said Chinley, sweating with irritation. "I'm late for my talk."

"It's your bicycle," said Feng. "The sign which you've locked it to says: 'if you do not put your bicycle in the proper place, the college wardens will let all the air out of your tyres'."

"*Jesus!* He stopped me to tell me *that*?"

"It's just for this week, Professor. For the visit." Feng was starting to whine.

"Fuck the visit!" said Chinley. "And fuck Mr Deng."

A group of grinning students had gathered, which angered him further. He caught sight of Mr Hu, also smiling now, and wondered whether it was this man and his colleague who had somehow prevented Belinda from visiting him again at the guest house. Spreading rumours, maligning both of them. He had not seen her since their trip to the East Lake. "Your Mr Wu and Mr Hu," he continued, "are just like two little gremlins, snooping around where they're not wanted. Pains in the arse. What do I care if they let the air out of my fucking tyres?"

"No," said Feng. "That is not his job. Letting the air out is the college warden's job. Or rather the college warden's assistant's job. Mr Hu is not the college warden, or the assistant. He is a Party Secretary. He is trying to help. He does not do the dirty work. Gremlins? How do you spell it?"

Chinley was about to turn his back on Feng and continue on his way up the steps to the lecture theatre, when he saw Terry cycling slowly towards him. He looked tired, grey-faced and cold. He did not notice either Chinley or Feng, but as he drew level Feng called out:

"Get off and milk it!"

Terry braked, rested with one foot on the kerb, and looked at the Foreign Affairs official.

"What?" he whispered.

Chinley had not heard anyone say this since he was in his teens, almost forty years ago. If it had not been for the Chinese pronunciation and the fact that Terry had also heard it, he would have been worried that he was hearing voices from the past, reminding him of England. He was already being haunted by *faces* from the past: Samantha, for example. The one with the legs and the Chinese mother, whose face he saw, unfortunately, whenever he looked at Silvia Li.

"I beg your pardon?" said Terry, pressing the Foreign Affairs official.

"Get off and milk it," repeated Feng. Then he turned towards Chinley and said: "Correct expression, Professor? I am compiling a dictionary of idioms in English, you know, to boost my income. And you are a native speaker to help me. An expert on such matters."

"I'm not a language man," said Chinley. "I'm a waterways man. Mr Fox is your language man."

"So what's your opinion Mr Fox? Am I correct?"

Terry propped up his bicycle and massaged his hips. He was

shivering.

"Your expression," he said, "is archaic. Out-dated. Some decades ago, as I'm sure Professor Chinley will confirm, it functioned as a mild insult to anyone whose means of transport was painfully slow. But today, we don't use it. All right?"

Feng seemed satisfied with this.

"Ahh...*Thank* you, Mr Fox," he said, grasping the Irishman's hand in both his own and shaking it over and over again, as though he was trying to detach it. "So you can say it to anyone on a bicycle, suitably, or on a slow coach?"

"Well, you *can*," said Terry, pulling his hand free and losing his smile. "But we don't. Not these days. I've just told you."

To save his friend from further interrogation Chinley crossed the road and stood by him. He could see his imminent audience looking down from the windows of the lecture theatre.

"I have to give a talk now Mr Feng," he said. "And Mr Fox is coming to listen in. So we'll be leaving you."

Feng gripped the handlebars of his bicycle, and Chinley escorted Terry across the road to the Ecology Department building.

"Mr Fox!" shouted Feng.

"Yes?"

"Can I also say get *on* and milk it?"

"Of course you can, you pillock," said Terry, walking away. Mr Hu was pointing limply at the bicycle, which the Irishman had left propped on its stand, in the middle of the road.

"Didn't get much sleep last night?" asked Chinley, when he and Terry were beyond the swing doors of the Ecology Department.

"What do *you* think?" said Terry. "Tempers are getting frayed all round. I can do without any lunatics like that one this morning. And Gladys, well Gladys looks like a big angry boil about to burst open. But I suppose all *you* need to do to keep your cool these days is to get stuck in to your *t'ai chi*?"

"If only," said Chinley. "I must be in the wrong country after all, you know. I can cope with being deprived of sleep, and I can cope with the racket, but what I hate most of all is lack of privacy. I go to the bathroom now, you know, when I don't need to. Just to be on my own for a bit."

He heard a hoot of laughter from above, looked up, and saw several familiar faces watching from the second floor banisters.

"The Chinese are a patient bunch, aren't they?" he said. "Especially the women."

"On the surface anyway," said Terry. "And in the short run, maybe. But they're bound to explode eventually. Especially the women, as you say. So what are you treating them to this morning, your fans up there?"

"Sluice-gate maintenance."

"Sluice-gate maintenance? Good God. I think I'll give it a miss, in that case."

"Is it true," said Chinley, making a move towards the lecture theatre staircase, "that you and your wife have been banned from holding your barn dances until his nibs has been and gone? That's a bit of a joke, isn't it?"

"You know Gladys," said Terry. "Or maybe you don't. If her routine is interrupted she just goes to bed. If there's a bed available. Otherwise she dozes off as well as she can wherever she is. She's either full of life, or unconscious. If she's woken up like she was this morning, she'll yell for a bit, then drink herself to sleep again. So this week she'll have a good rest, and leave the likes of you and me to argue about how daft it all is."

"Sounds admirable," said Chinley. "I can see similar traits in Lisa. If something isn't to her liking and she can do nothing about it, she closes her eyes and keels over."

"Lucky Lisa."

"But don't you sometimes feel as though you're in an open prison here? A sort of funny farm. On days like this."

"Oh yes," said Terry. "But I think there's more to all the fuss now than Mr Deng's visit. I think it's the old guard trying to lay down the law while they still can. Controlling the mavericks. Before the whole country goes mad, out in the so-called real world beyond the campus gates. Or maybe half a mile down the road."

"What's that?"

"*Madame Klimbams.* Haven't you seen it yet?"

"*Madame Klimbams? Madame Klimbams.* Yes, I've seen that somewhere. It's a sign over a building site, or something."

"A building site no longer. It is now a night club, my friend. A night club for Chinese dreamers. Dreams of faraway places."

"That's what Astrid said," interrupted Chinley.

"Who's Astrid?"

"Oh, nobody."

"Just half a mile down the road," continued Terry. "Come with me tonight and we'll check it out, why don't we? With a name like that, who knows what might be on offer?"

Chapter Ten

The security officer saluted, that evening, as Chinley and Terry left the grounds of the Huban campus and walked amongst the cyclists pedalling downhill towards Wuhan town centre. The dual carriageway was damp and bleak; low-powered street-lamps turned the smog-polluted air a greyish-brown colour. As they walked, the two men checked for open manholes and stray bricks, before they stepped into any shadow.

Terry stopped outside a fairy-lit two-storey building which Chinley just about recognised from a week or so ago, having walked past there on his way to a drugstore which he had located, where he could replenish his stocks of insect brew. Then it had been a shell: a derelict warehouse perhaps, or a gutted factory. It was only the illuminated silver sign *Madame Klimbams,* glowing then in isolation, which caused him to look twice and investigate. Inside it had seemed like a vast mausoleum of cement-spattered floorboards and echoing vaults, with long planks, doors off their hinges, and row upon row of folding tables with tubular metal legs, left leaning against the putty-coloured walls. There was a high platform at the far end of the hall, as bare as an outcrop of rock. When he first saw the place it had looked intimidating, more like a setting for political speeches and dreary Party functions. But now, just one week later, the silver sign of *Madame Klimbams* though not self-explanatory, looked appropriate, and the interior was transformed: the naked bulbs had been replaced by a canopy of red, green, yellow and blue festive lights stretching across the ceiling; and the polemical platform was now a carpeted stage, softened by old-fashioned lamps with glowing pink shades.

The two young door-ladies peering out from the entrance now escorted Terry and Chinley to a distant corner table behind a beaded curtain. They could have been twins: both as tall as any Chinese woman Chinley had ever seen, and with identical moist and fleshy night-club smiles, and a thick black even fall of hair reaching down to the small of their backs. They wore red and gold ankle-length reception gowns which were split to the thigh. A turquoise sash with the words *Madame Klimbums* - an intentional mistake from a hopeful management perhaps

- embroidered in silver letters slanted across each small-breasted chest and looped over a bare shoulder.

Half a dozen Chinese couples were dancing a languid two-step to the plaintive voice of an austere female singer accompanied by soporific flute harmonies. Through the beaded curtain Chinley could see a bar, shining like a grotto in a cave, where two young girls in black tights and black pullovers sat with their heads close together, smoking, and drinking beer straight from the bottle. He stretched out full-length on the low-lying soft leather chairs, until he was almost horizontal. It was like reclining in a psychedelic planetarium, gazing up at multi-coloured stars; and the darkness at floor level, where long shadows from the dancing couples met, seemed like a black groundmist shifting around the ankles.

Lisa had declined his invitation to join them that evening, her reason being that she did not yet feel Chinese enough to go dancing as a daughter. Chinley then telephoned Mr Wang, who said he had to stay at home because his wife was seeing one of her doctors. So Lisa suggested that he should invite Silvia instead, as a substitute daughter. He did so, using Lisa's words, but discovered she was already booked: Jeffrey Ward had invited her for dinner.

As the evening progressed however Chinley found that there was no shortage of partners. At one point he even found himself dancing with a tall Chinese man, who claimed to be a reporter for the Dong Hu campus newspaper. Dressed in a white shirt and a ruffled black suit, and with his broad forehead, pointed chin, and stiff boney limbs, he reminded Chinley of a marabou stork unable quite to lift itself up into the air.

As they waltzed together the young reporter pestered Chinley for details of life in the West. Chinley tried to get him to be specific, but he kept interrupting, saying how much freedom and how much wealth there must be there, in the West; then, when the dance tempo quickened he shook his sleek and fashionably-waved hair from side to side, and demanded a demonstration of disco dancing.

Feeling in a buoyant mood, and as only Terry was with him, Chinley obliged, and was immediately surrounded by a ring of applauding onlookers. He then merged once more with the crowd, and danced to everything the DJ chose to play, even launching his heavy frame into *a paso doble*, at the invitation of an equally large woman wearing a thin white cotton blouse, which was short enough to show a taut and slender naked midriff. She told him that she was a postgraduate student of Physical Education from a nearby college, and he said that he could well believe her. Meanwhile the reporter was busy with his camera, and he persuaded Terry on to the dance floor as well, to pose with the two young women who were now sharing his veiled corner table.

Shortly before midnight Chinley stood in the open air below the *Madame Klimbams* sign, waiting for a taxi. When Terry appeared, he was with one of the girls from his table. Her cheeks were the size of buttocks; and when she smiled, they lost their slackness, and rounded into shining golden globes.

"When you get home," said Terry, "can you by any chance sneak in without Gladys hearing you? That way she won't know I'm not with you."

The Irishman's eyes were as animated as when he played the harmonica. Even in the dim street lighting Chinley could see that his face was flushed red, highlighting the haemorrhaged veins, and the tip of his nose was glistening. He was not drunk at all, just exuberant, and each time he spoke the rum-flavoured condensation from his breath drifted towards Chinley and hovered, like a cloud of ectoplasm linking two believers in spiritualistic communion.

"But if she spots you," continued Terry, "tell her the truth. No point having her worry. She knows I'm on a final fling out here, and for a wife you couldn't meet a more broad-minded woman. She only worries if she thinks I'm getting over-excited. But what a way to go, if I was, hey? Anyway, it's you who should be getting excited, with your bridal chamber juice. Isn't it working? I mean, you're not *tempted?*" He turned to the girl whose head was now resting on his shoulder and said: "This is Doris, by the way. She's on the game."

"Doris?" said Chinley. "No. She can't be called Doris, not if she's on the game. She needs something a bit more... a bit less... you know." The name Doris was too close to his own wife's name: not appropriate at all.

"You're right," said Terry. "I'll work on it overnight, and by tomorrow morning we'll have her christened... what?"

"Erm..."

"*Molly*. Yes... *Molly*. That will do. Come on, why don't you come with us and we'll do a double act?"

"What?"

"Or grab one of the others before they all go home."

"Well," said Chinley. "I don't think... hmm. But there's Lisa, you see. She might... she might raise the alarm. She does that sort of thing."

"As you wish." Terry looked at the ballooning cheeks of his escort and said: "What are you grinning at? You're not supposed to be listening." They linked arms and twirled off into the fog.

The long birch-lined boulevard leading to the guest house formed a tunnel, full of opaque light from a hazy moon, the pale tree trunks curving like a wall of upended bones. Chinley walked on home at an energetic pace, now and again pounding the fist of one hand into the palm of the other. He was sweating all over. The slower dance rhythms at *Madame Klimbams* had given him the licence to move close up to his partner, and his head now reeled with after-images of swaying hips and tight bellies, and the provocative tossing of thick glossy youthful hair. He remembered Wang's classification of Chinese women, and wondered how many of his partners tonight might be exceptions to the allegedly highly-moral norm. One solution to the present urge, obviously, was to be honest about it and follow Terry's example; but such a business transaction did not appeal to him, although he was not sure why.

It was a conundrum. There was a nagging urge, he had to admit. If he did nothing, the urge would not go away; if he followed Terry's lead, the urge would also not go away. Maybe if it was a woman who didn't ask him directly for any money for that sort of thing: then he could pretend that she was virtuous enough not to be sharing him with other men. His wife, he remembered, always had a virtuous look about her. He could still recall his surprise at discovering, just before they were married, the private passion which lay beneath her public reserve.

That was twenty-four years ago. Twenty-five in the coming New Year. He wondered if they could still claim a silver wedding anniversary, if they were living apart but were still together on paper. Lack of privacy again, yes, that was another reason why he was no longer with her. In the months before he left England he was in the habit of snapping at her routinely whenever he sensed that there was no pressing cause for them to be in the same room together. He was tired of being constantly watched: watched while he was preparing a pipe; watched while he was brushing his teeth; and watched while he was watching television, watching her reflection on the screen, watching her watching him watching her. True, he was under constant scrutiny also here in China, in a way; but this, he told himself, was only because the Chinese were fascinated by foreigners: he was not under *surveillance*.

"Why the rolling eyeballs?" said Lisa, when he arrived home, walked into the sitting-room, and gave her an uncharacteristic hug.

"Just try a drop of this stuff as a nightcap," he said. Thankful that his daughter could not read his mind he opened a bottle of ginseng root wine. He had come quietly up the stairs as requested so as not to bring Gladys into the hallway. He glanced at his watch and wondered if Doris had become Molly by now.

"Well, as the tolerant child waiting up for her father to come home," said Lisa, helping herself to another glass of ginseng wine, "aren't you at least going to tell me how it was?"

"How what was? The evening?"

"Of course the evening. This stuff is supposed to put lead in your pencil, isn't it? What would it do to me?"

"It was fine." Chinley coughed and felt in his pocket for his pipe.

"Did Terry have a good night?"

"Oh yes, yes."

"Where is he?"

"Who?"

"*Who*? Terry, of course."

"What do you mean, where is he? In bed with Gladys, I suppose. Where else?"

"Only I didn't see him come in with you."

"*See?*"

"What's wrong with you tonight? When you look out of a window, in case you haven't noticed, you very often *see* something. I look out of the window, and I see you, and no Terry."

"He would have been coming up behind me. Hasn't he come in yet? There's been all sorts of doors banging downstairs. We bumped into Mr Feng, of all people out in the road, with his language questions. This time of night, I ask you. Can you believe it? Can you say this, can you say that. *I* managed to escape. I'm the water man. But Terry's the language man, so he was lumbered."

"Hadn't you better tell Gladys that he's on his way home?" said Lisa.

"No. No. Not to worry. Feng won't keep him long, and Gladys might already be asleep."

He tapped the loosened gunge from his pipe bowl into an ashtray, and blew a blast of air down the stem. Images from the dance floor of *Madame Klimbams* once more crept into his mind. He tried to concentrate on refilling the pipe.

"Silvia says hello," said Lisa. "She called in after the dinner with Jeffrey."

"So it's Jeffrey now, is it?"

"Why not?"

"How is he treating her?"

"She says he's good for her English. And he tells her about life in America."

"Ah yes, of course. The ways of the West."

"What?"

"Never mind. You know, she always looks disgruntled to me that girl. Dissatisfied with life. At her age. You weren't like that."

"She's just a more serious person, that's all. Ambitious maybe. She thinks her sisters are wasting their time and their talents working in a hotel, even if they *are* in Beijing. Beijing for her, she says, would be just the beginning. The very beginning."

"Her sisters are delightful. So's her father." Chinley rested his head on the back of the chair, looked up at the ceiling, and pointing with his pipe he said: "Still, if she's a compulsive complainer, she's found a kindred spirit. Up there in the attic."

"Come on," said Lisa. "You hardly know the man. Give him a chance."

"What's going on there then?"

"Where?"

"Between those two." Chinley now jabbed a forefinger in the direction of the overhead apartment.

"I don't see that it's any of our business, but I've already told you. He's helping her."

"Helping her what?"

"Helping her with her English. Giving her a few books and things. That's all."

The booming echo of a loud female voice carried up the stairwell. Chinley and Lisa sat listening, sipping their ginseng wine, astonished by the power of the woman's vocal cords. The reverberations from the outburst made it sound as though there were several voices, rather than just one.

"That Gladys?" said Chinley.

"Who else? Must be Terry back."

"No. She's on the telephone." It occurred to Chinley that Gladys might be somehow trying to track Terry down. The less Lisa overheard now, the better. "She's certainly got the lungs to call a ceilidh," he said. "Yes, I must wander over there one day, to Building Ten, and see her in action. After Mr Killjoy has gone back to Beijing."

"She's perfect for a ceilidh," said Lisa.

"And to think she's a librarian," said Chinley. "Listen to that volume. It must be the frustration coming out. Having to whisper all day and shuffle around in the stacks. She could have had lots of careers, with a voice like that. She could have been a policeman, or a politician. Or a teacher. Or..."

"Shhh! I think she said: 'don't worry, mother'. What could that be about?"

"You shouldn't be listening."

"Shhh..."

"*Her* mother? She must be ninety."

"It could be Terry's mother," said Lisa. "She'd be even older."

What a night to choose to ring her son, if it is, thought Chinley.

"Or it could be a nun," he said. "A Mother Superior."

The operatic level of decibels continued for a while, then a door on the upper landing was heard to bang open and slam shut again. A rapid succession of heavy thumps descended the stairs.

"There he goes," said Chinley, raising his glass towards Lisa in a mock toast, and eliciting a smile. "The Professor in the attic is not amused."

As they drank they heard the ping and clatter of a telephone being knocked off its stand, then three full-throated screams followed by several loud slaps.

"Jesus," said Lisa, her smile fading.

Chinley went to the apartment door, and opened it in time to see Jeffrey Ward sprinting back upstairs, barefoot, in a dressing-gown. Catching sight of Chinley down below he stopped and glowered at him over the banister, his bearded chin raised and his ruddy forehead gleaming with sweat under the bare bulb outside his door.

"Verbal elephantiasis," he said, dribbling spittle over the hand-rail. "The old nelly. Some of us here are trying to get some sleep. Noisy old bag."

He padded into his hallway and slammed the door shut. Lisa was already down on the ground floor, knocking and calling for Gladys to let her in.

Chapter Eleven

"Yes," said Feng. "He has a reputation for being a what? A volatile character. He's in no mood to be dallied with. Tangled with. Tampered with. What is it?" He sat pen in hand, his notebook on his knee, He was in the guest house, in Chinley's apartment, at Lisa's insistence. He sniffed at the air and said: "There's that smell again. So your wife *is* coming out?"

"Can we keep to the point?" said Chinley, shifting in his seat to avoid Lisa's sideways glance.

"What point?" said Feng.

"Jeffrey Ward."

"Ah yes."

"He's *dangerous*," said Lisa.

Feng smiled.

"He *is*," she insisted. "Last night he knocked the telephone out of her hand, slapped her across the face, and chased her down the stairs."

"Actually..." began Feng.

"He *did*!" shouted Lisa. "We heard him!"

"Actually...I've just seen Mrs Fox. She was very calm. Apparently it was the other way round. It was *she* who slapped *him*. Across the face, yes. She told me so herself."

Lisa looked at her father but they both realised that this could be the case, as they had only heard the blows, not seen them.

"But what about Mrs Fox *now?*" persisted Lisa. "Is she okay? She wouldn't even let me in last night. She must have been scared stiff. What right has *he* got to intimidate her like that?"

"She's very calm," repeated Feng. "In fact she wants me to check that Professor *Ward* was all right this morning."

Lisa raised her arms in disbelief, and puffed out her cheeks to release a prolonged and exasperated blast of air.

"Then she's obviously had a serious blow to the head," she said. "Either that or she's been on Terry's rum."

Her father leant back in his armchair and stroked his chin. He needed to know. "And *Mr* Fox?" he said. "How is *Mr* Fox?"

"Yes, Mr Fox," said Lisa. "None of this would have happened if you hadn't held him up in the lane last night. He was nearly home, when you stopped him with your daft... questions." She pointed at the notebook.

"*What?*" Feng kept his smile, but his eyes narrowed in wonder.

"Lisa," said Chinley. "I think you've asked Mr Feng enough questions yourself, for now. Things are getting confused. So tell us, Mr Feng, how is *Mr* Fox?"

"He's asleep," said Feng. "In bed. Not ill it seems, just sleeping in. That's why Mrs Fox was talking to me so quietly just now. For a change. Shagged out, I think was the way she put it. Correct sentence? She didn't want to disturb him. She knows how loud her voice can be."

"So it's all right for *you* to ask questions," said Lisa to Chinley. "But not for me?"

"There are questions, and questions," said Chinley. "My question was a request for information. Yours was, in effect, an accusation."

"You say *I* delayed Mr Fox?" said Feng. "When? *Where?*"

"Please don't be offended," said Chinley. "My daughter's upset. She's very fond of both our downstairs neighbours."

"No matter," said Feng. "No problem. But can I ask you a big favour? Can I ask you, as leader of the house, to be patient with Professor Ward? Then we can have a harmonious society. Especially this week, as Mr Deng is arriving later this morning. You're all invited to lunch with him."

"Community," said Lisa. "Harmonious community."

"Harmonious community," said Feng. "Yes of course. Thank you." He opened his notebook and scribbled.

* * *

Chinley could not recall the English name of the Chinese woman in the missionary-grey pleated skirt. Sitting next to Belinda, who today looked uncharacteristically dishevelled and whey-faced, but was nevertheless once again wearing her gold-spangled scarlet jacket, the woman in grey looked just as frumpish and severe as she did in Beijing. Presenting a demeanour compatible with Mr Deng. He was dressed like an undertaker: white shirt, almost black tie, and black suit. Together, they exuded a funeral formality, which was no doubt their intention, in keeping with their status as inspecting officials from the State Education

Commission.

But Chinley was hoping that Wang, with his monstrous grin and his tendency, after a couple of drinks, to make loud personal remarks, would help to enliven these proceedings in the campus restaurant side-suite reserved for the reception.

Before Feng could usher him elsewhere Chinley settled himself in a space between Terry and Gladys. Lisa, either unaware of or disregarding a breach of protocol, immediately took a seat between the guest of honour, Mr Deng, and the Dong Hu university President, a dapper though podgy academic with no neck and a twin sprouting of pale hair over his ears, which gave him the look of a koala. To the President's left, places were reserved for Mr Wu and Mr Hu, who were not yet seated but were busying themselves flitting around the table and getting in each other's way with bottles of wine and cans of beer.

Jeffrey Ward was the last to arrive. Feng took his bulky brown overcoat and placed him in the one remaining unclaimed seat, between Gladys and Mr Deng's female colleague. Ward watched closely as Feng re-positioned his overcoat on the stand so that the lining was clear of the propped-up dripping umbrellas below.

Terry's ageing blue eyes were watery today and unfocused. But they sprang to life as soon as Belinda drew him into conversation, her mouth now curved into the misleading half-wit grin, which Chinley assumed she adopted, for some reason, at semi-social gatherings like this one. Gladys leant over in Chinley's direction and in a loud whisper she said:

"A lovely woman that. She's been getting on famously with Terry in the past couple of weeks, so I've noticed. He's been winning her over with tales of his old Irish home of course, cheering her up no end. I think she's not as daft as all that; I think she's only *pretending* to believe him. Just his type. Something's bothering her these days though, don't you think? But she hasn't said what it is. And he's told her that whenever he has the chance he'll bring her there. To Ireland, you know. And why not?"

She turned for a moment and smiled at Jeffrey Ward, her mouth opening and closing like a trap, then she came back to Chinley's ear, minimising her whisper. "The boot man, just look at him. Belinda goes rigid at our place whenever she hears him clopping past the front door. He's got a temper, but so did my father, and I know how to handle that sort of thing. Fight fire with soap suds. After the first blow. Women find that much easier than men of course, so for God's sake don't tell Terry what happened between me and Boris over there. He'd kill him if he knew."

She frowned, pursing her lips, and Chinley stared at her, fascinated by the passing resemblance to a gargoyle about to spew. He wondered how much she knew of Terry's philandering. Shagged out, she had said. But that way of putting it could have been what? As Mr Feng would say, just a coincidence.

"How's life at the guest house?" Mr Deng wiped the grease off his lips with a steaming napkin, and spoke to Chinley. The man's thick black eyebrows, from where Chinley was sitting, looked like an upwardly mobile extension of his heavy spectacle frames. "I hear you're the Foreign Expert representative, Professor Chinley. Congratulations."

"Thank you. Yes. Life at the guest house? Well... *fine*."

"Everything in harmony? Good."

"Yes. Well..."

"Yes," chipped in Feng. "Harmonious community."

"I was thinking," said Lisa. Mr Deng turned his head towards her and took off his spectacles, to study her at close range. "Maybe it's about time we all had - an outing," she continued. "All the people from the guest house, I mean. Get to know each other a bit better. Consolidate the harmony."

Chinley looked at his daughter with admiration. She really does have a talent, he thought, for lying through her teeth.

"Perhaps while you're here, Mr Deng," she continued. "And your..."

"Hilda." His colleague spoke for herself, and softened the expression on her face.

"And Hilda. You can both come with us if you'd like to."

"Yes," said Belinda. "We can all go to my pagoda."

Wang laughed loud and long, and said: "Please excuse my wife."

"No," said Lisa, "I think that's a brilliant idea. It's no distance at all and I've always wondered what it was like up there. How about this afternoon, right after lunch?"

There were murmurs of approval. Wang stared into his glass of beer, then drained it in one draught.

"Won't it be slippery in the wet?" said Gladys, but no-one was listening to her.

"You have a very impressive daughter Professor Chinley," said Mr Deng, replacing his spectacles, as though his evaluation of Lisa was now complete.

"I've got an appointment this afternoon," said Jeffrey Ward. "So I won't be able to come."

"*When?* Who with?" shouted Wang, standing up, his teeth flaring.

"In half an hour."

"Who *with?*" Wang insisted.

"With a Chinese friend. It's none of your business. Sit down."

"Well bring him along," suggested Mr Deng, gesturing for Wang to sit down.

"Yes," said Lisa. "We need you there especially, Mr Ward. Excuse me asking, but is it with Silvia? Your appointment?" Jeffrey Ward nodded slowly, under the gaze of the entire table, and prodded limply at a large chunk of fish with his porcelain spoon. "That's all right then," continued Lisa. "I'll have a word with her on your behalf. I'm sure I can talk her into coming with us."

"Bloody big bones in this local fish," said Wang. "You're very wise, Professor Ward, to treat them with caution. We don't want one of our foreign experts choking on a bone."

Good for you, said Chinley to himself. Good for you, Wang. True to form. A laugh at last in this mournful gathering. Mr Wu's head was bent low as though in worship, close to his side plate, on to which he was dribbling whatever he could not swallow. Chinley caught Mr Hu's eye, and indicated that Wang's glass needed a refill. Mr Hu immediately went over with a bottle of *baijiu*. Wang's cheeks were already ablaze; his lips were puffy and swollen from the passage of hot chilis and alcohol. He would be singing soon. Belinda fidgeted. Ward raised his beard and scratched at the fish flakes caught in his hairs. He checked his watch, and drummed his fingers on the tablecloth.

Belinda paired off with Chinley to lead the two-file column through the drizzle and up Pagoda Hill. She told him she remembered her offer of three weeks ago, to take him to the place which they were now about to visit.

"This was not exactly what I had in mind," she said, looking over her shoulder at the disciplined ranks marching close behind them. "Apart from anything else, people get in each other's way on the spiral.

There's no rail to hold on to you see, so it's like walking around the edge of a big empty well. The only light is the daylight from the gaps, so most of the climb is in the dark. You have to feel your way forward, and that's much easier if there's no-one on your heels, breathing down your neck, trying to squeeze past."

"When did you last go in there?" asked Chinley. "Maybe it's safer now."

"I'm there all the time," said Belinda. "It's my pagoda. It's my retreat before sunrise. When even Mr Wu and Mr Hu are still in bed. Come sometime then, if you don't believe me, and you'll find out."

Unwelcome fantasies began to play once more on Chinley's senses, but another possible scenario came to mind, helping to check his libido: a vision of Wang on the balcony, his teeth working in mockery, in the company of Mr Wu and Mr Hu perhaps, handing them a pair of binoculars and saying: "Have a look at this. Top floor of the pagoda. He believed her, the old fool." But now Chinley heard himself saying: "Yes, Belinda. Good, I'd really like that. I'll come and join you here one morning."

He glanced behind to see who might have been within earshot. Closing on him, with mud streaked across the toe-caps of his dress shoes, was Mr Deng, paired off with Lisa.

"The new Yangtse dam, Professor," he said. "Your daughter tells me she's not interested in going there with you to see it."

"Not over-keen," said Chinley. "I don't understand it. I thought she'd jump at the chance. Who wouldn't?"

"Does she know all about the location of the new generators?" continued Mr Deng. "And the revised distribution network proposals? Maybe if she knew more about it all, she might change her mind."

"No thanks," said Lisa.

"So an interest in waterways and hydro-electric power does not run in the family?"

"Waterways yes," said Lisa. "For looking at and messing about on. Hydro-electric power plants and dams, no. He can go on his own and leave me to my own devices."

"You'd be alone in your big apartment."

"Terrific! I'm desperate to get rid of him for a few days."

Mr Deng looked from Lisa to Chinley, and back again, then slowly parted his duck-like lips, as though ready to wail with misery. But no sound came out, and when his lips clamped shut again Chinley guessed that this was the closest Mr Deng would come, in his company, to having a good laugh.

When the group reached the top of Pagoda Hill they rested on a circle of low barrel-shaped stone seats, and changed partners. Terry made his way towards Belinda, and Gladys squatted next to Chinley.

"I know all about *Madame Klimbams* by the way," she said. "And I know all about Molly."

Chinley said nothing, then gave a start as Gladys slapped him hard on the knee and shouted: "*Grand!* Isn't it? Keeping his pecker up at his age. *You* might take a tip or two from our Terry instead of... what *is* that stuff they gave you at the drugstore?" Terry, hearing his wife, broke off his conversation with Belinda and grinned at Chinley. Then he swelled his chest and gave it two sharp thumps with clenched fists. Belinda relinked her arm with his, and hugged it to her.

Gladys lowered her voice. "All that worries me," she said, her head bent to the ground, "is the excitement of it. His heart. Some people would say at his age he's had a good run. But me and him together, we've only just begun. I was on the telephone to his mother the other night. She's a bit hard of hearing, which is why I had to yell. And if I'd known then where he was and what he was up to, and if I'd told her, do you know what? She'd have been *delighted*. That's all. Delighted. That's his mother for you. And that's Terry for you." She tapped her forehead and said: "Mental health, you see. Balance. Some of us have it, some of us don't."

"How old is she?" asked Chinley.

"His mother? Ninety-two. One of those ageless old Irishwomen. Tough skin, soft heart, never refuses a drink, and not afraid of turning a mangle. Not afraid of *any*thing. She's certainly caught Belinda's fancy. She's been asking so many questions you'd think she was going to write the old woman's life story."

Chinley was distracted by the sight of Hilda sitting with Jeffrey Ward; he wondered what they could possibly find in common to talk about. Or had she heard something?

"Old folk are more tolerant than young folk think," said Gladys. "I've seen Terry mellow just in the time I've known him. Don't let anything slip about the incident on the stairs though, will you? The only thing that gets him fired up the wrong way these days is if he thinks someone is having a go at *me*. As if I can't look after myself. Here she comes look. Bo Peep."

Silvia was making her way up the hill towards them.

"I'm not going to ask her any questions," continued Gladys, "or give her any advice. Unless she wants it."

Silvia sat down beside them, keeping her back straight, as usual, as though someone had told her to be careful with her posture, and she placed her hands on her knees. She was wearing a wide-brimmed transluscent light-blue rain-hat, and the older maxi-skirt, and had switched her high heels for calf-length black leather boots: sensible, for the occasion.

"I came here with Professor Ward the other day," she said to Gladys. "Just for a walk."

Chinley wondered if she still called him 'Professor' to his face.

"Ah," said Gladys. "So you've already been up to the top then. Is it worth the effort?"

"I didn't want to come back here at all," said Silvia. "But Lisa asked me to, as a special favour. It's a bit of a nuisance. What's it all about?"

"I think," said Chinley, "that she just wants to have an agreeable get-together. For a change."

"And she especially wanted your boyfriend to be here," said Gladys.

"My *what?*" Silvia gave a strange laugh, and held a hand over her mouth. "No no. He's my teacher."

"Don't take me so seriously," said Gladys. She jerked a thumb towards the pagoda. "So what's it like from the top, this place? The view?"

"We never went up," said Silvia. "We stayed at the bottom." She began tapping her toe on a stray limestone chipping. Terry's mannerism, but Chinley felt that in this case it was more of a nervous tic. "Professor Ward..." she checked that he was still occupied with Hilda. "Professor Ward told me then that he's not easy with heights. Unless there's a good railing to hold on to. But in there there's nothing." She looked up to the top of the tower. "And you see, up there there's hardly any railing at all. Just a footrest."

"Well what's the big fuss?" said Gladys. "We didn't come here to see who's got a head for heights and who hasn't. We came here to get to know each other better. No-one's going to force your... teacher up to the top. No-one's going to force anyone to do anything."

"I know that," said Silvia. "But I don't think, now he's here, that anyone could persuade him *not* to go up there."

"Well in that case he's an idiot," said Gladys.

The pagoda was stark and derelict, and higher than it seemed from the road to Belinda's apartment. Chinley counted seven levels, each with narrow spy-hole slits in the stonework. At each level there was a primitive look-out ledge, no more than a protruding slab, with a thick iron rung at its edge, no higher than a brass fender skirting the bar of an English pub. He could see that this iron rung may offer little reassurance to someone like Jeffrey Ward: something to trip over rather than a safety measure.

He saw Mr Deng hand Belinda some money, which she passed on to a scruffy attendant who was sitting on a chair by the entrance to the tower, and he guessed she was making a block booking. Mr Wu and Mr Hu now led the way, holding hands, to Chinley's amusement, but they were forced into single file as they walked into the darkness of the interior. Next to go in was Jeffrey Ward, followed by Silvia, then Mr Deng and Hilda.

Gladys was already short of breath from the exertion so far, and as she waddled in front of Lisa, Chinley wondered how she would cope with the climb to come. He gestured for Belinda to go in front of him, then for her husband, but Wang insisted that Chinley precede him. All Chinley could see now of Belinda was the shine on the back of her shoes, and he used this as a guide to which direction he should follow during the climb. He looked over his shoulder, and beyond the bobbing outline of Wang's head he saw Terry, still outside, take a gulp of rum then disappear like a shadow as he stepped out of the raincloud and into the inner gloom. Feng took up the rear.

Inside it was as black as a cave. The only relief came from the seven squashed rings of daylight high above them. Belinda was right: the steps were steep, uneven, and clammy. There was a musty smell of damp earth and decaying vegetation, and a stream of condensation could be heard dripping all around them in a constant trickle. Nothing could be heard from the rest of the party except for an irregular panting, the creaking of shoes, the scraping of unsteady footfalls, and the swish of clothing. Chinley could see no-one ahead of him and no-one behind him, and he stopped to listen more carefully for a while, in case he had taken a side-turning, then he realised that this was improbable as he was inside a vertical cylinder. When he stopped, Wang bumped into him from behind, and his high-pitched laugh echoed upwards and down again. Chinley could imagine Wang grinning at his discomfort, knowing that he was struggling to keep his footing. Like walking around the rim of a big empty well, Belinda had said, and remembering this Chinley now tentatively tapped a foot sideways to feel how close he was to the edge of the spiralling steps.

He counted four out of the seven levels as he passed upwards through the shrinking patches of sky, and he decided that he would have a rest when he reached level five. He stopped by a block of light and Wang, whose close presence and hot breath was beginning to unsettle him, went on ahead, with a chuckle of apology. As he passed by Chinley had a glimpse of his buck-tooth grin. Devilish. Terry and Feng caught up, and stood near Chinley by a slit in the wall. Feng then fearlessly took a step out on to the protruding stone slab, then turned to face Chinley and Terry, his back towards the drop beyond and his heel resting loosely on the low iron rung. This man deserves more respect than I have so far shown him, thought Chinley. Terry took out his bottle of rum, drank a good measure, then passed it on to Chinley.

"Holy Mother of God," he said. "Are we doing this for *pleasure*?"

"Is Mrs Fox all right now?" asked Feng.

"What do you mean *now*?" said Terry. "Why shouldn't she be? She's always all right, God bless her. She's up there with that lot. Ask her yourself."

"I mean after what happened on the stairs the other night," continued Feng. "With Professor Ward. There's been no further... violation?"

"What in God's name are you talking about this time you pillock? What stairs? What violation?"

"You know that Professor Ward is disturbed by voices?"

"What?"

"Mr Feng -" began Chinley.

"Well he is," continued Feng. "And it was your wife who disturbed him the other night. When she was shouting on the telephone. Didn't she tell you? It was your mother she was shouting at, wasn't it? Is she deaf? Your mother, I mean."

Chinley, his knees trembling now, was too worried by the vague black hole inches behind him to further interrupt Feng's flow.

"Never mind my mother," said Terry. "What are you getting at?"
"Well, he ran down the stairs and forced her to be quiet."
"Who did?"
"Professor Ward."
"Jeffrey Ward? Him up there?"
"Yes."
"*Forced* her to be quiet?"
"Yes. Didn't he, Professor Chinley? She put up a fight though. As much as a woman can. Gave him a few hard slaps back in the face, she must have told you? Don't worry, he came off worse than she did in the end. She's a tough old bird, isn't she? Just as well."

Feng chuckled, and the Irishman's eyes went cold. His nose crinkled like that of a tormented dog. He stared for a moment at the grinning Foreign Affairs official. Then he grabbed the bottle of rum back from Chinley, gulped down all that was left inside it, and flung it high over Feng's head.

"*Forced* her to be quiet did he?" he whispered. The bottle smashed in the courtyard down below, and the watchman wailed a lengthy complaint.

"Well in that case," continued Terry, "I think I'd better have a quick word with him." He ran off up into the darkness of the pagoda, shouting "Let me at the bastard! The *bastard!*"

Chinley heard the clumsy scuffing and scraping of Terry's metal-tipped boots circling above him; then Wang's loud laugh rang out, followed by hisses of protest and caution. Two men were now yelling at each other, and Chinley heard the thud of a fist, then more yelling and thuds, and the scream of a woman. Then there was total silence, and a succession of muted cracks and thumps. He stiffened in horror as a heavy bundle of cloth fell past him in the darkness, brushing against his outstretched hand.

Part Three

Chapter Twelve

It was more of a wake than a funeral. The reception was held on the ground floor of Building Ten, in the room used for the dancing lessons, and there was an open invitation for anyone to attend, whether colleague, friend, acquaintance, or stranger. Gladys decided that a bequest of one of Terry's suitcases, the one which was still half-full of bottles of rum, should go to Chinley. The suitcase was now on the floor in the hall of Building Ten, open, behind a makeshift bar.

Gladys was busy and seemed untroubled, now. The post mortem concluded that her husband died of heart failure, and as they walked away from the hearing she told Chinley that she would not dwell on questions which could not be answered: questions of the pain he felt, the exact moment of unconsciousness, whether he was aware that he was falling. The only time her voice faltered in fact was when she said how sad she was that the last thing Terry saw in his life may well have been the smirk on Jeffrey Ward's face, as he grinned at the sight of the older man flailing out at him.

She located a Roman Catholic priest in downtown Wuhan, who arranged a service in his church and a burial in a small western-style cemetery overlooking the Yangtse river. It was during the burial ceremony, when Chinley was gazing absent-mindedly at the wide expanse of grey water and grey sky to the west, thinking that it looked more like the runway of a major airport than a river, that the idea came to him to secure a token for Gladys, a token of his brief but warm friendship with Terry. A gesture, which he was sure she would for once appreciate.

He would need to have a word with Mr Li and Silvia about that, as soon as he returned from the schedule which Mr Deng had organised for him at the new dam construction near the Sichuan border: beyond the blurred horizon of cloud and flood plain which now formed a suitably sober backdrop for the lowering of the coffin.

Outside the door of Building Ten Chinley could see a gathering of young Chinese men and women, students who, Gladys told him, were from her Tuesday and Thursday dance class. They were clearly reluctant to enter, peering over each other's heads and shoulders at the threshold of the hall. He guessed they would be unsure how to behave on such an occasion, which must also have been why Mr Li had not turned up: perhaps they could not understand why this jolly music was being played, or why Lisa and Gladys were dancing together, each with a broad smile on her face, to an up-tempo mazurka.

He beckoned to encourage them to make their way in. They shuffled through in shy groups of twos and threes, and stared in wonder at the light-hearted antics of the chief mourners. The music stopped and Gladys bowed ritually, like a man, while Lisa curtsied and tittered. The Chinese guests took their initiative from Chinley, and joined him in a muted round of applause.

"And to think," said Gladys, taking up her position behind the drinks table, and lifting the caps off a few more bottles of beer and lemonade for her students, "only a few days ago I told his mother not to worry about him. It's her though, I feel sorry for, not being able to join in the fun. She's on her own out there in the sticks. Maybe she's having a knees-up down the pub. After it all happened, I didn't see the point of going into too much detail, what could I say, so I just told her he died peacefully while he was out walking with his friends. That's more or less how it was, really, wasn't it?"

"Yes, Gladys, spot on," said Chinley, putting his arm around her shoulder. Lisa nodded, with her eyes gleaming but her lips now pressed tightly together.

"Apart from the fracas with Jeffrey Ward, of course," added Gladys. "Where is he then? Hasn't he got the guts to show himself? I don't mind. A time like this is a time for forgiveness, isn't it?"

"It is," said Chinley. Lisa said nothing.

"When I told her, Terry's mother," continued Gladys, "there was this long silence at the other end of the line. I thought we'd been cut off, or she'd broken down or something, or hadn't heard me properly. I don't know. I was dreading having to say it all over again. Then she came back on. She sounded fine, and asked me when and where the service would be. He wouldn't mind being buried in China, she said. He loved the place, and he loved the people. Then she said, typical of her, have a good funeral and let me know how it went."

"Mrs Fox?"

Chinley recognised the voice, but it took him a moment or two to identify the young woman around whose shoulders Gladys had now placed a heavy freckled arm.

"Molly! Molly!" she shouted. "Thanks for coming!"

She kissed Molly's deflated brown cheeks, and brought a smile to her face.

"This is the famous Molly, Molly, this is Mr Chinley. But of course, you've met. And this is Lisa, his lovely daughter."

The two young women shook hands.

"So..." began Chinley.

"Word travels fast when a foreigner dies out here," said Molly.

"Oh he wasn't a foreigner," said Gladys, raising her voice as more people squeezed in on her. "But we'll leave that one. I'm so pleased you could come, Molly." She surveyed her audience and continued. "So close to Terry near the end, Molly was. You can't get much closer than that. I went to this *Madame Klimbams* place yesterday you know, just for somewhere to go, just to clear my head with a few drinks. Terry told me so much about it. Well, I'm half-inclined to be a Madame Klimbam myself. Yes. It's what he would want for me now, I'm sure, the old lecher. Every time I think about it, I hear his voice in my head, egging me on. Why not? It's a bit more me than fussing in a library. It's just a pity I didn't think about it a bit sooner, while he was still with us. Then he could have got a discount on the goods! Hey? Hey Molly?"

She squeezed Molly's shoulder and shrieked with laughter, and all those around her joined in. Chinley cast a quick look at his daughter, and wondered what she made of all this.

"Mrs Fox," said Molly. "There's a friend of mine outside who knows your husband. He's a photographer. Can he come in?"

"Of course he can come in," said Gladys, and she led her to the door.

"Who's this Molly then?" said Lisa, when they were out of earshot. "Close to Terry, near the end? How is it we never met her before, in that case?"

"Molly," said Chinley. "Is Molly."

"Molly," continued Lisa. "Yes, she looks a bit of a Molly. And who's Madame Klimbam?"

"There is no Madame Klimbam. It's a sort of...club."

"A club. All right," said Lisa. "So what's the problem?"

"Problem?"

"Why you're being so cagey."
"No problem," said Chinley. "Is Silvia coming?"
"She'll be here. Alone."
"No Jeffrey Ward?"
"No Jeffrey Ward."
"Lisa, are you sure you don't want to come with me to this dam? Change of scenery? Change of air?"
"Absolutely positive. What do I want with a dam?"
"It's not just the dam. You'll meet some more people. See a new town. It'll get you away from here for a bit."
"I don't need to be away. I've only just come."
"You'll be on your own."
"Terrific! And what about Gladys? I know she's good at giving the impression she's all right, but I'm sure she needs another woman about the house just now. And there's Silvia. Someone needs to keep an eye on Silvia. He's a monster. Can't you see?"

The high ceiling of Building Ten reminded Chinley of the premises at *Madame Klimbams* before it was transformed into a night club. The same bare and dusty concrete floor edged with flakes of plaster from the peeling walls, the same stacks of folding tables and chairs, and both of them with a stage more suited to politics than performances. One advantage this building could boast though, was its size. A fair crowd could assemble here.

"How did Terry manage to make himself heard in this place on a mouth-organ?" he asked Lisa. "Over Gladys's voice and all the stomping? Even with a microphone he must have been drowned out."

"You'll see in a minute," said Lisa. "As soon as Gladys organises her formation groups. Here comes the photographer."

Photographs, Chinley had discovered, caused great excitement amongst the Chinese, regardless of who or what was in the picture. An expectant throng was following Gladys and the photographer over to a corner table on which they spread a selection of large black-and-white prints. Chinley now recognised him as the modish young man he had waltzed with. His triangular head jerked up and down in response to the relentless interrogation from the crowd, and through the laughter and the shrieks Chinley saw that quick glances were being thrown in his direction, and he heard the words 'Madame Klimbams' and 'the foreigners' bar'.

He was glad that Mr Deng and Hilda, unable to attend the wake because of what for them was more pressing business in the capital, were by now hundreds of miles away, back in Beijing. He was also pleased that there was no sign of Mr Wu or Mr Hu making an appearance, to snoop around and finger through the photographs, the innocent photographs, and interpret them as scurrilous detail from his personal life, to be added to the file which was no doubt kept on him at the Foreign Affairs Office.

He noticed that several heads now swivelled more openly in his direction, and the youngsters kept their eyes on him as they exchanged palmed whispers. He beamed at them, and with this reassurance a gang of giggling girls approached and presented him with the prints in which he appeared; then they backed away to watch his reaction from a distance.

"You're a professional dancer Professor Chinley," said one of the bolder ones. "You're an expert."

"What's this?" said Lisa, grabbing a photograph. With her mouth wide open, she looked at her father and shook her head slowly in disbelief. The Chinese girls were huddled together, staring at her, their arms hooked around each other's waists and shoulders. One of them said: "Your grandfather's very talented."

"For his age, yes." said Lisa. "Aren't you, granddad? It must have been the rum."

Yes, but not just the rum, thought Chinley, recalling the patches of naked swaying flesh, the long long hair, the excited black eyes, the buttocks of Molly's cheeks. That was enough.

"So what does Molly do for a living?" asked Lisa, with a sideways look at her father.

"I've no idea," said Chinley. "Gladys might be able to help you there. Or you could ask the girl herself."

"I'm sorry about your friend," said a voice behind him. He turned and saw Silvia.

She looked now very much the high school pupil: her hair unclasped and unfussy, out of the pony-tail and falling loose over the collar of her pale grey jacket. She wore a plain black ankle-length skirt, a yellow blouse buttoned high, and a maroon v-neck pullover: "My father sends his condolences," she added: "He couldn't come, he's busy with his bean curd."

"Please tell him," said Chinley, "that I have something urgent to discuss with him when I come back from the dam. In two or three days at the most. It also concerns you, and your grandfather."

"My grandfather?" said Silvia.

She was interrupted by an announcement from Gladys, who bawled down a microphone saying that she had no intention of making a speech of any kind. She thanked everyone for being there; then she extended a special welcome to her dancing class students, and told them to select their partners for Mrs MacLeod's Reel without any further delay.

"See," said Lisa, as four young men climbed on to the stage. "This is how he did it." Two of them had harmonicas, one had a guitar, and one a flute. "Terry's backing group," she explained, as the tune started. "They helped him to make himself heard over Gladys."

In keeping with their teacher's regimental glare, the pupils' faces remained stern and obedient as they executed the steps she had taught them, but Chinley could not help suspecting a burlesque intention behind the hyper-stiff upper bodies and the exaggerated bounce in the legs. An English teenager, he reflected, would certainly not be taking this as seriously as they might appear to be, under the eye of a fierce instructor like Gladys.

He watched Silvia looking on. Dressed this way she reminded him again of Samantha: of his teenage curiosity about her and her Chinese mother, and his dejection when he realised they would have nothing to do with him. Gladys caught his eye and sent a signal for him to join in with the action. He used the excuse of a door banging open and closed behind him to look away from her, and he turned to see Belinda and Wang standing together by the entrance.

A little late, but Chinley had no doubt they would come. Wang kept his head bowed down towards the floor; Belinda scanned the room with no apparent interest, until she rested her eyes on Silvia. Her lips now shaped themselves into a smile, and she walked over and tapped her on the shoulder. Silvia had not taken her eyes off the musicians, but now she turned with a start. Belinda said something to her and, her mouth for once gaping open, Silvia shook her head and shrugged her shoulders. She made as though to move away, but Belinda rested a gentle hand on her arm.

When the dancing stopped Silvia extricated herself and went quickly over to Gladys. She touched the Welshwoman's hand, and spoke to her briefly, then made her way past Wang's bowed head and out of the hall. Belinda's attention was now focussed on the musicians, who were leading into the tune for the next dance. Chinley walked over and stood by her side.

"See?" she said, taking hold of his arm and pulling him close to her. "The harmonica players. They could be his own boys."

The two young Chinese men were wearing flat tweed caps, and as they played they cocked their heads to one side and tapped a foot, in unison, along with the rhythm.

"Do you know where he is?" said Belinda.

"Who?" said Chinley.

"Professor Ward. I went to the guest house. Either he's not there or he's not answering the door. Do you know?"

"I don't," said Chinley. "I've no idea. But why..."

"Silvia says she doesn't know, either. I could run back there but my husband won't let me out of his sight. Look at him, guarding the exit. Will you do something for me?" She moved a cheek close to Chinley's ear. "Please give him a beer or something and take him off to the other side of the room so I can get out." Wang now caught Chinley's eye, grinned an automatic horsy grin, seemed about to laugh but didn't, then flung back his head and stared at the ceiling, his teeth, in profile, curving over his lower lip like the prongs of a garden fork.

"Please," said Belinda, pressing against Chinley now with the whole length of her body. He went over to the drinks table, ordered two bottles of beer, and waved one at Wang. But Wang would not move from his position by the exit, so Chinley joined him there, leaving Belinda to glare at the floor now, prowling and agitated. Outside, flicking their cigarette ash into puddles in the road, were Mr Wu and Mr Hu.

"Us women can stick together too," said Lisa to Chinley when he came back into the room after finishing his beer.

"What?"

"Did you ask him to back off?"

"Who?"

"No, of course you didn't. You're both men."

She went over and spoke to Gladys, who gave Wang a long look, then nodded at Lisa, as though she was consenting to a request.

Chapter Thirteen

"An escort agency?" said Chinley.

"Not what you think," said Lisa.

She and Silvia were lounging on the floor amongst a spread of ink-mixing stones and calligraphy charts. They had spent the late afternoon down in Gladys's apartment, where she was now preparing dinner for Belinda. In Building Ten, on a plea from Lisa, Gladys had gone over to Wang and told him that she wanted the pleasure of Belinda's company for the evening. Just the two of them for once, in private. She needed to talk to a woman of mature years right now, she said.

He muttered something about mature years meaning nothing, but agreed, on condition that Belinda was not given anything to drink. "Quite right too," said Chinley when Lisa told him this, but he did not tell her how clearly he remembered the blow to his arm in the boat. He was now busy stocking the sideboard, which had become his drinks cabinet, with the remainder of Terry's rum.

"It's all above board," continued Lisa, talking through her hair. "There are escorts and escorts, as you might put it yourself. And Gladys needs a project like this, to stop her from getting morose. She can hear Terry's voice in her head she says, driving her on. I think she deserves our support. Your support."

"How can I support something I know nothing about?"

"By giving it a chance. It will start off as a kind of hot-line to *Madame Klimbams*. So that if more dancing partners are needed anytime for the customers they can phone Gladys, and she will provide them."

Procure them, thought Chinley.

"Who can phone Gladys?" he said. "Monsieur Klimbam? Grandmère Klimbam?"

"There are no Klimbams. You know that. Just a manager and his wife. Entrepreneurs. A young Chinese business couple."

"So where did they pick up a name like *Madame Klimbams*?"

Lisa looked at Silvia.

"They didn't say," said Silvia. "They probably saw it in a western newspaper or a western movie, from Japan or somewhere."

"What does it matter?" said Lisa. "Gladys is the obvious choice for someone to help them out. She's sociable, she has a... a remarkable presence. And she's a westerner, which Silvia tells me is the single most important pull factor for a place like that, both for the customers and for the investors. *And*, she knows all the most talented dancers around here."

"Does she think then that hornpipes and jigs are suitable for a night club?"

"That's where I come in," said Lisa. "While I'm still here, I can tutor Gladys's lot in disco stuff, extend their repertoire, and then they can all register with the agency pool. Earn some money. Actually, come to think of it, judging by the photographs I've seen of you and what people who saw you in action are saying, there's no reason why you shouldn't help out yourself. As one of the instructors."

Chinley stared at the bottles of rum in Terry's suitcase. In an hour or two his daughter would be on her own here: if he told her now that he wanted her to have nothing to do with Gladys's scheme, that he thought it was not only ridiculous but dangerous, she would be more attracted to it. He decided on a light-hearted approach, persuading himself that this flight of the Welshwoman's fancy would be forgotten by the time he returned from his trip to the dam.

"Why not rope in Belinda?" he said. "She wears the right kind of jacket."

"See?" said Lisa, to an imaginary audience. "I knew you wouldn't take us seriously."

Chinley felt like banging his head on the edge of the suitcase.

"Anyway," she continued, "judging by the look on her face this morning in Building Ten, when she thought no-one was watching, Belinda would be better off employed as a bouncer. She was still singing, though. Opera stuff this time." Lisa looked at Silvia. "But that's a squawk, a tormented wailing, a dying goose, to my father. Not proper singing at all as far as he's concerned. I can see his point, I suppose. She sounded much better one or two weeks ago."

Silvia concentrated on the calligraphy.

The telephone rang on the stairs. It was Feng with details of the arrangements for Chinley's journey. A Foreign Affairs Office car would be arriving in one hour, to take him to the railway station. He replaced the receiver and gave himself a few moments to think, before returning to the girls. Although he would be out of town for only a few days he now felt reluctant to leave.

Outside *Madame Klimbams* Terry had been quite explicit about the nature of Molly's role. And Gladys not only seemed not to mind, she wanted to join in and make a business out of it. A woman with a strict Welsh chapel upbringing, so she claimed; perhaps her real intention was to clean it all up. You couldn't tell with Gladys. He was fairly sure that such services as Molly's were not only illegal here but carried with them severe penalties for anyone apprehended. On the other hand, he knew that Wuhan was described as a special economic zone; so perhaps the police were turning a blind eye, accepting that more business meant more brothels. It all went hand in hand, as it were. He looked out of the bay window at the empty lawn. In ten minutes or so, at dusk, the *t'ai chi* group would assemble there, like a primitive cult performing a ritual dance to the setting sun. He would have time to join them for a while, to soothe his anxiety.

He gathered together what he would need for the journey to the dam, then changed into his *t'ai chi* clothing. A quarter of an hour later, he returned from the group on the lawn with a less troubled mind. He chose a pipe from the rack and gave it to Silvia.

"For your father," he said. "He's taught me a lot."

"I told him this afternoon you wanted to have a word about my grandfather."

"Yes. Well as I said, it concerns all three if you. It's about that old sword of yours. If you don't want it, and if I offer your family a fair price..."

"You want to buy it?"

"Yes."

"What for?"

"For Terry. For Gladys, in memory of Terry. To add a personal touch to his collection."

"I know he wanted it," said Silvia. "He was always asking me if I could persuade the old bugger in Sichuan to part with it. What's a bugger?"

Chinley took a breath, but as he was formulating what he judged to be an appropriate definition, Lisa said: "We'll talk to Mr Feng about that, Silvia. If he hasn't got bugger written down in his notebook yet, then he should have."

"Don't tell Gladys about this," said Chinley. "Either of you. It's a surprise. If the old bugger lets it go."

"I'll find out while you're away," said Silvia. "But how will you get it? He never comes here, and we never go there. It's not the sort of thing you can put in the post."

"If the answer is yes," said Chinley, "I will go to your grandfather personally and collect it from him."

A display of trust towards his daughter was needed now, he thought. He locked the sideboard door and gave her the key, refraining from suggesting that she limit her intake of rum. Then he gave her the key to his safe, assuring her that there was more than enough cash in there to cover any conceivable emergency. He checked his papers and his tobacco supply, kissed Lisa goodbye, then shouldered his bag and went down to the porch accompanied by Silvia, who was returning home to cook her father's dinner.

In her new shoes she struggled along the driveway trying to keep her footing, her high heels sinking deep between the egg-shaped pebbles, and she left him waiting at the porch for the Foreign Affairs Office car. He watched her walk off down the gravel path in stops and starts, her back held straight as ever and almost motionless, as though she were balancing an invisible object on her head. The gravel became sand, and the going became easier for her; the only perceptible movement now came from her legs and her swinging pony-tail. As the trim figure and the belted white raincoat merged with the pale bark of the birch trees at the far end of the guest house boulevard, Chinley became aware of a presence at his elbow.

"A little cracker, hey?" said Jeffrey Ward. "What a body, but most of all what a face. Perfect. Have you ever seen skin like that before? So why should I take the old hen when I can have the spring chicken? Not as much between the ears of course, but she's better for bed. I don't know where she's picked it all up from. A virgin she was. Western movies, I suppose."

Ward's face was bone-yellow in the moonlight, and his lips and beard glistened with saliva. He turned towards the guest house porch, then looked at Chinley over his shoulder and said: "You know something, you really should invest in one of those for yourself. While you still have the wherewithal."

He crunched his way indoors. In the silence, which followed, Chinley heard the latch of a window being pulled to, on Gladys's side of the porch. She must have heard everything that was said. The headlamps of the approaching Foreign Office car now illuminated the guest house façade, and he sneaked a look at the window. But it was not Gladys with her nose pressed against the pane and her eyes straining against the beam of light. It was her dinner guest. Belinda.

Chapter Fourteen

The centrifugal force at the hub of the surging mass of passengers disembarking at Yi Chang railway station caught Chinley in its wake, and swung him towards the exit barriers. Here, he was pushed into railings dividing everyone into channels, like sorting pens for cattle at a country market. A young man with a steady grin and large black-framed spectacles thrust himself forward as far as he could across the intervening obstruction, and grabbed Chinley's bag, at the same time trying to shake his hand.

"Welcome, Christ," he said. "My name is Barry. I'll see you at the bottom of the steps."

Chinley was left once more to the whims and the whiplash of the crowd as Barry pushed his way back towards the exit. Feeling as though he was sailing in a strong wind he steered a course towards a turnstile, which released him into a more open space. Here he was besieged by a coven of old women, with faces like dusty brown figs. He had no idea what they were selling, if anything, and whenever he stopped to try and find out he was encircled by them. They all looked much the same age and appealed to him with the same shrivelled lips and undernourished complexions. He was reminded of gypsies years ago back home: old crones who put a curse on any household which sent them on their way without first making a modest purchase, or passing over a coin or two. So out of superstition he chose one of the quieter women and exchanged a crumpled low-denomination note for a small package of satsumas, which she produced from somewhere close to her bosom.

At the bottom of the steps he looked again at the scurrying old beggarwomen. If Lisa was here her first move would be to extract a plan from this Barry chap to do something for them, before she followed him anywhere. Her own plan to liberate Belinda from her husband for an evening had backfired: though perhaps Belinda had not heard everything that Jeffrey Ward said about her.

Chinley wondered whether, once she realised what was happening at *Madame Klimbams*, his campaigning daughter would befriend Molly too, and try to persuade her to abandon the coop. He could imagine

Molly's response: "I'm only doing it for a few weeks, just to give myself a start in life".

A hand grabbed his arm, bringing him back to the present, and pulled him by the sleeve towards a minibus parked in the station forecourt. A stubble-pocked driver grunted in response to Chinley's greeting, and the three men drove off down a steep hill towards the town centre.

Chinley had been given no warning of the size of his audience at the College of Water Technology and Hydro-Electric Power. During the past month or so the numbers attending his lectures had varied from a dozen or two to perhaps just over a hundred. But this morning, with his head still fuzzy from the overnight train journey and a breakfast of rice cooked in a wine soup, as they approached the entrance to what was no less than an indoor stadium, Barry proudly informed him that more than two thousand students and staff from various institutes in the region had gathered to hear his speech. It was far too late to decline the invitation: even before they entered the vast auditorium he could hear the premature applause, no doubt triggered off by advance notice of his arrival. Marshals with megaphones and name-badges saluted him, and he was directed by them towards a bank of cameras from the Hubei Province Television company, and onwards into the arena and on to the podium.

The theme of his talk was 'The Inland Waterways of Britain', and he was baffled by the apparent popularity of this topic amongst the locals. He put it down to the Chinese dream: they were finding out as much as they could about places they were never likely to see. But he imagined that to hold the interest of a crowd like this he would have to forego the didactics and attempt to be purely entertaining. Technically, for a smaller gathering, he was well prepared: he had slides, a projector, wallcharts, maps, a short video, and some postcards; but here, none of this was of any use.

On the way to the podium he caught a glimpse of his reflection in a full-length mirror. In the bedroom of the Double Rainbow hotel on his first night in China he had looked overweight yet civilised; but now he was a fat hillbilly, red-nosed and greasy; his hair was ruffled and standing on end. In normal circumstances he would have groomed himself a little before facing the public, but in his present mood and the present situation he decided that a slightly comic deportment might be an advantage, in helping to keep his audience awake.

A good start would be for Barry to tell everyone that Christ had arrived on an overnight sleeper, and was now ready to talk to them; but Barry took himself off into the background, leaving the introductions to the President of the host college, who read his foreign guest's full name out more or less accurately from a slip of paper.

Because of the age and magnitude of China's rivers and canals, Chinley knew he would not be able to impress anyone with dates and distances. So he began by emphasising the point that although the rivers and canals in Britain were much smaller than those in China, they could be found just about anywhere. He went into great detail describing his own area of Birmingham, glorifying the underground water network, and he raised a few laughs by making it clear that he was not referring to the sewage system. He found that gestures were necessary to clarify the distinction.

Partly as a consequence of the mild alcoholic haze which was numbing his brain, he began to enjoy himself, throwing in jokes and mimes which received an increasingly enthusiastic response from the smiling and apparently satisfied ranks in front of him. He noticed that one of the cameramen was heaving his shoulders with unsuppressible laughter, and kept bobbing up from behind his zoom lens, with his mouth open and his eyebrows arched, ready for more wisecracks from the visiting Professor.

The allotted hour went by quickly and, as far as Chinley could tell, successfully. The President now joined him on the podium and led the applause, every so often turning and bowing to the speaker. He then spread his hands on the microphone table and addressed everyone in Chinese. Chinley assumed that questions from the floor were being encouraged, but as he listened carefully to the unfamiliar accent it seemed that this was not the case. He had no idea what was being said; the only phrase he thought he caught was 'The Carpenters'. At last the President turned round to face him.

"We would like to invite you now, Professor, to sing a song. If you would be so kind."

"But I can't sing," said Chinley, finding it hard to believe what he was hearing.

"Don't worry about that," said the President. "Neither can we." He clapped his hands slowly to reinforce the collective request.

If he had been sober Chinley would have tried to find some way of evading the entreaty, say by giving a demonstration of an alien's attempt at *t'ai chi*. Or doing his party piece from years back: walking across the stage on his hands. But as the wine was still working on his system and he felt somehow bolder these days, he said he would oblige, and a fanatical cheer went up around the hall, as he dredged his mind for the lyrics of something which would be loosely relevant to the theme of his talk.

Ignoring shouts for *Yesterday Once More* and *Moon River* he opted for *Loch Lomond*, but he could only remember one verse, or it might have been the chorus, he was not sure which, so he switched to *The Banks of the Ohio*, of which he also knew only one verse. No-one objected to the geographical incongruity, and now in fact he could hear voices singing along with him. Finally, he sang *Dirty Old Town*, which he was fairly sure made a brief reference to a canal.

His medley was over, but an encore was demanded. He thought for a while. Something Irish. Something Terry had come up with. There had to be something Irish. In the kaleidoscope of names and places which mingled in his brain, all the Mollys, all the tunes, the bars and the brothels, thoughts of the fate which might be awaiting his daughter found him a focus, and after describing to his audience, as well as his imagination would allow, the deprivation of prison life by the banks of the Royal Canal in Dublin, he sang all six verses of *The Ould Triangle*.

The performance caused such a stir of hand-clapping, foot-stomping, and seat-banging, that what had started as a formal educational gathering now transformed itself into more of an African-style political rally.

He waved to his supporters, bowed to the cameras, then took his seat beside Barry, leaving the perspiring President to bring his house to order. On cue two female undergraduate students walked over to the stage, one with a bunch of flowers, the other with a carrier-bag containing something obviously fragile, packed securely between two polystyrene blocks. Chinley went back to the microphone to offer his thanks, and the audience watched in silence as he carefully extracted the contents of the carrier-bag. He prised apart the polystyrene blocks far enough to see that they contained a porcelain figure of some kind. It would have been within Wang's power of revenge to arrange for a reciprocal pot Buddha to be presented to Chinley in public, a figure which Chinley actually felt a growing kinship towards, as his own hair thinned and his belly expanded like a gradually inflated innertube.

But under increased pressure from his grip, the polystyrene clamps snapped apart to reveal not a Buddha but a foot-high porcelain figure of a Tang dynasty horse, painted in its traditional colours of pale brown, green, and yellow. He held it by its buttocks, thinking of Molly, kissed its mane, then for the cameras raised it high over his head, like a trophy.

"It has been suggested," said Barry, as he poured some more beer into Chinley's glass, that the Chinese should modify their eating habits."

"Really?" said Chinley. "And who said that?"

"Oh... people," said Barry, his dimples deep and his eyebrows lifting. He stared at the couple at the next table in the dimly-lit restaurant where they were having lunch. The couple could have been planted there as an audio-visual aid giving strength to his argument: the man, tubby, middle-aged, and surprisingly rosy-cheeked, was slurping his soup with gusto from a raised bowl, while his female companion, a young woman with tangled hair and vacant eyes, cleared her throat and stooped elegantly towards a spitoon, over which she dribbled and spat. Chinley pretended that the couple were not there.

"I've always found," he said, "that the people I eat with, here, eat quite normally. By and large."

"You're very polite, Professor," said Barry, pushing out his naturally-protruding chin. His lower jaw sagged, and his lips curled backwards over his immense spade-like teeth, like two pink slugs. "Very diplomatic."

"Well, my daughter makes up for that," said Chinley. "She's far more outspoken than I am. I suppose she might improve as she gets older. There again... Barry, there isn't a telephone in here by any chance, is there?"

"Yes."

"Yes?"

"Yes. There isn't."

"And you don't have a mobile phone?"

"Yes. I don't."

It was Chinley's second day with Barry. The visit to the dam had taken place that morning, so Chinley's local obligations to Mr Deng were now fulfilled. But he was not left in peace to recover from the demands of being the guest of a proud community. Last night he had fallen asleep with Barry still in his hotel room. He remembered thinking how remarkable it was that someone would try to carry on a conversation with a person whose eyes were closed, and who was obviously in need of a rest. Even Betty on the aeroplane had stopped talking, in similar circumstances. He was relieved to find on waking that Barry had at last left him alone, but he wondered how long the man had stayed there listening to his own monologue.

He went downstairs to the foyer, found a sleeping receptionist, and coughed in her ear. She opened an eye, and he pointed at the telephone. She shook her head. He pointed again, and again she shook her head, and closed the eye, so he went back upstairs to bed.

A new customer now arrived in the restaurant: a young woman on her own, dressed startlingly in close-fitting brown leather hot pants over fluorescent pink tights and slender scarlet shoes. Her high heels caught in a crack in the concrete floor. Chinley and Barry could not help but stare at her as she steadied herself, minced across the room, and settled on a stool in the shadows of a corner table. Barry's head swung back in Chinley's direction.

"Is she charming?" he asked. "We don't often see women like that in here. I bet she's from Sichuan. Over the border. They've got a reputation you know, these women from Sichuan. It's the spice."

"Quite charming," said Chinley.

After a further spell openly ogling the girl, Barry said "It's not easy for a man like me. To find a suitable woman friend in China."

Chinley was reminded of Silvia once saying much the same thing, from a woman's point of view.

"Chinese women are always changing their minds you see," continued Barry. "Every ten years."

His chin was getting closer. He rested his head on his fists and propped his elbows on the plastic tablecloth in a mixture of sauce and oil.

"In the nineteen-fifties," he said, "the most eligible bachelors were the heroes. The war heroes. Back from Korea."

Barry's gaze was so intense now that Chinley eased himself back a little in his chair.

"The tough guys. The fighters. But in the sixties, the women looked for someone from their own social class. And the best men then were supposed to be the poorest men. Ten years later they were looking for men with brains, and ten years after that, in the eighties, they decided that money was the most important thing, not brains, and ten years after that they went looking for rich businessmen."

He paused to look at the girl in the corner, hoping perhaps for a comment from her, or a smile, but she remained unresponsive to his penetrating voice and his penetrating eyes.

"Go on," said Chinley. "What about now? What about the new millenium?"

"Now? Who knows? Maybe the best thing for a man now is to be a foreigner."

His predicament, whether real or imagined, caused him to howl with laughter, and he swivelled around in his chair, to glare for a while once more in the direction of the corner table. Then his head came back to Chinley.

"They think a foreigner is a passport to a better life. Old or young, it doesn't make any difference. In fact the older you are the more money they think you've got. So you, for example, you should be of prime interest. You have power."

"I'm a married man," said Chinley.

"No matter," said Barry, sounding for a moment like Feng. "Where is your wife then?"

"In England."

"Why?"

"It's a long story."

"There you are then."

"There I am what?"

"You can do what you like. You could certainly afford a mistress. String her along. Let me see. Who do I know at Dong Hu? Well, there are thousands of them. Is it a mature woman you're looking for?"

"I'm not looking for any woman."

"That narrows it down a bit," continued Barry. "Most of the mature women are married too, of course, so you would have something in common from the start. But you should take heed of what happened to some of your predecessors."

"What's that then?"

"You may not always be as safe as you think. Your power to choose may go to your head. You may choose carelessly."

"Choose what?"

"Choose a mistress. You'll know Mr Wang at your place for example, the one who deals with all the foreigners?"

"Mr Wang? Of course. What, are you suggesting I should take him as a mistress?"

"No. But his wife is notorious."

"Belinda? Notorious for what?"

"Belinda?" laughed Barry. "Is that what she's calling herself nowadays? That woman changes her name as often as she changes her hairstyle. Last year it was guess what? Cleo! And before that, what, Suzie or something."

"What are you trying to say?"

"She's a nutcase."

"I have met her," said Chinley. "I think she's a wonderful woman, and no more loony than you or me."

"No, I mean she's a real nutcase," said Barry. He looked at the corner table and lowered his voice. "You know, she knew this foreigner once, and there must have been some misunderstanding. They say, she tried to cut his thing off. With a pair of scissors. Cut his *thing* off! She's being watched now though."

"Aren't we all?" said Chinley.

"She would have been locked away by now," continued Barry. "If her husband didn't know the right people. Has nobody told you about her?"

"No," said Chinley, struggling with an urge to stand up and shout the man into silence.

"No," said Barry. "I can do better than that for you. Or why don't you just go straight down to the girly bars?"

"The girly bars? I'm not... I don't... "

"They're everywhere these days. I can give you a list."

"No no," said Chinley, at last seeing a way Barry's ramblings might be of interest. "But isn't it true, that the authorities in China take a dim view of such places?"

"Yes, of course they take a dim view. If you're caught."

From the static grin on Barry's face it was impossible for Chinley to tell whether his sympathies lay with the authorities or with the girly bars.

"So theoretically," said Chinley, "theoretically what would the punishment be? If you're caught?"

"Why, are you thinking of starting one? Importing women?"

"For God's sake no. I mean, what are the risks from the woman's point of view?"

"Oh, for the woman prison. If she has no familiar. No connection. And for whoever was running it, big scale say, execution. Depending on their circle. Depending on who they know."

The man might be talking nonsense, but there again there might be something in what he had to say, Chinley reflected. He would find a telephone that was useable and call Lisa that evening. He would scotch Gladys's plans at the outset, just in case. But would someone somewhere be listening in, to a telephone conversation to the campus? In a way, the less said the better, until he was face to face with them all. He could not even be sure about Barry. Looking and behaving the way he did, he would be the perfect spy. Better to steer clear of the girly bar topic completely.

"What about Chinese men then?" he asked. "In general. They must be just as interested in foreigners as the women are. Assuming of course that there's any truth in what you've been saying about the women."

"Yes, Chinese men too. Why not? Did you say you have a daughter in Wuhan? English?"

"Yes of course she's English."

"Why didn't you bring her with you?"

"What? She didn't want to come."

"She'd be no good for me anyway," said Barry.

"*What?*"

"Too tall I suppose. Does she take after you?"

"Yes," said Chinley. "Actually she does. In some ways."

"Women in China," said Barry. "Women in China used to be chosen because of what they looked like, *and* because of the way they cooked. Nowadays, not many women like that one over there go anywhere near the kitchen, so now it's just down to what they look like. She'll be all right." Barry gave her another long look. "Your Chinese is quite good," he continued. "The bit I've heard you use. But you need to work on your tones."

"I see," said Chinley.

"The first tone, for example, is a level tone. Like this." He made a Chinese sound and accompanied it with a thrust of his broad forehead and a craning of his neck. "Then, the rising tone." This had him easing his shoulders forward, and bobbing out of his chair to a half-standing position. He sat down again and said: "Number three. Falling-rising." He dipped his head then heaved his chest out. "Now," he said, "we have the fourth and final tone, the sharp fall." He sat upright in his chair, then as he spoke he jack-knifed himself, with an energetic downward sweep of the whole of the upper part of his body.

"Thank you Barry," said Chinley, thinking yes, the perfect spy. "I will practice that."

At this point he realised that Barry, whether by guile or by chance, had eventually managed to hold the attention of the girl in the pink tights. She froze in mid-mouthful. At the corners of her lips, dangling like distended vampire teeth, were two thick yellow noodle strands. Now that she was looking at him, Barry leant over the back of his chair to get as close to her as he could without leaving his seat, and for some reason choosing to speak to her in English he said:

"We're going to the ballet this evening, Miss. Would you care to join us?" He nodded towards Chinley as if to say: "Look, I've got a foreigner in tow."

The girl retracted the noodles with the speed of a lizard whipping in its prey. Then she bent her head and shook her hair loose, so that her face was well hidden from view.

Early that evening, before he was collected for the trip to the ballet, Chinley made a call to the guest house in Wuhan from a different hotel, where he pestered the receptionist until she screamed and slammed the telephone in front of him across the desk. He heard the receiver being lifted at the other end, but for a while there was no answering voice. He could hear music, which sounded like Lisa's, whoops and cries and frantic rhythms, and he heard the clinking of glasses and bottles. At last there was a Chinese voice at the mouthpiece: a woman, whose accent was so strong that Chinley understood nothing of her response. She started to laugh, so he just repeated the word 'Lisa' several times.

"Yes, Lisa," said the woman, laughing again. A few moments later his daughter came to the telephone and cleared her throat.

"Hi dad," she said. "What's up?"

"Everything okay?" he asked, wondering why she suddenly sounded American.

"Sure. How're you doing?"

"Having a party?"

"Are you?"

"No. Are you?"

"We're celebrating. In the apartment. A night for the girls, so you're well out of it. But even if you were here, you wouldn't have been invited."

She cleared her throat again, and laughed hoarsely.

"Celebrating what?" said Chinley.

"Our sisterhood," said Lisa. She hiccupped, but Chinley resisted asking the obvious question.

"Who's we?" he said.

"Not many you know, I guess. Although you may well have danced with some of them. Caught on camera. Can't deny it. They all sound American, it's weird. Molly's here. And Gladys of course. No Belinda though. We can't expect miracles with a husband like that. I'm sure everyone sends their love."

Chinley swallowed down his anxiety and changed the subject. "So what about our upstairs neighbour?" he said. "No more trouble?"

"Oh that creep? No. Nothing we can't handle. Nothing we aren't *handling*. Silvia's here with us by the way. Have I already told you that? No? We sneaked her in."

"Sneaked her in?"

"Under one of your overcoats. So she wouldn't be seen by the beast."

"What?"

"He's bought a new doormat." Lisa was chortling again now. "Out of his own pocket, I think. At least, he didn't ask any of us to chip in. Just as well, as it happens. And he's got a new obsession now. The carpet on the stairs. He says it needs nailing down for safety. That was when we were still on speaking terms."

"So he has been bothering you?"

"No. Not any more. He's impotent now, as it were. What an arsehole."

"Good. Any post?"

"Nothing. Just one for me."

"What, from home?"

"Yes. Sorry dad, no message for you this time. Not even a few grains of coffee."

"Money's lasting okay? No disasters?"

Chinley heard Lisa joining in with some distant laughter, which sounded like the cackle of a magpie.

"Money?" she shouted, as the volume of the music was turned up. "Yes. Well... I'll explain when you come home."

"Explain what?"

He was sure he heard the strained baritone yells now of a man in the background, followed by a communal shriek of protest, then the call was interrupted by a high-pitched female voice, possibly an operator, howling in rapid Chinese as though there was an emergency to be dealt with, and whoever was on the line was causing a hindrance. Then there was a click, silence, and a dialling tone. He went back to his soulless hotel and satisfied his urge for a draught of insect brew. The daily dose must be doing him some good, he told himself, otherwise his body would not be calling out for more. As no hot water was available in his room he braced himself for a cold shower, and while rubbing himself down he imagined grabbing both the hotel receptionist and the telephone operator by the neck and banging their heads together. He laughed out loud, glad to discover his old temper was there if necessary, and a spasm like a hunger pain passed through his stomach.

Rising the next morning early enough to avoid Barry, Chinley meandered through the Yi Chang back streets until he was a safe distance away from his own block. He sat alone at a pavement café, breathing through bunched fingers to block out some of the traffic fumes, and eating dumplings from a dark-green charcoal-stained steaming-drum. He stayed out of doors because he was mesmerised by the skills of the passing cyclists.

They glided by like dragonflies, in their hundreds, weaving across each other's path with a gift for avoiding disaster which seemed preordained. It was already early November, though there was little sign of winter approaching. The mountain air was drier than in Wuhan and the mid-morning sun provided just enough warmth for him to laze back on his well-sprung bamboo chair in barefoot comfort, wearing a pair of flip-flops, an open-necked shirt, and thin cotton shorts. The female cyclists reminded him of the dancers on the stage last night. He felt a sudden bachelor sadness that these women out on the street, whose eyes occasionally met his with a brief curiosity, were as inaccessible to him as the ballerinas on the stage. As inaccessible as Samantha was, at the beginning of lust.

He didn't share Barry's faith in the powers of the foreigner. One passenger, with an exquisite ivory mask of a face and a haughty look in her large black eyes, riding side-saddle in a thin white belted raincoat, reminded him of Silvia, and with a momentary feeling of panic he was also reminded of Jeffrey Ward's whispered advice that he should think of her, or somebody like her, as a worthwhile and timely investment.

* * *

Under a sodden sky the colour of an old grey dishcloth, Chinley climbed into a taxi on the forecourt of Wuchang railway terminal in south Wuhan, and unzipped his shoulder-bag. The polystyrene blocks which protected the Tang Dynasty horse when it was presented to him were too bulky to squeeze in amongst the rest of his belongings, so he had extracted the porcelain figure from its packing case and swaddled it with his own clothes, reinforced by a dozen or so satsumas from the old women in Yi Chang. Now he checked the condition of the horse, and saw that it was still intact. His head was still humming with tunes from the West: *Auld Lang Syne, Yesterday Once More, Moon River, Jingle Bells, The Tennessee Waltz*, which were played on the train from Yi Chang as a kind of breakfast serenade.

But the music troubled him: now that he was back in familiar territory his brain was invaded by insistent images of Terry, sliding the harmonica back and forth across his lips, wiping the spittle on his thick woollen Donegal trousers, and tapping his foot along with the dance.

A large fist seemed to be inside Chinley's guts, the knuckles clenched and kneading the walls of his stomach; his throat became dry and hard, then the spasm passed, and gave way to a rush of hatred. He lowered his head, studied the buttons on his overcoat, and pressed the flesh of his thumbs down hard on to the sharp pointed ears of the model horse.

The taxi driver chose a side-street route to the Dong Hu campus.

With his hand on the horn he hurtled across dusty intersections scattering the shoppers and the schoolchildren, disrupting the huddle of fruit vendors weighing oranges on vintage hand-held scales, and forcing the bicycles and the pedal rickshaws into the gutter. The strangest thing to Chinley was that no-one seemed to object to the bullying. He could see the main road running parallel a few blocks away, and the bottleneck of rush hour traffic inching off the Yangtse River bridge, and he felt he had returned too quickly to the din and the sorrow; he could have taken a boat instead of a train from Yi Chang, and drifted downstream to Wuhan over two or three days; but he was nagged by a concern for Lisa.

No-one was outside *Madame Klimbams* as they drove past, but the gaudy sign was illuminated, and he saw to his dismay that several enlarged and familiar black and white prints were on display, on a notice-board outside the fairy-lit entrance to the night club. He felt that the driver was looking at him now so as to confirm that his passenger was indeed the middle-aged raver on the poster. But he only wanted to know if they had reached their destination.

The Dong Hu students and the auxiliary staff at the university were carrying their enamel breakfast bowls and their chopsticks back from the campus canteen, eating as they walked. The guest house cleaners grinned and waved at Chinley as he passed the caretaker's lodge at the entrance to the Foreign Experts' grounds: he wondered if they were signalling their amusement at his daughter's antics during his absence. From the outside, the apartment seemed to be empty. He wiped his feet on the new mat, glanced at Gladys's door, and as he rounded the stairs at his own landing he saw Jeffrey Ward's latest ground for complaint, according to Lisa. The dusty purple carpet had lost its tacks, and was billowing around the flaky wooden banister supports. But it added character, you might say.

He let himself into the apartment and his nostrils filled with the combined odour of joss-sticks, dregs of booze, stray socks, and stale cigarette smoke. There was a note on the sitting-room table. It read:

Dad,
  Welcome back. Am spending the day with Silvia to lift her spirits. Some developments. Don't worry about the empty safe. Will explain later. See you for tea. Normal tea. Hope the dam lived up to your

expectations.
Love Lisa XXX

Although he was well aware that Lisa was prone to exaggeration, when he unlocked the door of the safe he found it as she had said: completely empty apart from a wad of travellers' cheques. Hundreds of pounds had gone. Thousands of pounds. He made himself a black coffee, then stood in the kitchen porch watching the *t'ai chi* masters going through their gentle but potentially lethal sequences on the lawn, between the sycamore trees. They were eerily blurred into green-shaded puppet-like figures by the mosquito gauze. Two swordsmen, newcomers to the group, were facing each other with huge ceremonial blades held vertically in front of them, the steel flashing in the sunlight which had at last broken through. He started to unpack, and pulled the presentation horse out from amongst the clothes and orange wadding. He wandered around the apartment wondering where best to place it on show, finding that this pursuit and the physical act of swallowing the black coffee helped him to force thoughts about Lisa and the money to the back of his mind.

But the tranquility was disrupted by a violent hammering at the front door. He opened it to find Jeffrey Ward hopping from one foot to the other, as though under instruction from Gladys. The veins on his forehead stood out like worms trapped and throbbing under his skin. His beard was soaked in sweat and raised high, and his dark red cheeks puffed in and out like a pair of bellows.

"No-one speaks to me that way!" he yelled. "Little bitch."

The madman's hearing voices now, thought Chinley.. He stepped on to the landing and pulled the door shut: Ward was hunching his shoulders and looked ready to muscle his way into the apartment.

"You put her up to this," he said.

Spittle from the frothing mouth sprayed over Chinley's cheeks. He was still holding the Tang dynasty horse loosely in both hands. Ward grabbed it from him by its hind legs, and jabbed its ears at his face.

Chinley jerked himself to one side, and heard a door banging down below: Gladys came running part-way up from the ground floor and stood open-mouthed as Ward raised the porcelain figure on high and brought it sweeping down through the air past Chinley's weaving head.

Chapter Fifteen

Hardly thinking, but needing to do something, Chinley took a firm grip on Ward's free arm and tugged him, as smoothly and easily as Silvia's father had shown him how, in the direction of the descending staircase. Ward staggered backwards down the first two steps, and as he tried to right himself, his boots caught themselves up in the loose carpet. Chinley looked on with a strange thrill as Ward slipped with the ease of a polecat between the banister stays, and came to a halt with his immense head jammed between the uprights. Gladys, oddly silent now, ran out of the way and back into her apartment. All Chinley could see of Ward was the hairy top of his apparently disembodied head, and his flailing arms. He had heard a sharp crack, which could have come either from the splintered wood or from Ward's neck.

He had a fleeting vision of Terry in the Beijing taxi, the Irishman's freckled fingers tightening around his own throat as they drove past the Hanging Bridge. Ward's bloated body was limp; the grunts had ceased and the groaning was now faint, and he hung there like an overloaded sack. At the turn of the stairs, lying on its side in a fold of the ruffled carpet, was the Tang Dynasty horse, gleaming yellow brown and green in the light from the bay window, but minus its head, and minus its tail. The only noise now came from inside Gladys's quarters: a succession of full-blooded roars, which gradually subsided, then gave way to piping hoots of what could have been hysterical laughter.

Lisa came home singing a Chinese operatic air loudly to herself in the manner of Belinda, long after Ward was removed and the guest house disturbances had quietened down. When he heard her voice down below Chinley opened his apartment door, expecting her to stop and stare at the wreckage. But she bounded blindly on up the stairs, past the jagged hole in the banisters, through the sunbeam highlighting the curled chippings on the carpet and the air-suspended dust, then she ducked under his arm and danced on into the sitting-room. She flung her coat on to the sofa, saw the broken horse on the table, and said: "Oh. Accident?"

Removing Ward's dangling body had not been easy: an electric saw was needed to cut away the wood which trapped his head, and four men, including Chinley himself and Mr Feng, were called on to manouevre the sweat-sodden Professor out of his hanging position and out to the Foreign Affairs Office ambulance.

Chinley felt like a pall-bearer, carrying a corpse without a coffin. The saw had cut the side-whiskers of Ward's beard, giving it an elongated doggish look; his flesh was a bluish-grey colour, but Chinley heard someone say they thought he was still breathing. Gladys, calm again, pushed her door open a little as the four men passed through the hallway; Feng shouted through the gap and asked her if she had witnessed the incident.

"He just sort of tripped," she said. Then she pushed her door open further and stared at the gaping hole in the banisters. After an intake of breath she asked if she could be of assistance in any way, and offered to make a cup of tea for anyone who was not in too much of a hurry. Chinley remembered wondering at that point what the punishment was in China for manslaughter: perhaps as a Foreign Expert, a Professor with connections, he thought, he might be given special consideration, if the accident proved to be fatal.

He looked at Gladys as he passed her door, speculating on exactly how much she had seen or heard, but he could read no message in her eyes. He offered to accompany everyone to the hospital casualty unit downtown, but was unsettled by Feng saying that it would not be necessary: a comment which he interpreted as meaning either that he had some explaining to do before he could circulate freely in public again; or that Ward was considered to be beyond help.

"Sit down," he now told his daughter. "And tell me where the money's gone."

"To Silvia," she said, unshelling a peanut.

"What?"

"To Silvia. So she won't need to humiliate herself any more with the man upstairs. That's what you wanted, wasn't it?"

"There was two thousand pounds in that safe. More than two thousand pounds. And you just handed it over?"

"Not exactly," said Lisa.

"Don't be ridiculous. Either you did or you didn't. And who's upset Jeffrey Ward?"

"If you'll just let me explain."

"What?"

"Silvia spoke to her father after you left. About the sword for Terry. It's okay now, for you to buy it. I told her we could go up to two thousand pounds, and she said that's about what it's worth."

"Did she now?"

"Yes."

"Jesus Christ."

"She's a *friend*. She wouldn't cheat us. She's almost one of the family."

Chinley was speechless. Years back Lisa had pestered him and Dorothy for a brother or sister. And now here she was, more or less buying one.

"He's old enough to be her grandfather good God, you know that," she continued. "I've told him as much. And he was doing whatever he wanted with her. Dirty beast. I've told him what I think about that, too. Anyway, I left a message under his door this morning, putting him in the picture. Straight from the shoulder."

"Yes, you certainly put him in the picture," said Chinley. "And now he's out of it."

"Sorry?"

"Come outside here with me a moment. Something you missed, while you were dancing up the stairs."

He pushed her ahead of him out on to the landing.

"Good God!" she said. "What's that?"

"That," said Chinley, "is roughly the shape of Jeffrey Ward's head."

He told Lisa what had happened, then went back into the apartment and unscrewed the cap off a bottle of rum. Lisa stood near him, looked out of the window, and tightened her lips. "As long as we can show that it was him who went for *you*," she said, "and not the other way round. That's how it was. Wasn't it? Was anyone watching?"

"Gladys came out. Sort of. But I don't think she saw much."

"It's not that catastrophic, is it? How bad is he?"

"I wish I knew," said Chinley.

"All this with Silvia," said Lisa. "It's not just charity. We could think of it as an investment."

Chinley winced at the word.

"Everybody gains if you think about it," she continued. "You get the sword. Silvia gets -"

"*Shut up!* And what other *investments* have been made while I've been away?"

"Sorry?"

"The escort agency. For example. *Madame Klimbams.* The happy-go-lucky ménage outside the main gate."

"Ah, we had a talk the other night about that. Gladys and me, and some of the girls. The night you rang it must have been. A serious talk."

"What I heard over the telephone didn't sound like a serious talk," said Chinley. "It sounded to me more like a launching party. All systems go."

"If it's people like Molly and that sort of thing you're worried about," said Lisa, "don't. We've come to an agreement. No sex, all right? The girls, Molly included, will be there strictly as dancing partners, not as hookers. They'll get their money from the management for being sociable, providing above-board entertainment for the guests. Otherwise, Gladys and me will have nothing to do with the place. Okay? People like Molly need protecting. Think what Terry would have wanted."

Chinley was about to say that he knew exactly what Terry wanted, but he stopped himself, because Lisa fixed him with one of her knowing glares.

* * *

"All your friends seem to be having accidents Professor Chinley," said Mr Deng shortly after mid-day, on the telephone from Beijing. "Who's next on the list? Mrs Fox? I suppose you've been to see Professor Ward in hospital? He might benefit from the presence of another native speaker close at hand, you realise that? A friend?"

"I'm no... I believe he's in no condition to receive visitors as yet," said Chinley.

"Well can you be available to see him as soon as he is in that condition? Mrs Fox I'm sure has enough on her plate already, so perhaps you are a more suitable person to keep an eye on the injured man. As the guest house representative."

"Oh yes, I'll be available," said Chinley, suspecting that this was Mr Deng's way of ensuring he did not move far from the campus. "Let's hope for the best," he added.

"Yes, I would," said Mr Deng, leaving Chinley to contemplate the possible ambiguity in these three words. "Mr Feng called me earlier," he continued. "But he was unable really to clarify the circumstances of the incident. It was just you and Mrs Fox in the building at the time, was it?"

"I suppose it was, yes," said Chinley, noting that both Feng and Mr Deng referred to the happening as an incident, rather than an accident. He decided it was time to say something, indirectly at least, in his own defence. "Did Mr Feng mention the loose carpet on the stairs, Mr Deng?"

"The what?"

"The loose carpet. On the stairs. It's been like that for some time now. Did he mention it?"

"No."

"Yes. Not nailed down properly. Lost its tacks. Mr Ward must have got entangled with it somehow. He was always bounding up and down the stairs you know. Energetic chap. In his boots. Sometimes, with the laces undone."

Chinley felt this approach, which presented part of the truth, would be far less complicated than telling the whole truth, and would prevent the enquiries developing into an interrogation involving Lisa and the Li family, and God knows who else. The more he thought about it, while half-listening to Mr Deng, the more he was sure he was doing the right thing: if the whole truth came out unnecessarily, then Silvia - if Barry were to be believed - could be imprisoned for her illicit romps with Ward; and her father would also be implicated, as he was the source of Chinley's skill in dealing with an armed assailant.

Then, closer to Mr Deng's heart perhaps, the trail would also lead to Belinda. Instead of probing, and opening cans of worms, it was better surely to blame the loose carpet, and Ward's boots.

"So you heard the noise of someone falling down the stairs?" Mr Deng was saying. "And then you came out of your apartment to see what was happening?"

"That's more or less it," said Chinley. If lies had to be told so that half the truth would be believed, he told himself, then they had to be told. After all, this was not a trial. He was not on oath. He was protecting the innocent. And Jeffrey Ward, as far as Chinley knew, was anyway not dead, so why all the fuss? There was a pause at the Beijing end of the line: Chinley could hear Mr Deng's wheezy breathing, a sound like that of a bass concertina with ruptured ribbing, and he could imagine the thick eyebrows arching in frustration:

Mr Deng was a factual man, Chinley knew, which meant that now there would either be a relentless barrage from the bureaucrat, or a speedy conclusion to their dialogue.

"Well," said Mr Deng. Chinley heard another deep intake of air, and in his mind's eye he saw the man's barrel chest expanding to its limit. He wondered if Mr Deng was wearing his funeral suit. "Let's keep our fingers on the pulse." Quite a clever remark to finish with for Mr Deng, thought Chinley, if the irony was intended.

"Yes certainly, Mr Deng. I'll let you know how things progress."

"No need," said the brusque administrator. "Mr Feng will see to that."

And Mr Wu and Mr Hu no doubt, added Chinley, to himself.

Later that afternoon he heard a quiet Chinese knock on the door of his apartment. It was Silvia. The contemplation which she interrupted concerned her family: Chinley was considering whether or not it would be better for everybody if he quietly removed himself from the Dong Hu campus for a few days. Then no-one could ask him any more questions. Also, if his intended token to Gladys were to be meaningful, it should be collected as soon as possible from the grandfather in Sichuan. Yes, it would be expedient to be incommunicado for a while so that the Dong Hu campus ferrets - Feng, Wu, and Hu - would not unearth more than they needed to. If Ward recovered, or did not recover, Chinley would return home soon enough to deal with the consequences either way; at present he felt as though there was a gaggle of Chinese officials waiting to interview him, with more inquisitors from the American Embassy no doubt on their heels. Neither his pipe, his rum, his ginseng wine, his insect brew, nor his Foreign Expert's armchair helped him to think straight. A week ago, half an hour's *t'ai chi* on the lawn below the window would have been therapy enough to organise the mind, but the present circumstances demanded the lowest possible profile. He should not show himself on the lawn: if Feng or some other spy saw him toning up his body, they may well begin to suspect what had caused Ward's acceleration in momentum as he crashed through the banisters. For similar reasons he refrained from practising his exercises even in the sitting-room: someone might have an ear to the front door or an eye to the keyhole; or they may be monitoring his movements in some less obvious way.

Silvia walked with royal stiffness to the sofa, seated herself, and asked for a cupful of hot water. Her quiet knock was misleading, reflected Chinley; so was her choice of drink. They were no more than Chinese habits suggesting modesty. It was too late for a negotiation on the price of the old sword: the money had already changed hands. He could ask for the money back, for the time being, but that would mean more delay. He was angered not so much by having had no say in the transaction, but more by Silvia's present silence on the matter.

She sat on the sofa sipping her hot water infuriatingly, her eyes undrawn by his glare. Was Astrid right after all? *Was* he a pushover? Did Silvia think he was a pushover too? These young women. They don't know as much as they think they know. But they look as though they think they know everything. Sucking their yoghurt. Swinging their legs. Sipping their ridiculous hot water. He did not actually mind that she had his money. She needed it more than he did: he agreed with his daughter at least on that point. And it would secure the sword, which Terry had wanted. That was the important thing. But he would insist on a reaction of some kind, an acknowledgement at least that preparations were in hand for her side of the bargain to be met.

"Well then," he said, imitating Gladys by placing his hands on his hips, and making no attempt to disguise his irritation.

"Yes?" said Silvia, with what seemed to Chinley a taunting smile.

"I believe we have some arrangements to make, young lady," he said, imagining how satisying it would be to grip her by the shoulders and give her a good shake.

"You mean a replacement for Professor Ward? So soon?"

Chinley took a deep breath, as Silvia's father had instructed him to do before dealing with an opponent, then he exhaled slowly, convincing himself that he was exorcising the tension which was tightening his chest and pressing in on his rib-cage.

"No," he said. "I mean your grandfather."

"When would you like to visit him?" said Silvia, gazing through the window. "He'll have my letter within a day or two, telling him to expect you. It's already been sent."

Yes, they do things differently in China, Chinley told himself: Silvia was not goading him, then. She clearly had every intention of honouring the agreement. A blurted western-style reassurance from her, he could see now, may mean to a Chinese mind that she thought he did not trust her. It was true he had only half-trusted her: her notion of the sword's value coincided too neatly with the total cash available from the safe. But now in her taut face he could read no feelings one way or the other.

A taut but startling beautiful face, unquestionably. Transluscent, delicate; like rice paper. Not a blemish. But it was so odd, the way she comported herself. Even while sitting down she held her head in the pot-carrying posture. She kept both her high-heeled shoes flat on the floor now, and her hands rested motionlessly palms down on her maxi-skirt.

Chinley felt as though he was giving her a tutorial, and wondered if she adopted the same saintly pose when sitting at home with her father. If Ward were to be believed, she could not have remained so rigid with *him*... but Chinley dismissed these troubling thoughts from his mind and said: "Has he got a telephone number, your grandfather?"

At this Silvia took her eyes away from the window and looked at Chinley. Her mouth fell open. "Of course not," she said. "He can't afford a mobile, and the land lines are coming up. Feng Jie's being run down, not built up. You of all people should know that. Your dam project -"

"It's not *my* dam project," said Chinley. "It's *your* dam project."

"Well whatever, it means that my grandfather's town will be flooded."

"Yes," said Chinley. Was this a grudge reflected in the price of the sword? He moved closer to her.

"So the place is being run down," she repeated.

"And how does your grandfather feel about being de-housed? Or rather, re-housed?"

"He's looking forward to it. It can't be worse than the place he lives in now. You'll see that when you get there."

"*Come with me!*," said Chinley, unable to prevent the words coming out, unable to prevent his fingers reaching out to brush against the rose-marble cheeks. He stepped away from her and said: "To see your grandfather, I mean."

"Thank you," said Silvia. "But I'm needed here."

"Ah yes," said Chinley. "Yes, of course."

"You're not leaving before the opening night are you?"

"What opening night?"

"*Madame Klimbam*s Cultural Centre."

"*Madame Klimbams* what?"

"Cultural Centre."

Silvia said this so seriously that Chinley had to laugh. The wording had to be Lisa's. Something she had inherited or learned from her mother, he realised, was a belief in appearances. Change the name, and you change the nature. Drape something in virtue, and it becomes virtuous. This was why Dorothy, he suspected, whenever she bought herself a new coat, always bought a virtuous-looking one, slightly on the large side, and with lots of buttons. Fifty or sixty years ago, he imagined, she and Lisa may well have come here as missionaries, believing that a quick baptism would conjure a Christian out of a Buddhist. Out of whatever.

"*Madame Klimbams* Cultural Centre?" Chinley repeated.

"Yes. My father asked me to check that you'd be there on the opening night. Lisa and Gladys invited him to give a special demonstration, which he thought you might be interested in."

"Why? What demonstration? With me?" said Chinley. "Not a demonstration with *me?*"

"No, of course not with you," said Silvia. "It's a *special* demonstration. Not for beginners. Tomorrow night, if you can make it. He's hoping to see you there."

"Does he know...?"

"About the money? Oh yes. He thinks it's a good price too. For me."

"And does he know all about Jeffrey Ward? *All* about Jeffrey Ward?"

"You know, Professor Chinley," said Silvia. "My father is a quiet man these days. He rarely asks any questions."

* * *

"You haven't joined me for sunrise at the pagoda yet," said Belinda. She was on a sofa next to Chinley at *Madame Klimbams*, her hair now swept high and fashioned into a nest of black eggs. He was content just to look at her now and again. But her words were painful to him: whatever she said right now would be painful: the last person to speak to him from that seat was Terry.

Wang was not there at the moment but according to Lisa was coming as soon as he could, at least to make sure his wife got home safely, as he put it.

"What do you think of when you're up there, Belinda?" said Chinley. "Up the pagoda. The spirit or the flesh?"

"I think about my poky apartment for one thing. You haven't been *there* yet either. I really must organise an evening for you."

"Fine. And what else do you think about? Up there."

"I think about Terry."

"Yes."

"I think about all sorts of things. Or sometimes nothing at all. Sometimes I just look at the mist, and go floating in it. It's always misty in the morning. Mist from the South Lake. Silver cloud."

She crossed the legs of her embroidered white silk suit and adjusted a scarlet hair ribbon.

"How can you enjoy the sunrise if there's always a mist?" said Chinley.

With wide unblinking eyes Belinda looked at the empty space at the other side of their table, and said: "It's the mist of the sunrise."

Chinley was again intrigued by the close match between what she said and the way she said it: indistinct classical Chinese images spoken in a quiet lisp, although the lisp seemed to come and go. He wondered how much truth there was in Barry's account of her way with foreigners, and for reasons which he could not understand he hoped that the accusations were true.

"Come and look at it with me tomorrow morning," she said, "and you'll understand what I mean."

"There's nothing I would like to do more," said Chinley. "But I won't be here tomorrow morning."

He predicted, accurately, that she would not ask him where he *would* be. That, he realised, partly explained the pleasure he took in her company: she showed no inclination to chronicle his whereabouts. So different from Dorothy. So different from Lisa. He was also taking secret pleasure from the knowledge that, at last, he had out-manoeuvred the campus spies: only Lisa, Silvia, and Mr Li knew his plans for tomorrow, knew where he was going.

He heard a squash of compressed air, and felt himself rising a centimetre or two. His last experience of such a sensation was on the hotel minibus in Beijing. Now he heard again the squeak caused by Gladys's clammy bottom as she fidgeted into position alongside him, on the imitation-leather upholstery.

"Where's the culture then, Gladys?" said Chinley.

"Coming up, coming up," she said, snuggling down like a hippopotamus drying out on a riverside ledge after feeding. The dance music stopped. Molly, dressed in a plain pea-green blouse over baggy white shorts, and a tall thin man, a foreigner, a stranger with cropped fair hair, joined Chinley at his table, which was close to the stage. Whoever the blond man was, when Molly looked at him her face came back to life, an enormous grin reinflating her cheeks.

Lisa positioned herself centre-stage under a spotlight, looking informal, even sloppy, in the same jeans and pullover, which she had on when she arrived at the security lodge on her first night. Her hair though, Chinley noted, was now as lustrous as it had ever been and took the spotlight well.

"Ladies and gentlemen," she said, in her mother's compère voice. "I would like to thank you all for coming to our opening night here at *Madame Klimbams* Cultural Centre."

There was an enthusiastic round of applause from a thin audience.

"I am pleased and proud to introduce to you tonight," she continued, "our first guest artistes, two very dear friends of mine, Mr Li Yang, who I'm sure actually needs no introduction to most of you, and his lovely daughter, known to you locals as Li Zhao Di, and to us foreigners as... *Si*Ni*a. Mr Li and Silvia! Thank you."

She initiated a further round of applause, then took her seat next to the club's manager and manageress.

Father and daughter faced each other from a distance of perhaps ten yards, their broad ceremonial swords unsheathed now, held vertically from waist to forehead, and flashing red, green, and yellow as the metal caught the *Madame Klimbam* fairy lights. They wore identical costumes: loose-fitting functional white silk suits, looser than the one worn by Belinda, and each with a wide crimson cloth belt. Li Yang, appearing rejuvenated in the strong light, pirouetted and weaved his way towards his daughter in slow *t'ai chi* motion, finally accelerating his last few steps and bringing his blade to rest against hers.

She circled her father, her plimsoll-clad feet wide apart for balance, her knees bent slightly, and her weapon vertical again. Suddenly she lunged and froze, with the tip of her sword just short of her father's chest. The audience stirred and Chinley noticed that Molly's companion was rapt, hunched forward in his seat, his fingers interwoven and wriggling like those of an excited child. Perhaps after all, thought Chinley, as the pace quickened and the possibility of a mishap seemed more likely, there might be an audience for this sort of thing, although he wondered what guests thought they would find in a place called *Madame Klimbams Cultural Centre*, which to him sounded like a contradiction in terms. Meanwhile, the skirmish complete, Mr Li and Silvia bowed to each other and to those watching.

Then the crowd fell silent again as Silvia, keeping her back straight as always, lowered herself on to her knees and placed her sword on the floor in front of her. The manager and manageress now came on to the stage. The manager was carrying a plastic shopping bag. He reached into the bag, and passed the manageress a narrow white scarf. To Silvia he passed a padded cloth skull-cap, which she adjusted on the crown of her head. Then, to the amusement of the audience he dipped his hand once more into the bag and pulled out a large and glossy dark-green watermelon. He handed this to the kneeling Silvia.

Mr Li stood close by Silvia and watched her balance the watermelon on the skull-cap. She had the perfect posture, her only posture so it seemed, to enable her to hold it steady. The manageress walked behind Li Yang with the scarf and gently blindfolded him. Chinley looked at Belinda and at Molly, but their eyes did not waver from the two performers, and he could see that Molly's western friend had set his jaw in a bizarre grimace of anticipation, as if bracing himself for a blow.

The room fell silent as Li Yang raised his sword high in the air, hesitated ever so briefly, and brought it swiftly down towards his daughter's head. The water melon split neatly in two; Silvia caught each half as they slid down the chute of her parted hair, then she stood up to take a final bow with her father. The audience clapped and cheered, and the man with the short blond curls put his arm around Molly's shoulders and hugged her. Belinda was nodding, and mumbling something out loud to herself. Chinley rested his hand lightly on her knee; but as he leant over in her direction to ask for an opinion on the performance, he felt his own knee being grasped not at all lightly by the brawny snatch of Gladys's fingers.

When Li Yang and Silvia were changed out of their costumes Chinley invited them to have a drink with him at his table. They wanted nothing more than a glassful of hot water each. Li Yang waited until

Gladys was busy on the other side of the room, then with a chuckle of conspiracy he gave Chinley a photograph of his father, to help him identify the old man at the Feng Jie dockside. Grandfather Li's eyesight was poor, said Li Yang, and there may be other foreigners disembarking at the river port, so there might be some difficulty picking out Chinley's face as it was not very white.

"Is there an address for Grandfather Li?" said Chinley.

"Not really. But if you don't find him just call out his name a few times. It's that sort of place. If he's not there waiting when you arrive, someone will be looking for you on his behalf and they'll take you to his home." Li Yang was rising early for his bean curd deliveries the next day, so he and Silvia left quickly, their hot water hardly touched, and Lisa got up to leave with them.

Chinley noticed Belinda slip out of her seat and catch up with Silvia. They stood looking at each other in silence. Both women were in high heels, but Belinda was shorter by several inches and oddly stooped, whereas Silvia maintained her rigidity. Belinda reached out to rest both hands on Silvia's collar-bone. Then she bowed to the younger woman, but it was a cold bow, as though granting only partial absolution. Silvia's features stiffened. She twisted her shoulders free, and followed her father and Lisa out of the door.

Gladys must have told the manager that Chinley was fond of rum, because he insisted that "the Professor" share a quarter-bottle with him before going back to the guest house. Wang called in briefly while Chinley was sipping his rum. He hustled Belinda into leaving, and most of the other customers then also made their exit.

The tall fair-haired foreigner, Chinley discovered, was from Holland, a visiting businessman. He and Molly were nowhere to be seen. Gladys had another whisky and the manageress went outside the club to call a taxi for her two remaining guests. As Chinley and Gladys were driven home they saw Molly and the Dutchman in the distance, standing close together under a lamp-post. Chinley told the driver to pull in alongside them, and he wound down his window.

"Anyone for a lift?" he called.

"No, we're fine thanks," shouted Molly, her joyful cheeks ballooning out.

The Dutchman, also grinning, came closer to the car and whispered to Chinley: "I hope she's not going to take me to the cleaner's, this woman. What do you reckon?"

Chinley wound up the window, and the taxi continued on its way.

"I know how it looks," said Gladys, after a while. "But we have to be patient. We can't turn *Madame Klimbams* into a Cultural Centre overnight, can we?"

She rested a stout hand once more on Chinley's knee-cap.

"In the meantime," she added, rolling her fist into a pudding shape and thumping it down on his thigh, "business is business. Right?"

He stayed quiet and stared out of the window.

"And as for Jeffrey Ward," she continued, "you can trust me on that one, too. Whatever you need me to say, I will say."

Part Four

Chapter Sixteen

The hard narrow bunk throbbed with the pounding of the ship's engine. It was gone midnight, but each time Chinley fell asleep he was awoken by the magnified reedy whine of a mosquito hovering around his ear. The mosquito reminded him of Feng, and Feng reminded him of the shroud and the white flowers. In the berth on the opposite wall of the cabin a hunched and bulky figure, a kind of Chinese Quasimodo with a stiff toothbrush moustache, was snoring gently. The cabin was cheerless: cold and frugal, a cage of tarnished alloy and soiled timber.

The ship bumped and rattled like an oil tanker as it chugged its way upstream towards the Sichuan border and Feng Jie, the home town of Grandfather Li. Out of consideration for the sleeping Quasimodo, Chinley lowered himself as quietly as he could down from his bunk, raised the latch on the cabin door, and inched it open so he could escape once more out of the smelly cell and refresh himself in the night breeze coming off the Yangtse river. He made his way along the greasy deck past a litter of squealing piglets crammed in a large wicker basket, their owner tormenting them with a long pointed stick, perhaps out of spite for not having been allocated, or not being able to afford, a cabin. A cockerel squawked in a shadowy recess, then flew straight at Chinley's head, fanning his face with its wings as it made for the ship's rail, where it aired its chest feathers and tested its claws.

It was a starless night, but the urban river banks were illuminated now and the ship's conning light swung from side to side as though from a watch-tower in a concentration camp, picking out a dreary dockside complex of steep concrete embankments and the last of the Soviet-style high-rise residential blocks at the western edge of Yi Chang. Barry's town. Chinley lurched towards the now dormant rooster as the boat slowed down. Finally, the engines were cut and they drifted to a near standstill, chains and ropes dragging and straining somewhere out of sight. He stepped forward over several ragged bodies to see what was happening; then he stood in awe as the boat moved into a dark chasm, a ship lock, an enormous nightmarish vault with vast steel walls towering high on all sides.

The massive sluice-gate which they had passed through began

slowly narrowing its aperture until its vertical rows of teeth were jammed together, blocking out the riverside illuminations and leaving him and his ferry trapped at the bottom of an echoing black chamber. He watched in reverence to his trade as the water in the ship-lock rose, and the grey-green nightshade tips of the Yi Chang buildings came once more into view.

He guessed that Feng, Mr Wu, and Mr Hu would sooner or later notice his absence, and confer. No doubt Feng would then find a precedent to visit his apartment, and Lisa would concoct a convincing cover-up story. She was good at that. She would probably say that he was staying with the Li family for a few days, which was almost true.

The water level in the ship-lock had now risen to its full height. The sluice-gate opened and the ferry surged forward, leaving behind the riverside lights and the night-shift workers cycling along the damp concrete of the dockside tracks. Chinley marvelled at the magnitude of the engineering and, strangely, felt his own loins being fortified.

He set off on another round of the decks. Then, having nowhere else to go and nothing else to do, he went back to the cabin, wondering how to pass the approaching seven hours of darkness if he was to be kept awake by the mosquito and the snores of his cabin mate.

He was also disturbed by the recurring thought that Jeffrey Ward might be dead. Only Lisa knew the full truth about what happened on the stairs. How much Gladys knew was, so far, anybody's guess.

The loose-fitting wood veneer of the bunk rattled noisily along with the thrust of the engines, but in the absence of the mosquito, which seemed to have moved off elsewhere, and in a lull from the man opposite, Chinley subsided into unconsciousness. His final thoughts were of relief at being at last out of the public view, or at least being in the company of strangers who held him accountable for nothing.

The night sky was fragmenting into dawn as the boat pulled in to dock at Feng Jie. The searchlights were still flicking from bank to bank but now, instead of illuminating dull concrete flood barriers they picked out smooth purple and blue rocks at the foot of the sheer riverside cliffs. Feeling ever more like a fugitive Chinley stood amongst the unkempt passengers waiting to disembark, with their ragged belongings wrapped in knotted cloth on shoulder-poles. He left it to those around him to push their way forward, and he let himself be carried with them into a narrow exit, a bottleneck, to be disgorged at the rim on to a flimsy metal bouncing gangway.

Off the ship but not yet quite on land, they all shuffled in single file along a disintegrating man-made causeway of tilted wooden planks and corrugated iron sheets, across muddy river flats towards a high sandstone outcrop. Here there was a steep climb up a rough natural stairway, now sparkling with quartz as day broke, leading to tumbledown shanty dwellings on the edge of the settlement and a few abandoned market stalls. Chinley tagged himself on to the trail of passengers, and while scanning the phalanx of locals for a face matching Grandfather Li's photograph, he followed them and their swaying bundles into another century.

The straggle of disembarkees, in the dawn shadows looking like exhausted and pox-ridden pirates, with their hitched-up trouser-legs and silt-spattered naked ankles, made their way slowly and quietly through the fortified gate in the old town wall, and into the cobbled lanes of Feng Jie. Here, the commercial day was just beginning. Shutters clattered open, men and women in chefs' hats appeared on the pavement, as silent as wax models in a museum. They rolled their lumps of dough near huge steaming pots illuminated by antique yellow gaslight; while the older folk, crippled seemingly with cold and arthritis, jogged as well as they could up and down the high street, or just stood on the spot swinging their arms and doing their early morning breathing exercises.

Just call out his name a few times, Silvia's father had said, and he will come to you. Chinley could not bring himself to stride up and down like a town crier, shouting for Grandfather Li, but he imagined that some of the senior citizens here may know where he was, so he stood near an old couple who were running on the spot and asked them. Perhaps his peculiar Chinese accent was incomprehensible to them: they looked at him briefly, and at the photograph, which he held out, but they made no reply, just continued skipping on the flagstones.

Chinley sat on a stool at a roadside stall and ate a breakfast of soya milk and dumplings. Then he stayed where he was, wondering what to do next. A young girl dressed like a budding gypsy dancer cocked her head at him and spoke to the cook, who nodded. The girl then faced Chinley again, and beckoned for him to follow her.

She guided him through a network of winding rubbish-strewn

passageways out into a back yard, then up a rotting open staircase of grey wood to a single room on the top floor of a whitewashed tenement block. An electricity cable without a bulb dangled over the bed; the internal paintwork was slapdash and scarred; and the one token window was simply a cube cut out of the wall, creating an unprotected opening to the outside world, like the gap left by a missing air-conditioner.

The room was musty and damp, and the early morning sunlight, slanting in through the hole in the wall, highlighted a drift of dust, which had settled thickly and comprehensively on all available surfaces. Chinley assumed he was being offered accommodation.

It was basic, but it would save him the trouble of looking elsewhere. The teenager screeched something down into the yard and a younger girl of perhaps twelve years of age, another gypsy type, came running to join her at the top of the frail stairway, shrieking just as loudly as she ran. But as the youngster rushed across Chinley's threshold the sight of him brought her to an abrupt standstill. The older girl ushered him out of the way on to a balcony, then both the girls, coughing and sneezing as they worked, attempted to dust and clean the place.

The balcony looked down on to Feng Jie's main street. No fussy little bridges and decorative streams here: just rough flagstone passing points over deep drainage channels. The market place was full of traders, but they seemed to have nothing to sell except oranges and satsumas. If they all have oranges and satsumas, he found himself thinking, who do they sell them to? He fumbled in his pocket for his pipe. This was beginning to feel like a place where he could forget everything. This was what he needed: a place where he could fill his mind with nothing more than a concern for the sale of oranges and satsumas.

The dusting and the coughing stopped, and the two girls stood shoulder to shoulder on the doorstep yelling at each other and at Chinley, but when it became clear that he did not understand them they disappeared. Soon afterwards he heard a familiar clanking noise outside his door, and he opened it to find two large thermos flasks filled with hot water. The girls had not, however, provided a packet of tea. On the bedside table he found a porcelain cup. He lifted its lid, and saw the remains of a drink left perhaps by the room's previous occupant: dark green leaves, long dried-out and encrusted like barnacles on to the cup's interior. Nevertheless, he poured the thermos flask water on to the seemingly petrified gunge and took the resulting murky brown liquid back with him to the balcony, so he could see how trade was progressing with the fruit-vendors.

Then he heard the dull clang of a heavy iron bell. Further up the high street, away from the river, he could see a shabbily-dressed trio, looking and sounding like three tragic minor characters from a Chinese folk opera.

Two women to the rear, with arms linked, were holding in front of them the long thin sticks of the blind; their leader, though to all appearances also blind, was tapping his way confidently towards the market-place, now and again striking the bell at his waist to warn others of their approach. They seemed like harbingers of the fate of their town: not just a defacing but an obliteration, to lie at the bottom of the ever deeper river.

Chinley, with his height and his good health, his long legs and his western clothes, felt guilty and over-conspicuous, and he went indoors, disheartened, to sit on the bed. He suddenly wanted to know exactly what Gladys had seen, and whether he really could trust her, as she said he could. Whether she would explain to everyone if necessary that he had acted in self-defence. There must be thousands of villages like this in Sichuan Province alone, he thought. But even so it would be impossible for him to hide in any of them: as a tall foreigner he was too visible, and if someone wanted to find him, if Jeffrey Ward was in fact dead, they would soon root him out. With his head resting on the hard thin pillow he decided to make the most of his own company and his freedom while it lasted: he would spend the rest of the day recovering from the discomforts of the boat journey, then tomorrow he would go off into the hills. But as he lay there he heard again the clanging of the heavy iron bell, closer now, followed by footsteps climbing the stairway leading to his balcony. The door juddered open, and the daylight was dimmed by the frame of the blind man from the market place.

From the balcony, looking down on the market square, Grandfather Li had seemed to Chinley much younger than he did at close quarters. While he was striding along, leading the two blind women with their long thin sticks scratching the flagstones, he looked as sprightly as his son, sprightlier even. His son had an occasional limp. But now, indoors and sitting on a bedside chair he was ancient, like an idealised reincarnation of an early prophet. Yet his skin - a blessing passed on to Silvia - was still smooth and tight across his face, despite his age, and shone like pale gold. He had a full white beard and his long hair was soft, grey, and ungroomed, like strands off a sheep's fleece caught in a bush.

As though he knew Chinley was looking at his eyes, which gleamed like polished resin, he said, in slow clear Mandarin: "I can still see a little, you know. But not much. So I guide those whose eyes see less than mine. The girl who cleans here read me the letter from Wuhan. You probably found her difficult to follow?"

"Impossible for me," said Chinley. He felt a sudden shame at wanting to take a valued possession, an heirloom, away from this man.

"Yes. How does the room suit you? Is it comfortable enough? We can look for another one if you like."

"Oh no, it's fine," said Chinley. "Just fine."

"I live on the floor below. After you've had a rest come down and see me. Have some dinner. Have a beer. And have a look at the sword."

"Are you sure..." said Chinley. "Are you sure you don't want to keep it?"

"*Me* keep it? What for?"

"Well... Aren't there any youngsters here who want to learn how to use it?"

"One or two used to come and pester me. One or two of the boys. But they've all left town now, and who can blame them? This place is going to be *flooded*."

The old man gestured at the walls as though the bare room represented the whole neighbourhood.

"My son got away from here a long time ago," he continued. "And now his daughters are leaving *him*. Fine. Two in Beijing. What Zhao Di has in mind is anybody's guess."

"Yes. I've got a daughter like that myself," said Chinley.

"Good. But at my age and in my condition," continued the old man, "I have time enough to sit and imagine what she *might* be up to. Still, who can blame her for wanting to use her brains, and her beauty, to better herself?"

His eyes levelled with Chinley's, so clear and apparently focussed that Chinley was sure his Chinese host could see more than he was prepared to admit.

Chinley now explained exactly why he wanted the sword and the old man, his face becoming expressionless, rested his elbows on the table. His hands disappeared into his beard, supporting his chin.

"The money's with Silvia," said Chinley. "Did she...?"

"I don't want to know anything about the money," said Grandfather Li. "That's none of my business. Do you have enough hot water? Did the girls deliver it?"

"Yes."

"And tea?"

"Yes," said Chinley, looking at the cooling mud-coloured liquid in the cup on his bedside table.

"The older one's called Xiao Lu. She's the one to rely on. She's never far away, so give her a shout if you need anything. It makes no difference what you shout. Just make a noise of some kind and she'll come. I'll be downstairs now. No hurry."

The iron bell clattered as he rose to his feet, and Chinley could hear the metallic clang punctuating his descent down the steps.

* * *

The blade of the sword was blunt and hefty, broader than those Chinley had seen paraded on the guest house lawn, and broader than the one used by Li Yang to cut through the water-melon on his daughter's head. Perhaps that was an indication of its antiquity. The brownish metal was pitted and lined with deep grooves, and it was surprisingly cold to the touch, but it glowed, Chinley imagined, with age.

Grandfather Li rested the join of the blade and the hilt on a single finger to indicate the quality of balance, and Chinley made ignorant noises of approval. Li then explained the symbolism in the carving and engraving: the dragon for vitality and superiority, the phoenix for completeness and harmony, the crane for longevity. Chinley made more nasal noises of admiration, but Li shook his head and said: "Bunkum. That's what Zhao Di calls it and maybe she's right. Useless myths and hocus-pocus to her. So she won't miss it. When's your boat back to Wuhan?"

"My boat back?" said Chinley. "I haven't been thinking about that at all."

After dinner Li asked Xiao Lu and the younger girl to show Chinley around and accompany him at least as far as the town centre. In a corner of the market place they left him at the fringe of a group engaged in what seemed to be a drinking game, and as usual he became the focus of prolonged intensive stares. He had become more or less inured to this and was ignoring it, until he realised that some of the men were trying to attract his attention. He had not fully awakened from his long afternoon siesta, and he did not yet feel capable of deciphering their accents, so he ignored their small effeminate waves.

Then Xiao Lu appeared again and gave him two cigarettes, saying they were from the three men who were signalling. Chinley acknowledged the gift and one of the men ran across with a lighter, then ran back cackling to his table. Shortly after this Xiao Lu brought over a bottle of *baijiu*, for which Chinley, to his own surprise, was developing a taste. She filled a small cupful for him. He turned to the three men and delighted them by draining the contents in one gulp, then holding the cup upside down in the usual manner to verify that it was empty. A little later two chocolates in a glossy green and red wrapping were sent over, and the three men continued grinning and staring at him, their eyes bright with amusement. Xiao Lu came over again and stood by his chair, and said, in English:

"Tonight very good. You go home."

He was mystified but entirely willing to co-operate, if this was the only condition attached to the VIP treatment he was receiving. He stood up and draped his jacket around his shoulders, with a nod of thanks to the three men.

"*No!*" said Xiao Lu, blocking his exit. "You go home."

"Yes, for Christ sake," said Chinley. "Let me get past you then."

"No," said Xiao Lu. "You go home with *them*."

She pointed at the three men, who were now standing, ready to leave.

"What? *Why?*" asked Chinley.

A babbling throng clamoured around him: the drinkers, Xiao Lu and the younger girl, and several passers-by, but it was only when one of them, a rough-looking character with bulging eyes and a hare-lip, began humming *The Wedding March,* that he began to understand what was being asked of him.

Yielding to the group pressure he was escorted through side streets and alleyways to the part of town where he had his room. Here, the whole procession ascended a fire-escape in a block near his own and walked on past a door which lay off its hinges into a festive crowd, Chinley being pushed to the front as though his presence were urgently required.

Feeling like a visiting dignitary he was introduced first to the bride and groom, an attractive young couple with long limbs and a wine-induced flush on their cheeks. The bride held her glass at a careless angle and the groom, in an attempt to show Chinley to the other guests, wrong-footed himself and stumbled, allowing Chinley to demonstrate his relative sobriety by steadying him and holding him upright. Chinley then passed around the room shaking hands and posing for photographs. He was being tailed by a video camera and every so often he heard its operator mumble, in English, as though he were practising an entry in Feng's dictionary, "Lucky omen. Charm. Talisman." When the ritual greetings were over Chinley looked into the video lens and said: "What are you mumbling about?"

"*You,*" said the cameraman, bowing low. "You are a lucky omen, a charm, a talisman, for the newly-weds. For their future."

"Me? Why? Good God."

"Because you are a foreigner simply from an outside country." The man then used his forefingers to trace a fat figure-of-eight in the air. "And, you look like a Buddha."

Xiao Lu brought Chinley a glass of red wine, and as he drank it he thought about the statuette, which he had bought for Wang in Beijing. He ran an exploratory hand over his skull: his hair was receding, but still there, whereas the Buddha, as far as he recalled, was completely bald. Then he remembered the bulging belly and the folds of skin hanging out of the loose blue robes. He looked down at his own stomach, which by western standards, he imagined, would be considered quite a normal shape for a man of his age. Here amongst the lean Chinese men, however, it appeared to be swelling with each sip of wine that passed his lips.

He sat down, to minimise the protrusion, and raised his glass to the staring ranks of well-wishers, thinking how fortunate it was that no-one there knew anything about him. A lucky omen. How could he bring any luck to any couple, after *his* twenty-five years of marriage? He was on the point of a divorce; he had a daughter who was a near-alcoholic, an impetuous philanthropist, very generous with money which was not her own; and by now he was possibly being hunted down as a killer. These were not qualities to bestow on newly-weds. There must be others in the town, other visitors from abroad perhaps, who could also convey the Buddha's bounteous nature: others, more obese than himself and with less hair on their heads. And with more promising family fortunes. He called the cameraman over to his side and said:

"Listen. You really should go out in the street again and look for someone else. Another foreigner. Just to make sure."

The cameraman stood silently grinning as though waiting for him to finish a joke. But Chinley just said: "You really should", so the cameraman went off to whisper to a number of people in the room, who stared over his shoulder at Chinley. He returned and said: "No. We want *you*. We see you are an honest man and a modest man. And also, the party is nearly over."

* * *

It was barely daylight but Chinley was already climbing the hills above Feng Jie, past khaki-coloured puddles and ponds, and drainage ditches flanked by screes of powdery red earth which glowed like burning cinders as the sun rose. He came to an amphitheatre of orange groves and thin green tiers of fig trees curving down the contours of the slopes. As he walked on it occurred to him that this was the first time since his arrival in China that he was in a place where no other human being could be seen or heard. Sensing the prospect of deeper solitude he took a narrow uphill side-track, and left the orchards, the woods and the fields behind him. He crossed a derelict bamboo bridge spanning a ravine, and climbed to a bleak moonscape expanse of bleached clay and luminous yellow earth. Then without warning, around a bend in the muddy upland track, the mass of land fell away from him into the hazy emptiness of a pale golden mist.

The hoots of unseen tugs and ferries told him that somewhere far below was the Yangtse river, with its overburdened boats; but here he was alone, and becoming increasingly feather-headed in the thin mountain air. He took a rest on a blackened limestone ledge, opened the hip flask which Lisa had reminded him to bring, and drank some of

Terry's rum.

Sitting at such a height, reflecting on his lot, his thoughts became wilder. He was free now. He needn't go downstream with the river back to Wuhan. He'd had to defend himself against Jeffrey Ward, he'd had no choice. Why should he risk people thinking otherwise? He could take a boat instead to the far west and slip out of the country. Take the sword back to Grandfather Li: Gladys would be none the wiser. Telephone Lisa and tell her to leave Wuhan and *Madame Klimbams* immediately, say goodbye to Belinda for him, tell Silvia she's a lucky girl, and make her way home to England as best she can. He took another large mouthful of rum, then gave way to an onset of drowsiness and spread himself out on the ledge, using a forearm as a pillow.

There was a chill in the air when he woke so he strode off downhill at speed, calculating that if he continued along the arc of the hillside he should eventually return to his starting point on the outskirts of the town. He felt detached and liberated, and was intoxicated enough not to care whether the route he was taking led him back to Grandfather Li's building or not. After maybe an hour or so descent he reached a crossroads, looked at the Chinese road-sign, and laughed aloud at his own illiteracy.

He sat on a stone bench and filled his pipe. Crisp fallen leaves blown along by a gusty breeze scraped by his feet, and a swaying branch of the hawthorn tree under which he was sitting caught on the sleeve of his jacket. He looked up and was startled to see half a dozen fat sparrows perched there wing to wing, staring down at him. Angered at being scrutinised yet again, albeit by the birds, he shooed them away. When they were gone he paused for a while, and shouted out:

"All right. Bugger off then Dorothy, if that's what you want!"

He laughed as a steamer boomed back at him from the wide unseen river still far below, and he drank the rest of the rum. He laid the empty hip flask on its side on the bench, and spun it round, then he lurched off in the direction the cap was pointing when it came to rest. But he had gone only a few yards when he was stopped by an elderly woman bent over a walking stick.

"Are you the man who's staying with Grandfather Li?" she said. He nodded, and she pointed out the road he should take to get there.

* * *

Unshaven and aching from his neck to his ankles, Chinley stood on the observation deck of the Yangtse river ferry. To cope with the journey he needed to empty his mind of all consideration of time and distance, so he had no idea what day it was, nor the hour, nor how far he had already sailed.

The presence of people around him on the approach to Grandfather Li's apartment block had sobered him somewhat after the tribal dance down the mountainside, and the sobriety brought with it a decree that whatever else he did he should not abandon his daughter. Abandon his wife, yes; that was different. He and she were abandoning each other. But abandon his daughter, no. As this meant going back to Wuhan, he took charge of the sword, had it packed and camouflaged in a suitable carrying-case, and picked up the remainder of his belongings from Grandfather Li's upstairs room. Ahead of him was a two-day journey.

The grey-brown river narrowed yet again to pass between dark shale cliffs rising sheer from the water and corkscrewing up and up into sunlit peaks high above the mist of the gorge. They coasted effortlessly past a small green trading junk facing the other way and labouring against the current, its crew stumbling over boulders at the water's edge, pulling on ropes to help their boat on its way upstream. Downstream the river was placid, its steady wind-raised ripples appearing from a distance motionless, like wet cobblestones. But the peace of mind this brought to Chinley was short-lived: he was being stared at again, this time by members of the crew, high-ranking members by the look of their uniforms.

They came one after another and pressed their noses against the glass pane of the entry to the observation deck. Several of them were nodding at each other, as though they were agreeing on his identity. As the ship reached its first resting point and pulled in to the harbour at Barry's town, Yi Chang, Chinley saw the blurred outline of a woman, a figure which put him in mind of a dimly-recalled Chinese folk tale, in which there is a recurring apparition of a stern old lady who is always there, no matter how far or how fast you try to get away from her.

Now, as the blurred image came into focus, he recognised her. He tried as before to recall her name. *Hilda*. That was it: Hilda. Her spectacles flashed as she turned her head towards him, acknowledging him with a small bow. The senior crew members were still staring at him from behind the glass panel. He felt like Dr Crippen: she must have called the ship to check that he was on board.

Chapter Seventeen

In the confinement of the cabin Hilda sat on a buckled swivel-chair with the club heels of her sensible shoes resting on the packing-case of the sword. A thermos of freshly-boiled water was delivered and Chinley prepared two cups of green tea, exercising his lips into a smile in an effort to hide his concern at her appearance.

"Professor Chinley," she said, solemnly. "Professor Ward is no longer with us."

Chinley's stomach contracted at the news, but he managed to feign an expression of limited comprehension, as though the man's name was unfamiliar to him.

"Professor *Ward*?" he said. "No longer with us?"

"That's right," said Hilda. "He is no longer a pigeon."

"I'm sorry?"

"He is no longer a pigeon. I thought you might like to know."

Chinley looked at Hilda, wondering if she too had been drinking.

"Now," she continued, her face still sombre. "He is being looked after by friends at an American convalescent home in Hong Kong. So he is no longer a pigeon in our hospital in Wuhan."

Chinley felt his tightened lips relaxing into a grin. As relief surged through his whole body, he pounded on the table in front of him with both fists, then hooting with laughter he jumped to his feet and threw his arms around Hilda's neck. She tried to release herself from his hold, without success, then she stopped squirming and pushed her spectacles back up her nose.

"I didn't realise he was such a good friend of yours," she said, shaking her head at Chinley's continuing chuckles. "In fact we were all worried that there was some growing animosity between the two of you for whatever reason. There were some incidents... not just the pagoda. But perhaps Mr Feng has exaggerated."

"Have a drink of rum," said Chinley, sliding open a panel below his bunk.

"Not for me," said Hilda.

"No," he continued, unscrewing the cap of a fresh bottle, "it's just a great relief to hear that he's pulled through. And he's quite all right now, you say?"

"No, I didn't say. But he was obviously well enough to travel."

"So when do you think he's coming back to join us?" said Chinley.

"He won't be coming back. You see, from reports, Mr Deng and myself were given the impression that Professor Ward was not completely suited to life in China, even at the guest house. We believe he had, or has, a volatile temperament, which he can't control. So we have written to him care of the convalescent home inviting him to have a rest for a while, back in the United States, for example."

"I see," said Chinley, wishing he knew exactly what was being left unsaid. About Belinda, about Silvia. About Gladys. About himself. "But why were you looking for *me*?"

"A coincidence in a way. I'm here to visit the Hydro-Electric Power university. You've been there."

"Yes. I've *sung* there."

"I know. Why was I looking for you? Mr Feng sent a message to Beijing, because he was worried. You hadn't been seen on your usual walks around the campus. He called to see your daughter, in case you were ill, and she advised him to visit Mr Li the bean curd salesman. Mr Li told him a strange story, that you were visiting his grandfather in Sichuan. And Mr Feng asked me, as I was coming here anyway, to find out which boat you were on so we could pass on the good news about Jeffrey Ward. About his recovery." Her eyes met Chinley's and she added: "In case you were concerned about that."

A voice crackled in the cabin speaker announcing the imminent departure of the boat, and Hilda stood up and stepped awkwardly over the wooden packing case.

"So this really is what you were after?" she said. "Can I have a quick look? Don't worry, your secret is safe. Mrs Fox has not been told, although we wondered... She thinks you're just visiting the dam again."

Chinley flicked open the catches of the case and eased back the lid. It was like emptying his pockets for a policeman, he felt.

"Oh," said Hilda. "A bit battered, but... interesting enough I suppose. Who knows what poor Mr Fox would think? *How* much did you pay for it?"

"Well," said Chinley. "How much would you say?"

"Well," said Hilda, "you might have to pay up to two or three thousand renminbi for an old sword like that."

"You mean two or three thousand *pounds?*"

"Good heavens no, I mean two or three thousand yuan, If it was in good condition. Especially as you're a foreigner."

She looked at Chinley and forced a laugh, but he said nothing, so she shook hands with him and left the cabin. Then she turned and said

"There have been some domestic changes in the Li family household, by the way. Mr Li is losing his youngest daughter. She's going off to Beijing to join her sisters. Soon, I believe."

"What, working in the Double Rainbow?"

"Oh no," said Hilda. "You know her better than that, don't you?"

Chinley said nothing, but shouted: "Say hello to Barry!" as Hilda walked away. "Barry at the Hydro-Electric Power place. Do you know him? The man who looks after foreign visitors here."

"Yes of course I know him," she called back. "He's my nephew." Heavy-coated gold-braided crew members were waiting for her, and they escorted her down to the landing stage.

Chinley went back into his cabin and threw away the remains of the green tea. He had a generous glass of rum, then felt an urgent need for his own personal draught of insect brew, which Lisa said she would pack for him but in fact had not. With a sick sensation in his stomach he calculated an approximate sterling exchange rate for three thousand *yuan*, Hilda's upper limit.

Yes, Hilda might be wrong; but if she was right, three thousand yuan being roughly equivalent to not much more than two hundred pounds, Silvia had earned herself a huge profit. The gift was for Terry so its monetary value, Chinley told himself, was irrelevant. But to be duped by someone who, as Lisa said, was almost one of the family now, that was relevant. She was not stupid, Silvia. She must have known what she was doing all the time. Using Lisa. Using *him*. He was just another foreigner for her, there to make some money out of. A pushover. Chinley could hear his veins pumping at the thought that *Astrid* had been right, after all. So it seemed.

The ferry chugged into the downstream flow of the river, and Chinley's mind darkened. He lay on the bunk and drank the rum straight from the bottle, hoping this would lighten his mood. But it had the opposite effect. No, he told himself, he had been generous too often in life. This time for once he would not shrug off the deceit and the loss and put it down to experience. He was too old to be putting things down to experience. This time he would insist on a satisfactory return for his investment. Business was business, as Gladys pointed out.

Perhaps if Silvia... perhaps if Silvia and he were closer. Now that Jeffrey Ward was off the scene. Dorothy was off the scene too. The more Chinley considered the possible new scenario, the more it appealed: Beijing. A young woman living there at his expense. That was what it amounted to. That was already set up. All very well, as long as she... what? Made herself available for him whenever he chose to call on her. And when she came to Wuhan to visit her father she would also visit the guest house and spend the night there. Lisa was sure to become restless soon and move on, so he could then use the apartment for any purpose whatsoever.

He looked at himself in the small round rusty mirror by the bunk, and was startled to see the manic sheen in the whites of his eyes. But vindictive plans, he told himself, were a natural consequence of having been duped. And two days later, when the ferry moored at the dockside in Wuhan, the notion of the higher return was still there, like a dark crystal shaping itself inside his head. But the first business to attend to was to off-load the packing-case with Gladys.

Building Ten was not in complete darkness, and Chinley could see a shadow flitting from wall to wall. It was a Tuesday evening, one of the country dancing nights. If Gladys herself was still there, perhaps tidying up, he could surprise her now. The door was open so he stepped quietly inside.

She was there all right, busy folding and stacking chairs. Unseen, he made his way towards the end of the hall and rested his luggage on the edge of the stage, near the piano. She was making enough noise to cover his movements, and he soon had the packing-case open and the contents exposed. He then raised the lid of the piano: a presentation like this one deserved an overture. He waited until she finished positioning one more chair, then he brought the fingers and thumbs of both hands down heavily twice on to the instrument's deepest register.

The reverberation of the powerful bass rumble died away, and he looked across the hall. Gladys didn't recognise him. She was standing quite still in the centre of the room, but another lighter vamp on the keys from Chinley brought her marching towards him.

"Who's that?" she shouted, stopping again. He tinkled on in a higher key now and she came closer, protruding her turtle neck to its limit. At last she recognised him.

"A sighting of the campus phantom," she said. "We've all been worried about *you*."

"I'm all right," said Chinley. "I wish I could have played you something more suitable for the occasion."

"What occasion?"

He pulled the open packing-case towards her. She stared at the contents for a moment or two, then held her hands out wide apart in front of her, palms upwards, in a silent gesture of amazement. Her head craned forward and her nose pointed at the shining metal, as though she intended to sniff it from a distance before moving any closer.

"This is for you," said Chinley. "A small gift, in memory of Terry. It's the sword he always wanted. The one he kept pestering the Li family for. What do you think of it?"

She reached out, and touched the blade.

"Beautiful," she said. "Beautiful. *Rough*."

Chinley remained seated at the piano tapping random notes, leaving her time to investigate her new possession; but as he tinkled on he felt her broad hand stroking his hair, and her vast bosom pressing against his shoulder.

"What a marvellous weapon!" she shouted. "Crude and powerful. Just like he was, in his prime. No drugs. Still, if they help."

"*What?*"

"And his prime lasted a long time, I can tell you."

"How is everyone?" said Chinley, shifting his body a little away from hers. "Lisa? Mr Feng? Molly, Belinda?"

"We can sharpen it," said Gladys, listing in Chinley's direction like a dinghy. "Have it like a razor. I've always been a bit of a tinker you know. Sharpen it so it looks good hanging on the wall. Eh?"

"Wouldn't that... detract from its antique quality?" said Chinley.

"Rubbish! Sharpen it! Let's have it *gleaming!*"

She rolled her shoulders, pressing the spread of her breast against him; to Chinley it felt like the stubborn flattened nose of a bulldog. As though reading his mind she brought her face close to his and lolled an enormous tongue at him. She began hopping from one foot to the other, like a lumbering old squaw doing a war dance. Let her dance out her excitement if that's what she wants, Chinley told himself, concealing his apprehension with a tired grin.

Then she pounced on him, dragged him backwards off the piano stool, and tugged feverishly at his coat buttons. In an effort to free himself he dropped to his knees and tried to crawl between her skipping legs; but she pivoted and straddled the small of his back, shouting "That's the way! Yes! Yes!"

The strings inside the piano were pinging with the vibration they were both making. He felt her hands roving his belly and gripping the belt of his trousers. He struggled backwards and forwards on his knees, but the more he wriggled the more she was encouraged, shrieking with delight and, he assumed, interpreting the thrashing of his limbs as his contribution to the foreplay. She slapped his now bare buttocks, and he became aware of items of her clothing falling to either side of him. Then he saw two huge and glistening naked knees pumping up and down like pistons, at the edge of his vision, and he decided that the only gentlemanly way to put an end to her caper before things went too far was to feign an injury.

He groaned loudly, placed a clenched fist on his rump, and fell prostrate on to the grimy concrete floor. She breathed hot air over his neck for a while, then rolled over and went to stand in front of him. He closed his eyes to the whale-like expanse of flesh, which hung before him, and he hoped fervently that if somebody heard the commotion and came in to switch more lights on, they would do so after Gladys readjusted her garments.

"Are you all right?" she said.

"I think I've twisted a muscle, or whatever you do with a muscle. Maybe I should lie here quietly for a moment."

"Yes, you stop right where you are, and I'll make you comfortable."

He speculated with dread on what kind of relief she had in mind, but she returned with a cushion and pushed it under his cheek.

"Don't try to move yet," she said.

For God's sake put your clothes back on quick, said Chinley to himself.

"I'll just take the sword over to the guest house," said Gladys, stooping to pick up a blouse, "and lock it safely indoors, so we have less to carry. Then I'll come back and we'll put you on your feet. There's a gash on your forehead I'm afraid, but it doesn't look too serious. I'll wash it for you later. Don't touch it."

When she was clear of the building he sat on the edge of the stage and dabbed his head with a paper tissue. If only it was Belinda tending his wounds again, he found himself thinking. Or Jane, or Alison, or Silvia. Or Molly. Molly *causing* his wounds.

This is the rum talking, he told himself. But it was not Molly wounding him, it was Gladys. He didn't want Gladys wounding him. Not Gladys. Not the personification of *Madame Klimbam* herself, but rather one of the young charges, one of those narrow twisting torsos...

The memory of Molly brought a picture of Terry to mind: a youthful Terry now that death had taken his age away; beaming and winking at what had just happened or nearly happened here in Building Ten. Chinley unzipped a well-padded pocket in his shoulder-bag, and took out the hip flask.

"To Molly and her ilk," he said, swallowing a mouthful of rum. Yes, his life would be different, he sensed, once his daughter was on the move again. He adjusted his clothing, shouldered his bag, and made his way with speed up into the woods.

Chapter Eighteen

"That's a very recent wound you've got there," said Lisa. "What have you been doing with your head?"

"Branch of a tree," said Chinley. "The price you pay for taking a short cut."

"How often do we need to tell you, there *is* no short cut out there. And even if there was... what's the hurry?"

"No hurry. It's a pleasant walk, through the trees, away from all the traffic and the muck."

"You're a masochist, you know that? Did you get the sword then? Let's have a look at it."

"I dropped it off already with Gladys. She seems to appreciate it."

"Good. I'll go down and have a look."

"No. Don't go just yet. She's ready for bed. Go tomorrow. How are things with the Li's? I hear Silvia's on the move."

"She is. Mr Li can easily find someone else to do things around the house for him, I suppose, if he can afford it, but it looks like an end to his cabaret life. There can't be many people willing to kneel at the feet of an old man wearing a blindfold, doing an oriental William Tell."

"She's really going then?"

"She is. At the weekend."

"Doesn't hang about, does she?"

"She doesn't. I admire her for that, she's remarkable. I'm proud to have her as a friend, almost a sister. She wants to find a place in Beijing before the rent gets any higher. We'll see her on Friday though. I've arranged for a farewell party at *Madame Klimbams.* Her final performance with her father."

"Let's hope it's not *too* final," said Chinley. "The old man has to lose his grip some day. As it were."

"She'll be all right. She always is."

"So the Cultural Centre's still above board then?"

"Well, you know," said Lisa. "Market forces and all that."

"As long as *you* -"

"Ah yes, there *is* some more news. Jeffrey Ward's on the mend. Isn't that good? He's been taken to Hong Kong."

"I know," said Chinley. "Fortunate for everybody, that."

"And I'm going there too."

"*What?*" Chinley stared at his daughter in total disbelief. Was there no limit to her compassion, to her naïvety, to her ability to forgive? No loyalty to Terry and her own father? He controlled his anger and said as calmly as he could: "Jeffrey Ward has got friends of his own out there to look after him, I'm sure. What does he need *you* there for?"

"You don't think - !" laughed Lisa. "Jesus, that bump on the head might be more serious than it looks."

"What, then?"

"Mum phoned while you were away. She wants me to meet her there so we can spend Christmas together. Then she'll take me back to England. Her treat, she says."

"Your mother's flying out to Hong Kong?"

"Yes. Want to come?"

"Me?"

"Never mind then," said Lisa. "Tell me about Grandfather Li. How does he feel about having his house flooded?"

* * *

The following morning Lisa and Chinley were sitting in the out-patients' waiting-room at the Huban campus clinic. She had taken it upon herself to book an appointment for him because, apart from the swelling on his head, he had been making what she referred to as unusually loud noises during the night.

The clinic was as morbid as he remembered it when he came to give blood there, only one grade up from a cave-dwelling. Clammy tiled walls along uncarpeted corridors; a stark concrete floor; and unwelcoming over-silent personnel sitting behind antiquated school desks, their rumpled white uniforms given a jailor's look by diagonal grey stripes, shadows from the high barred windows. Chinley noticed that now, as on his last visit here, all the staff, receptionists, doctors, nurses, cleaners, all of them, carefully avoided any eye contact with the patients. When he pointed this out to Lisa, suggesting that in a way it was a welcome change, she said that it was probably a sign of respect; but he was more inclined to take it as a sign that they all had something to hide. Something to be ashamed of, as though they all knew the place was a shambles but had done nothing about it.

Eventually Lisa was called over to an opaque screen and her father's prescription was pushed through to her by a pair of anonymous hands which crept out spider-like from underneath a grille, and were then retracted. She presented the prescription at the pharmacy, but Chinley was far from reassured.

"What were you whispering to that doctor just now?" he said.

"Only the truth. That you've been rumbling and hissing like a cappuccino machine all night. Believe it or not, that translates quite well into Mandarin. We obviously have more than your head-wound to worry about. My guess is, it's something to do with that vile stuff in the brown bag."

"No," said Chinley. "That's been no problem so far, and I feel quite well on it. But it could be some psychosomatic reaction."

"Oh yes? To what?"

"Take your choice. To your mother flying out to within spitting distance. To losing Terry. To having a barney with Ward. To what *you* might get drawn into at *Madame Klimbams*. Take your choice." To being ripped off by Silvia, he added, to himself. But there was no point going into all that with Lisa now: she was obsessed with Silvia's rice paper charms, and as she was off soon to Hong Kong she might as well leave with an untainted memory of the girl.

"Don't be so barmy," said Lisa. "And can we get out of this dump before I keel over?"

On the hill outside the clinic, Chinley held a half-pint sized greenish bottle up to the daylight.

"What is it?" he said.

"You're to take a dessert spoonful four times a day," said Lisa. "Either as it is or diluted fifty-fifty with hot water."

He unscrewed the cap and sniffed the contents.

"Smells like varnish to me," he said. "Mixed with creosote. What *is* it?"

"Snake bile if you must know," said Lisa. "Well, that's to say there's snake bile *in* it. An ancient remedy for indigestion and possible parasites, amongst other things. Held in high esteem."

"By who? And for what other things exactly?"

"By poets, for example. As an aphrodisiac. Gladys told me..." She was distracted by the sight of Wang, who was cycling past them with his eyes on the sky, and with several live hens tied to his handlebars.

"Gladys told you what?" said Chinley.

But Lisa called to Wang. His bicycle frame was too big for him to stop without dismounting, and it took him some moments to come to a halt. He cocked his leg over the saddle, rearranged the dislodged fowl, and said: "Ah, Professor Chinley. Welcome back. Excuse me. I've just been to the market."

"Please don't talk too much about food, Mr Wang," said Lisa. "My father is feeling fragile today."

Wang looked at Chinley, then prodded his swollen stomach and said: "What have you been consummating, Professor? You're full of gas."

"That's one way of putting it," said Chinley. "So... Professor Ward, I hear, is recovering. In Hong Kong?" He looked back towards the clinic buildings. "Lucky man. He'll be better off than staying around here. For the treatment, I mean. Better facilities no doubt, and friends around him."

Wang began to laugh.

"Sorry?" said Chinley.

"No, it's my wife. Down there in the waiting room. Did she tell you anything?"

"We must have missed her," said Chinley. "We were in the other bit. Nothing serious, I hope?"

"Just the usual. It keeps her calm you know," said Wang, with a chuckle. "Over in England," he continued, looking up at the sky again, "how do you buy blood? By the pound? By the litre? Or by the bagful?"

"What blood?" said Chinley.

"By the skinful," said Lisa. "We call it black pudding."

"When you buy blood here," said Wang, "it's safer to use the State market, like I do. Do you have State markets in England? These small butchers in the private market may not realise when they have a sick pig. You may have eaten a sick pig, Professor." Chinley nodded. Wang nodded back at him and said: "My wife keeps reminding me that neither of you have been over to our place yet for dinner. How about tonight? With Mr Wu and Mr Hu?"

"Certainly," said Lisa, with an eye on the now tranquil hens. Wang startled them out of their composure with a jangle of his bell, then he pushed away and cycled off, his trousers tucked into his socks and his black raincoat flapping in the wind.

* * *

"A bit of scum, a bit of filth, and a bit of broken glass," said Wang, poking his head out from the dark recess in the corner of his sitting room, which functioned as a kitchen. "It all helps to toughen up the system. Wouldn't you agree, Professor?"

"Oh yes," said Chinley, only half-listening. He was on the sofa with Belinda, who had been telling him again how much she enjoyed their day out by the East Lake, and how they must go there again together sometime, or alternatively up the pagoda, even though the golden season was as good as over now. He was trying to ensure that she kept her voice down, because Mr Wu and Mr Hu had now arrived and were well within earshot, giggling with Lisa by the sitting-room window.

Chinley had told the Wangs that he would soon be visiting Beijing, because, he said, there were a few matters he wanted to discuss with Mr Deng. Hearing this, Wang said he would put pressure on Mr Feng to ensure that the stair carpet in the guest house was seen to before Chinley's return. This was the closest anyone had come so far that evening to mentioning Jeffrey Ward, or the circumstances leading to his hospitalisation.

Belinda, looking pale and half asleep, sipped at an orange juice and stared unblinkingly, for minutes on end, at a female fashion model on the western calendar, which lent some colour to the otherwise plain walls. Chinley reflected that she herself was so adorned tonight that the bare house around her was, for him, a welcome relief to the retina. But her wide glaucomic eyes gave her a somewhat demented look, and as the smug Party Secretaries sat watching her, each holding a glass of *baijiu*, it seemed to him they were humouring her, like patronising warders.

"Nothing serious at the clinic today I hope, Belinda?" said Chinley.

"Sorry?"

"At the clinic. We were in there just before you. Me and Lisa."

"No. I wasn't at the clinic today. Who told you that? I've not been there for weeks. And then it was only for a cold."

"Not there?"

"No."

Wang stood in the middle of the room laughing loudly, and he summoned everyone to the table. He went back to the dark hole in the corner and, with each dish he brought out, his oversized lips curled back from his speckled buck-teeth in a wet and fleshy smile. At last he removed his pinafore, and settled amongst the guests, leaving Mr Wu and Mr Hu in charge of the spirit bottle.

"Now it's served its purpose," said Belinda.

"Sorry?" said Chinley.

"The stair carpet."

"Yes," said Wang. "I'll get on to Mr Feng tomorrow to tack it down for you." He turned towards Lisa. "And what about you, Lisa? Are you going to Beijing with your father, or staying here on your own again? He wouldn't be boring you with any dams up there."

"There's a vague plan to meet up with my mother," she said.

"Ah, excellent. In Beijing?"

"No, in Hong Kong."

"Hong Kong?" said Belinda.

"Hong Kong."

"To see your mother?"

"Yes."

"And you, Professor Chinley," said Wang, "you'll be alone in Beijing then?"

"More or less. I'll be seeing Mr Deng of course. And Hilda."

"Your wife won't be coming to join you then?"

"No. It doesn't look that way. But I'm sure we'll manage a phone call."

"Only a phone call?" said Belinda.

"Yes."

"What a pity."

"Yes."

The ensuing silence was broken by a staccato choking sound. Wang was bent low over his side bowl, on to which he had been disgorging chicken-bones, and he was now making what sounded like a sobbing noise. Chinley could see nothing of the man's face: just chimney-brush tufts of greying black hair standing out from the crown of his head, like fur on a frightened cat.

Wang heaved his chest in spasms, taking snatches of air, then a strangulated clicking noise could be heard coming from the back of his throat. Assuming that his host was having difficulty with his food, Chinley leant over and clapped him a few times between the shoulder-blades. But as Wang raised his face, it was clear that he was not suffocating at all, but weeping with the strain of holding back his laughter. He leant over and patted Chinley's arm.

"You westerners," he said, shaking his head. "You're all very interesting. Your wife comes from England to Hong Kong to meet your daughter. But she will not go to Beijing to see *you*. Ha! Haha!"

"No," said Chinley, beginning to enjoy the joke himself.

"So will *you* go to Hong Kong, Professor," said Wang, "to see *her*?"

"No," said Chinley. "Certainly not."

Both men were laughing openly now, and Mr Wu and Mr Hu joined in, grinning and swivelling their necks, like ventriloquist dummies, and taking the opportunity to top up the *baijiu* glasses.

Belinda and Lisa looked at each other in silence, then Chinley saw Lisa check her watch. Lately she was reminding him more and more of her mother, and of their combined strength against him when they got together. In a short while she would, he knew, decide unilaterally that it was time to leave; she would stand up and put on her jacket and wait for him to do the same. But in just over a week from now he would be running his own life again. Everyone in the room here, Lisa included, was under the impression that his only reason for visiting Beijing was to see Mr Deng. The idea amused him. An awareness that for some reason he now had an erection amused him further, and he continued smiling as he watched Lisa rise to her feet as predicted, put on her jacket, poke her nose at him and say: "Shouldn't we be going now?"

* * *

He was contemplating the scene on the lawn below his bedroom window. It was like a stage back-drop: the sycamores were so still that they looked artificial, and birds he had never seen before, winter birds presumably, with slender blue-black tails, were gathering on the branches, their long curved beaks pointing down at the two ghostly *t'ai chi* practitioners who stood almost motionless, rooted ankle-deep in a shallow weft of freezing mist which rose from the hoar-frost between the tree trunks.

The two men, in flimsy white robes with a scarlet sash around their waists, like the costumes worn by Mr Li and Silvia, stood facing each other, exhibition broadswords held out before them at chest level, aimed harmlessly up to the sky and glinting in the sunshine.

Chinley had seen these two swordsmen often, sometimes immobile as now, like two statues warding off evil spirits at a shrine; and at other times he had seen them in action, lunging at each other's throats. He had no idea whether the swords were as genuine and as lethal as they appeared to be, but he imagined they were, judging by the manner in which they caught the sun.

"Don't go in for anything like that by the way," said Lisa, approaching the window quietly. "Promise me. You're dangerous enough to yourself and others without a weapon."

Chinley turned around and saw that her face was wet with tears. He put his arm over her shoulders, and she nestled in close to him.

"What is it?" he said.

"Nothing. Well. What a family."

"I know. You're right. What a family."

"No, not us. Well us too, yes. But I mean the Li's. They hate it here, the girls. And it's their home."

"Really hate it? Are you sure?"

"They do. Look at them. All gone. And with their father's blessing."

"It's not all that far. Beijing."

"It is. And they can't afford to come back, only once a year, for a few days."

"At least they *do* come back. When they can."

"Jane and Alison do. I don't think Silvia will. The things she was saying to me when we were alone. *She* wouldn't have her father's blessing, if he knew what she was thinking. *She* won't be coming back ever, if she can help it."

"We'll see."

"Oh *no!*" Lisa pushed herself away from Chinley and stared down through the window. "*Good God almighty!*"

"What?"

"The stupid women!"

He moved closer to the window and looked down at the lawn. There were now four figures in identical silk suits, with scarlet sashes. Belinda had tagged herself on to the expert twosome, and watching the trio closely was Gladys. She had an obviously toy broadsword painted dull silver, and held it in the way a butcher might hold a cleaver while chatting to his customers.

"*Me* dangerous?" said Chinley. "I doubt I could be more of a liability than either of those two on the loose. Thank God it's a toy they're playing around with."

He scanned the perimeter of the lawn, expecting to see Mr Wu and Mr Hu watching from somewhere, but as far as he could tell he and Lisa were the only witnesses.

Belinda's hair seemed to have grown rapidly in the last few days: it was now splayed out on her shoulders, as he remembered it during their dance together in Beijing. Her legs and her mouth gaped wide open as she imitated the stance and the facial expression of the swordsman closest to her. But she is a natural, thought Chinley. He watched her aesthetic stylised movements, until he became aware that she was exciting him. He should go to see her soon, alone in the pagoda as she wanted, he told himself. Early one morning before the trip to Beijing.

He became aware that Lisa was talking to him: something about the morning dose of snake bile, but he should ease off the insect brew for the time being, even if Gladys did say it would do him a power of good. "What's it *for* exactly, anyway?" he heard her say. He shook his head and switched his attention to Gladys now. She was on her haunches, apparently taking a rest.

"God Almighty, no," said Lisa, as Gladys shifted her weight on to her knees, straightened her back, and handed the make-believe sword to Belinda. "You know what they're up to, don't you? They're playing at Mr Li and Silvia." Belinda was tapping the sword playfully on Gladys's neck.

Chapter Nineteen

At *Madame Klimbams* on the following Friday evening, Chinley studied Silvia's delicate expressionless face as she knelt before her father, perhaps for the last time. Her send-off party was also a public farewell to Lisa, but at this moment the attention of the audience was focused on Gladys. Word had just spread that the reason she was hovering near the performers, wearing her extra-large sports gear, was because she had offered to take over as Mr Li's assistant for the watermelon act, as Silvia would no longer be available, and she did not want him to be deprived of the income for this crowd-puller.

It seemed that Li had accepted her offer, as he was not objecting now to her proximity, but what Chinley was anticipating, along with the rest of the audience, was the possibility that they would see Gladys's debut *tonight*.

She stood watching Li and Silvia, leaning against the props table with her hands on her hips. Then just as Li was about to put his blindfold on she stopped him and pulled a cloth away from the table behind her, to reveal a wooden box, which Chinley now recognised as the packing-case from Sichuan.

She opened the case and picked up the old sword. Twirling it as though it was a walking stick, she raised it high to show off the now gleaming edge, then she handed it to Mr Li.

"Don't worry, I've tested it on my legs," she said, half to him and half to the audience. "They used to be rough as sandpaper my legs," she continued, encouraged by the laughter: "Now they're pure silk. Just like one of Belinda's stockings down there."

Chinley, feeling somehow implicated in this remark and wishing to distance himself from it, turned to Lisa and said: "What on earth is she talking about?" Lisa told him to shush and listen. He had the impression that Gladys was looking straight at him, and he hoped the room lighting was dim enough to hide the flush, which spread up from his neck.

Li fingered the sword, then mumbled something to Silvia, in Mandarin.

"It's too sharp," she said.

He handed it back to Gladys and waited until she had locked it back in its packing-case before passing the water-melon to Silvia. He picked up his own sword and put the blindfold on. The audience froze, and the melon was neatly sliced. Li then removed his blindfold and gestured for Gladys to replace Silvia kneeling at his feet.

As though getting the measure of her, he watched as she settled herself into position on the boards, like ballast on a ship. Silvia put the skull-cap on Gladys's wide head, brought another melon, and balanced it on the cap. Then she helped her father to put the blindfold back on.

He took up the so-called horse position: a solid stance with legs apart, feet flat on the floor, upper body motionless. I know you're a wobbler, Gladys, Chinley was thinking. But please don't wobble now. He watched and waited. The cut was clean and quick and there was audible relief from the rows of spectators, then sporadic titters as Gladys stood up, bowed, and held the melon halves at breast level. Chinley noticed that Belinda, pale and silent, sat with her hands held oddly in front of her, a foot or so apart, as though frozen in mid-applause. Her eyes were fixed on Mr Li.

Silvia changed and went on her own directly from *Madame Klimbams* to the railway station to catch the overnight train to Beijing. As she was making her rapid departure Chinley asked how he could contact her, and she told him that her sisters would know. No, she said, she would not be living in their flat. He knew she had a mobile telephone now, but she didn't offer him the number, and he didn't ask her for it. No, she said, she would not be living over her uncle's drugstore.

A few hours later, after an all-night vigil at the guest house with her father and Gladys, Lisa was also ready to leave, looking unsteady with her big blue backpack and clutching a full bottle of Terry's rum. She and Chinley went to the airport long before sunrise, for her early morning flight to Hong Kong.

Back at the guest house Chinley energised and rehydrated himself with some insect brew, and sucked at a spoonful of the snake bile lotion. A crutch for the crotch, Lisa had called it, though he pretended not to hear what she had said, one night while she herself was on the ginseng wine. An aeroplane now passed overhead and Chinley noticed orange veins of daylight in the sky. He licked the teaspoon clean, and thought of Belinda. Sunrise at the pagoda.

Within minutes he was out of the house. The golden season lingered in patches on the woodland campus: the squat plane trees by the guest house porch, by Gladys's window where Belinda had looked out and no doubt listened in to Jeffrey Ward's unguarded opinion of her, were now charcoal-grey. But the bracken leaves, on the birch trees lining the boulevard, had not yet fallen.

He left the road and stepping through the bamboo thicket, then the pine copse, he wondered what he was up to. He decided it was all part of the final throes of his passing prime, or, to put it another way, a sign of encroaching senility. Whatever, as long as Dorothy and Lisa stayed away he was accountable to no-one. He realised he was now talking to himself, out loud. All he wanted to do, he heard himself say as he gestured in explanation to the trees, was to find out if Belinda really *did* go up the pagoda to worship the rising sun. No, he admittted, there was more to it than that: he wanted to see if she would behave in an exceptional way, as Wang might have put it. Actually, her being there at all would be exceptional enough.

It occurred to him that he could have brought some wine along to see what would happen this time; some of the sweet red stuff, which she was prepared to drink. Just about. It didn't take too long last time for her to lose control.

There again, perhaps wine was not such a good idea. Up the pagoda. He was already giddy with lack of sleep, but the crisp air and the anticipation that she might really be there kept him awake; it was as though he had wandered off into the countryside and intentionally lost his way after an all-night revel. He felt completely and deliciously irresponsible. He took several deep breaths, and felt the stirring of long-since dormant muscles in his chest.

Only the lower half of the tower was visible as he stood by a gap in the fence at the bottom of Pagoda Hill. The low December sun shone like a polished brass button, through a pale-green early morning mist. He stood still and listened, but all he could hear was the wind, the birds, and the hooting and squealing of the distant build-up of buses and trucks. It would be less alarming for Belinda, he thought, if she was there at all, if she saw him down here now in the open, than if she heard someone climbing the steps: but so far he had no way of knowing if she was already in there or not. If he called out to her as he climbed she would surely call back, and their combined voices would echo and carry too far, amplified by the old hollow cylinder, and broadcast to the neighbourhood. But if she really did go up there in time for the sunrise, then she should already *be* there: the sun rose half an hour ago at least.

He walked on towards the steps at the entrance to the pagoda. If he waited too long the heat of the day would disperse the mist, and he, or they, would then be seen from the ground, or more pertinently, from the balcony of Wang's apartment.

At the entrance to the tower Chinley was about to tread on what he thought was a tangle of leaves and twigs blown together by the wind into the loose form of a bird's nest, when he saw that it was an intentional design, man made, a kind of simple wreath. He propped it up against the warped foundations of the wall, and stooped under the threshold arch. He had placed only one foot inside the pagoda when he heard Belinda's voice, whispering from above, "Who's that?"

Over the scratching noise made by his shoes on the debris, he whispered back "It's me. I've come. Don't worry." Then he began to climb, groping in the darkness against the clammy curving wall. He could hear her shifting and fidgeting high above him, but she said nothing more. When he reached the top ring he saw her, out beyond the spy-hole, out in the open air; kneeling on the jutting ledge by the low rail, as though in a church pew. Staring out into the thinning mist. He knelt beside her and gently put his arm around her waist, surprised by the dampness of her cotton garments: he hoped this was condensation from the air, and not a sign of her anxiety at his arrival.

She looked at him with a different and unfamiliar smile on her face, and he wondered if she remembered that she herself had proposed meeting here. Several times.

"Belinda," he said.

"Cleo," she answered. "It's time for a change. A change of life."

"You mean a change of life *style*?"

"No. I mean a change of life."

"*Cleo?*" said Chinley. "Oh yes..."

"What?"

"Nothing."

She rose to her feet and shouted:

"*What?*"

The odd smile remained on her face. But now that she was standing, there was nothing for her to hold on to, and she was swaying on the ledge. Chinley rested a hand on her arm.

"*What?*" she shouted again.

"I like the name 'Cleo'," he said. "And it suits you. That's all."

"You're *lying*," she said. "*Lies!* That's not what you were going to say. What were you going to say?"

"All right," said Chinley, trying to secure a light but firm grip on her fingers. "It's okay. I'll tell you what I was going to say. But please keep still while I tell you. I met someone a few weeks ago who knows you, and he told me he thought your name was once Cleo. A man called Barry. In Yi Chang. That's all."

She shook her arm free. "And what other stories have been going around about me? What have *you* been telling people?"

"Me? Nothing. Really nothing."

"Why did you come here? What do you want? Leave me alone!" Her eyes widened and her smile fashioned itself into the lopsided village idiot's grin. Making an unnatural ululating sound, half a moan, half a howl, she tilted her face up towards the yellowing sky and shouted:

"Terry! *Terry!*"

Then she pushed past Chinley and darted off the ledge into the blackness of the tower's well. He saw a flurry of pale clothing as she scrambled down the massive distorted steps, and he prayed that she would keep her footing. But her flight seemed to be halted on the floor below, and he heard voices speaking in soft Mandarin.

He saw three bobbing shadows holding hands and moving down ahead of him in single file, as though in a courtly dance, without music. From the foot of the tower Mr Wu and Mr Hu led Belinda across the soggy peat towards the barrel-shaped stone benches where Lisa had parked everyone on the day of Terry's death. Chinley sat with them and they all waited in silence for Belinda to regain her breath.

Feng gave no reason for calling in at the apartment early the following day, and while he was there he chatted about the weather, how well the cut on Chinley's forehead was healing, the approaching Christmas season, and how they all missed Lisa; and he checked on the accuracy of a few more entries which he said he was including in his dictionary. He was just passing by the guest house, he said.

But when he left Chinley noticed a thin brown envelope on the sitting-room table. Without directly pointing a finger at Chinley himself, the single typed sheet of paper inside the envelope detailed a code of behaviour, apparently the house rules of the campus, which according to the author all the Foreign Experts in China were expected to observe.

Two items in particular however, Chinley sensed, did point a finger at the collusion of Feng in the compilation of the text: one of these read 'All Foreign Experts are desired to show respect for Chinese traditions and customers'; the other read 'All Foreign Experts who take liberties with the local women will be in our black books. There is to be no illicit sex either. With the local men and/or no drunken frolics'. There were other more accurately-worded references to non-involvement in the internal politics of the country, and 'non-display of missionary zeal'.

After re-reading the page and chuckling to himself, Chinley filled his pipe and settled down to stare at the knuckled boughs of the sycamore trees, and consider the implications of the method and timing of this correspondence. He felt safe: he knew that despite the fantasies which were increasingly tantalising him, he had not actually taken any liberties with anyone, man or woman, local or otherwise. Not yet.

Feng was clearly embarrassed to have to deliver this code of conduct. But why, Chinley wondered now, had he and the Foreign Affairs Office taken so long to advise him of their expectations? All those weeks. Perhaps they assumed that because of his age and his status he would not be guilty of any indiscretion: they may even think he was one of those English gentlemen they hear about who know instinctively how to behave and therefore need no reminding. Until now. So why now? An early morning visit to the pagoda was not a breach of the code, even if it was obvious he knew who was up there. Yes, there were the photographs on public display for a whole week on the main road outside *Madame Klimbams,* parading him as a philanderer. But even if he *had* lured one intended victim after another into his apartment, nothing untoward could have happened, because Lisa was always there.

Of *course*. That was it. That explained the timing of the brown envelope. Lisa was now gone; and with her, as Feng and the others must have realised, gone too were the constraints on him to behave himself.

The consequence of ignoring the campus commandments was not indicated on Feng's piece of paper, though Chinley guessed it might take the form of a discreet deportation, perhaps in the guise of another invitation like the one posted to Jeffrey Ward in Hong Kong. Invited to spend some time back home in the United States, for example. But Chinley could not afford to be deported. Not yet. He needed his job, more so now that his safe had been rifled.

Little bitch. Beijing. Beijing would be a more suitable location for the satisfaction of growing needs: less conservative than provincial Wuhan. More open-minded, maybe. Now that Lisa had slipped into the future he was free to travel up to the capital whenever it suited him, and why should anyone here care what he got up to there? He felt like a teenager about to escape from his parents.

* * *

"Why are you trying to sneak past me like a common criminal?" said Gladys, as Chinley found himself once again with his head on a level with her knees. Since the incident in Building Ten he was wary of her proximity, and his intention now was to push a Christmas card under the door then slip away unnoticed, in good time for his train to Beijing. He had crept along the ground floor of the guest house, and when he reached in his pocket for the card he heard the vamping of a harmonica and several male Chinese voices. While he was listening at the keyhole Gladys jerked open the door to find him crouched on the coconut-hair doormat which Ward was so keen to have at the front door, and which she had moved inside for her personal use. Peering around the bluffs of her shoulders, and now looking calm and amused, was Belinda.

"Merry Christmas in advance, Gladys," said Chinley, his whole body creaking as he staggered to his feet. He passed her the envelope. "No, it's just that I didn't want to interrupt your... whatever. And a Merry Christmas to you too, Belinda. In advance."

"Get yourself in here and have a drink," said Gladys.

"But -"

"Get yourself in here and have a *drink*!"

Four more Chinese heads were now drawn close together in the hallway, staring at Chinley and grinning: the four young men, the musicians from Terry's wake.

"You must. Come in and have a drink," they chorused.

He looked at his watch but Gladys clamped a hand on his elbow, steered him into the lounge, and pushed him into an armchair. Hanging on the wall opposite him, polished and gleaming dark brown, was the Li family sword.

"Ah yes," he said. "Ah yes. That looks fine, up there. Why not?"

"You're just the man we need to see, as it happens," said Gladys, pouring him a large whisky. Belinda stayed at her side, looking down at the bamboo matting on the floor.

"Me?" said Chinley.

"Yes. Belinda here wants a word with you. I'll leave you alone together. I have some rehearsing to do in the back parlour. Christmas concert, you know." She went off to join the musicians, and Belinda sat by the window in a hard-backed chair.

"I owe you an apology," she said. "That business in the pagoda the other day. I'm so sorry about it all. I don't know what comes over me at times like that. I've been taking... I've been upset because of Terry and things."

"That's all right," said Chinley. "He was a good friend of mine, too."

"It was an accident, I know. And I can forgive an accident. But there are some things I *can't* forgive."

She stared at Chinley in silence for a while. Then she turned to look at the open window, the porch window, the one he had seen her looking out of that night a month ago, illuminated by the car headlights. It rattled now on its latch. He walked over to her and rested a hand on her shoulder.

"It's all right Belinda," he said. "He's gone. He won't be back. Gone for good. You'll never see him again."

"Banished from the land, yes," she said, with a quick laugh. "By emperor Deng himself. So I should rest easy I suppose. The further he is away from me, the better for both of us. You know. You were with him out there when he said those things about me."

"I know. It was nonsense."

"You've not told anyone?"

"Of course not."

"I believe you. And yes... I *was* in the clinic the other day. It was me you saw. But please understand, it was absolutely nothing to do with *him.*"

"I never imagined -"

"There was never anything like *that* between us. You know?"

"I know."

"No, you can't know. You can only believe. Do you believe *me*? Or do you believe *him*?"

"I believe you, of course. Anyway, you can forget all about him now. He's gone."

"Yes. Right. Thank you."

Chinley heard a creaking of garments in the hall. Gladys leaned her buffalo head around the door and said: "All sorted? Good. Come and join the others."

The musicians chatted in muted Mandarin and played sequences of notes to each other. Gladys elbowed Chinley in the ribs. "Perhaps, Christopher," she said: "you can help me to persuade these young men to join me tomorrow for Christmas dinner. I need company at this time of the year, we all do. I would have had *you* my man if you hadn't been going away. Can't your business with his nibs wait a while? Odd that you should arrange to see him during the festive season. Very odd. Doesn't it strike *you* as odd?" She swivelled to face him, hands on hips as though demonstrating one of her Celtic dance steps.

"Not at all," said Chinley.

She swivelled back to face the musicians and shouted: "Why can't the Chinese make their minds up? Why are they suddenly so worried about celebrating Christmas? Don't they realise they've been playing *Jingle Bells* through the speakers out there every week since they were reconnected? And *A Child Is Born*."

There was a knock at the front door. Belinda went to open it and Feng walked into the parlour. Gladys made a half-turn and rested her weight on the other foot. She glared at him, her complexion darkening.

"How about *you* then?" she said. "Are *you* willing to come here and spend Christmas Day with Belinda and me? Wang says he won't risk it, whatever he means by that. But maybe that's a blessing. Belinda can be herself for an evening, for a change. What's *wrong* with you men?"

"In China we are more interested in celebrating the New Year," said Feng, playing with the peewit crest of hair at his neck. "I mean *your* New Year. On the evil day we have an evil meal. And we let off steam at midnight."

There were a few chortles from Gladys, and the angry purple hue lifted from her jowls. "What the hell," she said, nudging Chinley. "*We* know what he means."

"If you want men there's always Mr Wu and Mr Hu," said Feng. "They might come."

"I *know* there's always Mr Wu and Mr Hu," said Gladys. "No. Belinda's had enough of them, it's time they left her alone. Forget it, Mr Feng. We'll have a girls' night. Just the two of us."

Chinley checked his watch again. Gladys impatiently pushed the telephone towards Feng and asked him to order the Foreign Affairs Office car now to take Chinley to the railway station.

"Company for Christmas, Gladys?" said Chinley. "How about Molly? Molly and her *Klimbams* mates."

"Molly?" said Gladys. "Yes, it's odd about Molly. Haven't heard a dicky bird. Maybe she's run off with the Dutchman. *He's* disappeared too."

Feng moved closer, and Chinley noticed his eyes flick like tadpoles towards Gladys. He seemed about to say something but checked himself and spoke instead into the mouthpiece of the telephone. Gladys topped up Chinley's whisky and glared at the musicians until they began to fidget and reach for their instruments. During the second repetition of the chorus of *Edelweiss* the headlamps of a car flashed across the window pane; Chinley finished his drink and shouldered his bag. Gladys and everyone gathered in the hallway to wave him off.

"Say hello to Professor Ward for me if you see him," said Feng.

"I'm hardly likely to, am I?" said Chinley. "Mr Ward is in Hong Kong. I'm going to Beijing."

"But didn't you know?" said Feng. "He is also going to Beijing. He too has an appointment with Mr Deng."

Belinda would not meet Chinley's eye when he reached her on his way to the door, and when he took her hand and pressed it he found that it was clammy and trembling. She dug her nails hard into his flesh and he could feel the heat carried from a dark flush, which covered her cheeks.

Like an icon representing the West, the facade of *Madame Klimbams* was a blaze of electronic decoration: a large and hairy Santa

Claus, which reminded Chinley of Jeffrey Ward, came to life in a flashing display of animated colour; reindeer lifted their hoofs and dilated their snouts; the national flags of several countries bordering the north Atlantic glowed over the entrance; there was a large photograph of the Eiffel Tower and half a dozen or so prints of sombre white-faced politicians with glasses and thin grey hair. All men, and to Chinley all bearing a resemblance to Mr Deng. Good God. So Ward was coming over to Beijing to see his ex-boss. To plead for re-instatement, or what? Chinley was sure Mr Deng would not reverse his decision: he was not that sort of man; and to do so would be not just a loss of face, but a loss of face at Ministerial level. And it would be a betrayal of Belinda. Deng must have heard *something* of that connection. And Ward would be aware of all this, thick-skinned though he might be. So what did he want?

The traffic was inching along just here, and Chinley's attention was caught by a Christmas tree, full of tinsel and winking lights, which reached from the pavement to *Madame Klimbams* upper floor. He wound down the window of the car and heard *Jingle Bells,* being played for once with seasonal accuracy, through a loudspeaker positioned over the doorway to the club, over the national flags. He looked again at the heads of the dancing reindeer, and felt his own nostrils tingle. The car moved on past all the glitter and as they turned into the station approach he began to consider his barely-formulated plan for the week ahead. He would book in at the Double Rainbow hotel.

At this cockeyed time of the year, he told himself, it should be easy to re-establish his footing with Jane: he would begin by securing her help in making it difficult for Mr Deng and Hilda to hunt him down: Feng was sure to let them know the date of his arrival, if not the exact hour. Perhaps all that was needed with Jane was a more explicit response from him while she was in the bathroom.

Then there was Alison, with the mass of curls and the mischievous smile. Perhaps the western fashion indicated she was an exception to the highly moral norm. Chinley hoped that now she knew him better he would not be restricted to just sitting opposite her in the cocktail lounge, admiring her split silk dress from a distance and watching her leg moving up and down on the piano pads.

And then of course there was Silvia. In the privacy of the back seat of the Foreign Affairs Office car Chinley reminded himself that Silvia was substantially in his debt. Gladys's whisky and the winter blast of air blowing through the open window were having their effect on him: he saw himself now as a kind of Santa Claus figure too, but on his way to be on the receiving end for a change. She owed him one. Drunkenly, he wondered what Mr Li would make of all this. Here he was on his way to seduce one if not all of his friend's three daughters.

Glorious freedom. His hand rested on a side pocket of his shoulder-bag and he felt the curve of the snake-bile bottle and the crunch of the softer package alongside it. He realised he must have laughed out loud, because the driver was looking at him over his shoulder as he pulled in to park on the station forecourt, amongst the thin old women clutching satsumas to their bosom.

Part Five

Chapter Twenty

In the north, the golden season was long since over. On embankments in the Beijing suburbs, as Chinley lay horizontal looking through the carriage window of his soft-sleeper compartment, he saw thin leafless branches quivering against a cold sky, as though reflected in a pool of shifting water. When they arrived at the terminus, out in the station square the city noise was muted by a padding of snow, and he walked over to the taxi rank to an accompaniment of muffled staccato bumps of unfamiliar dry thunder, which sounded like heavy furniture being rearranged in an upstairs room.

But he was in no hurry. He filled his pipe and leaned back against a concrete pillar, to watch the passage of what to him were now the bicycle nymphs. They returned his gaze curiously, with eyes like sugared brown dates. Silvia could well be amongst them, he told himself, if she could still lower herself to sit side-saddle, as it were, and he wondered how she would respond to his presence. Certainly, the most likely way to find her was through Jane and Alison at the Double Rainbow hotel. He clapped his gloved hands together, removed his pipe from his lips, and blew hot air into the woollen fabric to warm his fingers.

The driver at the front of the taxi queue stepped out of his car and shouted a Merry Christmas. He was an avuncular figure, gleaming with goodwill: his forehead rose in a double escarpment towards the summit of his hairless head, its higher ridge resembling the rim of a huge blister stretched tight across the scalp and ready to burst open. Chinley moved towards the car, still sucking on his pipe, then he stopped and pointed the stem at the *No Smoking* sign on the glass panel in front of the passenger seat.

"Don't worry about that," said the driver. "It doesn't apply to you. You're a foreigner."

That afternoon in the cocktail lounge of the Double Rainbow hotel Chinley sat on the sofa with an Irish coffee, looking at a piano without a pianist. Alison was on a late shift, he assumed. To one side of the main lounge there was a kind of conservatory letting in what was left of the daylight, so he went over there and relaxed in a bamboo-weave rocking-chair. He stared out through the honey-glazed panoramic window at the sooty leaves on the garden shrubs and the line of fountains spurting pale tints of pink and green drizzle.

The arching bridge over the ornamental stream reminded him of the causeway at the East Lake and the ride to Mo Shan, where Belinda sat close to him on a moss-tufted boulder in the middle of a cloud. With an intense desire now for the company of a woman, he swivelled in his chair and glared at the silent piano, willing Alison, wherever she was, to return to her stool and entertain him.

Then he saw Jane. She was at the centre of a group of young female receptionists, talking to a tall Chinese man with flared black trousers and an off-white belted overcoat with cape shoulders tailored like folded wings. At last Chinley caught Jane's eye and, remaining in his seat, he toasted her with his Irish coffee. Immediately she pushed her way out from the huddle of her colleagues and came over, bowing all the way. She took his hand and held it for longer than he expected, applying gentle pressure now and again to his fingertips. She seemed delighted to see him, and he wanted to throw his arms around her. She looked vibrant, as though she had just been under a hot shower: something, he reflected, that neither she nor her sisters could indulge in at their father's home, at least not in the same way as here in the Double Rainbow. Back on the edge of the Hubei countryside it was more likely to be a pan of hot water splashed over the head.

"Are you booked in, Mr Chinley?" she said, distancing herself from him a little. "Will you be staying here tonight?"

"No. Yes."

"You'd better book in straight away then, if you want to. We're filling up fast. It's Christmas Day! Merry Christmas!"

"Yes. Merry Christmas." He nodded towards the piano. "Perhaps Alison will play us some Christmas music later?"

"Alison?"

"Yes. Why - ?"

"She can't. She's not here any more."

"Not here? Not an accident, I hope?"

"An accident? Of course not. She's at home. Waiting for a baby."

"Ah? Waiting for a baby? I didn't know. I didn't know she was, er, thinking about that."

"Isn't it wonderful? But there's another pianist now. A replacement.

Let me introduce you to him."

She gripped his sleeve and they walked over to the reception desk. The man she had been talking to turned to face Chinley. He shook hands, and bowed his head, but not too deeply: Chinley was sure he had seen him before somewhere. The girls behind the desk were giggling and pawing each other, and one of them said: "Congratulations! Congratulations to Jane and Mr Liu!"

Chinley looked at Jane.

"We're engaged," she said. "We got engaged last night. As it was Christmas Eve."

"What, you and..." He nodded at the young man next to him.

"Yes. Mr Liu."

"Well, good, congratulations," said Chinley, shaking hands again. Another evil day, he found himself thinking. He smiled at Mr Liu as well as he could and said. "Haven't we met before?"

"No," said the young man. "Definitely not."

"Let's book you in, Mr Chinley," said Jane. "Before it's too late."

The bellboy reverently placed a footmat by the regal-sized bed, turned down the sheets, made a discreet inventory of the contents of the drinks cabinet, then saluted and left the room. Chinley's hand hovered over the telephone, then withdrew and dipped into his pocket instead, rummaging for his pipe. On Christmas Day, he reflected, even if Jane knew her whereabouts, Silvia, especially someone like Silvia, was unlikely to have nothing planned for the evening. He looked at the footmat. He and Jane had knelt on one of these together to look at the map, spread out on a duvet cover identical to this one, embroidered alike with an intertwined dragon and phoenix. He remembered she told him, as though she could wish for nothing more in a man, that he reminded her of her grandfather. But he was sure her grandfather would never travel five hundred miles to claim a pound of flesh.

He could not sit still, and to stop himself reaching out again for the telephone he reached out instead to twist the knob on the drinks cabinet, and removed a miniature bottle of brandy. As he was unscrewing the cap he realised where he knew the man downstairs from: he was the one lying on his stomach in that clinic, dressed in an ivory-coloured silk robe, with long painted fingernails, Jane's fingernails, resting on his collar-bone like a necklace of red beads. Chinley realised now with admiration why the young man had denied ever meeting him. Protecting Jane. Protecting her job. A quick-witted young man. He felt like a father passing judgement on a son-in-law presented to him by his daughter as a *fait accompli*.

He scanned the television channels, then switched off and opted instead for an organist playing *The Tennessee Waltz* on the radio. Christmas Day. He should at least telephone Lisa. A quick call to Hong Kong. But half his mind was on Silvia, and anyway Dorothy might be the one to answer. He thought instead of telephoning Mr Wang: check that Belinda was okay. Christmas evening with Gladys would be a rare treat for her: no husband; no Mr Wu, no Mr Hu, flanking her like bookends. Gladys was quite capable of keeping them all well away from her territory. Trying to recall the Wangs' number, Chinley stared at the telephone and was startled to hear it ringing. He picked it up.

"Mr Chinley?" It was Jane's voice.

"Hello Jane."

"Hi. Mr Deng is asking for you."

"Oh God, not him already. He's not downstairs is he?"

"No. He's on the telephone."

"He's not listening in?"

"No, of course not."

"Then can you tell him I've booked out... no, you can't do that, can you. Can you just tell him I'm not in?"

"Certainly. Anything else?"

"No. Thank you for, for..."

"Covering up for you? That's fine. It's my job, partly, and we've done it before of course."

"Yes."

"Also with Mr Deng."

"Yes." Chinley was getting agitated, imagining Mr Deng, or Hilda, or both of them, to have him bugged.

"Don't worry," said Jane. "I'll tell him there's no answer."

"Thank you. Oh, and just one more thing Jane..." he began, but she had gone. Curses. A natural opportunity wasted, to ask how Silvia was and wheedle out her whereabouts; but at least he had a friend in Jane. She understood.

Much less appealing than the prospect of spending Christmas evening alone in a hotel bedroom was the idea of spending it with Mr

Deng, a man who to Chinley was about as festive as a filing cabinet. He felt better-disposed towards Hilda: she had after all opened his eyes; but he knew that there could be no Hilda without Mr Deng.

It had taken little more than twenty-four hours, he calculated, for Feng and Mr Deng to work out between them when and where he could be tracked down. If the telephone rang again, he decided, he might as well not answer it: he could think of no-one likely to make a call of any consequence. All that mattered for the moment was Silvia. The dividend collection. The Christmas cracker.

Jane may have already told her that he was here in the hotel, and she may well try to get in touch with him. But the last thing he wanted from her was a telephone conversation: he wanted her here, in the room. He strode the length of the carpet from door to desk, then back again, and hammered his fists on the wall panelling, then he opened the wardrobe and took out the heavy white boxer-bathrobe, undressed, and ran a bath. He finished the remains of the brandy, cleaned his pipe, and looked at his watch: it was still early, only twenty past seven. It would do no harm to find out where she was. She might be sitting in a room alone somewhere with a book. Swaddled and relaxed in the towelling of the bathrobe, he dialled down to the reception desk.

"Ah, Jane," he said. "Sorry to bother you."

"Not at all."

"I was just wondering. As I've some free time tonight... is there a number for Silvia?"

"*Silvia?*" said Jane, as though she had forgotten her sister's English name. "Silvia's out of town. On the coast somewhere, I think. She's due back sometime but I don't know when. Did she know you were coming? Did you have an appointment?"

"No."

"Sorry."

"No, that's fine. Thank you Jane, and have a good Christmas evening."

"And you Mr Chinley. What have you got in mind? Are you going to a party?"

"Well, I'm... yes, in a way. I'm calling in on some friends at the Sheraton." It was the only other hotel he could think of.

"Sounds marvellous," said Jane. "Have a good time there, and I'll probably see you on your way out."

At half-past seven, fortified by a double dose of snake bile, washed down with the insect brew, Chinley went for a walk. The bridge-building seemed even further from completion than on his last visit. Corridors of rusty iron mesh marked out a rough passage through the construction site; freezing mud seeped through the hairline cracks in his shoes, and the unrelenting traffic spattered him with waves of gravel and slush. From the ankle to the knee, his trouser-legs absorbed the moisture in the viscous muck from the roadworks, leaving jagged brown veins like the outline of impossible mountains in a Chinese fantasy landscape.

To the unconcealed amusement of the commissionaires he called in for a drink at the Sheraton bar, and sat for a while listening to the laughter of the expatriates and their faction. A penetrating male voice said: "Thighland's what *I* call it. *Thigh*land." Chortling heads were rotated, and Chinley was certain that some of the white faces were smirking at *him*. He finished his beer and left the bar before anyone made up their mind to invite him to join the circle. Before anyone asked him who he was, and what he was doing in Beijing. Several commissionaires closed ranks at the exit, but as Chinley bore down on them they scattered like schoolboys in the sudden presence of an enraged headmaster. And they did manage to swing the doors open smoothly enough not to impede his accelerating momentum.

He tramped out into the sleet, pounding the fist of one hand into the palm of the other. Swinging his elbows like an excited medicine-man and, growling through his pipe-loosened teeth, he looked for an empty space where he could give full vent to his spleen. But this was China, and his long strides brought him only to the crowd on the pavement: a tightly-packed shuffling army. He strode on towards them, attempting to insert himself in their midst, and ready to clip the heels of anyone who got in the way. He growled at the backs of women's heads, at their pony-tails, so they would turn and confirm that it was not Silvia walking ahead of him.

Jane was no longer on duty when he returned to the Double Rainbow. Upstairs in the seclusion of his own room, for the first time in several weeks he changed into a pair of running shoes and went through all the *t'ai chi* which Mr Li had taught him. Apart from dosing himself with a medley of drinks from the mini-bar, he could think of no other way to control his temper. Everything was happening around him, but he was part of nothing. Husbands together with their friends and wives or whatever, at the Sheraton bar and at dozens of similar bars throughout the capital; Jane partying with her fiancé; Alison at home waiting for a baby; Silvia out of town doing God knows what on the coast with God knows who.

As he went through the *t'ai chi* motion Chinley recollected the ease with which he propelled Jeffrey Ward through the rotting banisters at the guest house. Or more precisely, the way in which circumstances joined forces against the American to make *him* a pushover. Chinley had no delusions about that. No loose carpet or rotting timber would come to his aid if he was ever again confronted by the man. Yes, Hilda had made it clear that Ward would not be reinstated in his post at the Dong Hu campus, nor would he be accepted anywhere else in the country, apparently: so it made no sense that he was coming to see Mr Deng. Chinley pawed at the air, and executed high kicks in slow motion until his mood improved. Then he opened up the mini-bar.

* * *

The following morning as he crossed the foyer, dazed by alcohol and groggy after a sleep disturbed by the intermittent ringing of a telephone, Chinley was surprised to see Jane stooped uncharacteristically over her papers, with her chin resting on her hands and her elbows resting on the desk. Her lips puffy and sagging, she looked out at him through the black tent of her hair and rubbed her eyes.

"Oh, good morning Mr Chinley," she said, brightening. "How was your night?"

"Excellent. And yours?"

"Marvellous. I've never done anything like that before. Stayed up all night dancing and drinking. I suppose I'll have to get used to it, if that's the way things are going to be."

"Have you got time to come for a walk with me?" said Chinley. "Help you to freshen up?"

"No, sorry. I have to stay here." She lifted a few papers. "There's a couple of messages for you somewhere though. It's all in such a mess.

I'm not my normal self this morning. One from Mrs Fox, I wrote it down myself, where is it? She's been trying to get you all morning. Haven't you been in? Very sad about her husband, wasn't it?"

"Yes. Silvia told you all about it then?"

"No. Not Silvia. It's not the sort of thing she likes to talk about. My father told me. Here we are. Message from Mrs Fox." She passed him a sealed envelope. "And the other one, here we are," she continued, "is from Mr Deng. Again."

"*Already?* This morning?" Chinley gave her a Chinese smile, to indicate he was not blaming her for Mr Deng's persistence.

"Yes. But he insisted that he did not want to be put through to your room. He didn't want to wake you up." Didn't want to warn me that he's closing in, thought Chinley. "Here's the note, anyway, with his number. He wants to meet you for breakfast, and if he doesn't hear from you he will call here later this morning, he says. Are you still trying to avoid him, Mr Chinley?"

"Oh yes. Like the plague. I'm on holiday, and Mr Deng can talk about nothing but work. I wonder what he means exactly by later this morning?"

"If you really don't want to see him," said Jane, "you should leave here right now."

"When's the next erm... shuttle bus into town?"

"Half-past eight. What...twenty minutes."

"I'll walk," said Chinley. "Get out while I can. Have breakfast somewhere on the way."

"Where will you go? For a walk?"

"What? I don't know. I'm happy just to walk and walk and walk. Down the backstreets. I might call in on your uncle if I recognise the shop, to renew my prescription. Remember?"

Jane looked down at her shoes.

"I'm sorry," she said. "I only took you there to bring him some business. I didn't know you then."

She looked up.

"*Renew* your prescription? You're not still *drinking* that stuff are you, after all this time?"

"Yes. Why not? It goes well with the snake bile."

"Snake bile?"

"Yes. Why not?"

"It was just a temporary measure, to release the fluid, to help... You should stop taking it. If you have too much of it your body may, your urges may become... unnatural."

"I can handle that."

"Throw it all away. The snake bile as well. And don't go back to my uncle."

"All right. I'll go somewhere else then. And if Silvia calls, will you let her know I'm here?"

"Of course," said Jane. "She should be told."

The doormen fanned out as Chinley approached, and he walked between them with his eyes on the floor, brooding on Jane's latest turn of phrase regarding her sister. Out in the fresh air he opened the envelope. The message inside read

Please call soonest. Urgent. Gladys. That could wait, thought Chinley. Everything was urgent to Gladys. He screwed the note into a ball, together with the one from Mr Deng, and threw them both away.

Chapter Twenty-One

Chinley leant on the railings outside a Buddhist temple and stared at the man at the gate: he was like Grandfather Li, though maybe twenty years younger, and judging by the sentry-like attention he was giving his surroundings, obviously keener-sighted. Chinley in his turn soon came under scrutiny, and the man wagged his full white beard at him, as though he had long been waiting for Chinley to pass by. His skin was like pale varnished oak; his hair wild, with silver-grey ringlets bouncing like metal springs with each movement of his head. He didn't speak, but gestured for the foreigner to enter the temple grounds, as though he was ushering in a venerated guest. Chinley felt compelled to accept the invitation.

Perhaps this meandering through the Beijing back streets was after all fortuitous, Chinley reflected, as he entered the grounds and the noise from the outside world faded. A tranquil interlude to calm his cravings. Now, shuffling towards him, like a confessor from a bygone epoch, was another old man, wearing the rich ochre robes of a Buddhist monk. His head was completely bald, and shining, and his eyes were round and youthful. Quietly-spoken, he introduced himself as the head of the temple.

He looked at Chinley in silence for a while, told him that he had the appearance of a generous and fortunate man, then he tottered away, like a vintage clockwork toy. Not knowing how else to address him, Chinley called out: "Thank you, Father", to apparently deaf ears. But surely this is good tidings, he thought, to hear just as the year is drawing to a close: the word of somebody well-positioned in the hierarchy towards God should not be taken lightly.

But the good humour was short-lived. The skinny bare-armed novices in the temple were not so benign as their superior, Chinley found. They were ill-tempered and fidgety. They seemed to have no interest in his questions and no time to help him understand the inscriptions on the walls. It was not long before they infected him with their tetchiness. Out loud he said, in tones, which the acoustics of the building rendered resonant and supernatural, "Listen you little shits. It's no use being abstemious if it's going to make you waspish. Perhaps you are not cut out for this kind of life? Have you considered that? Or perhaps you are too young for it? What you need is a barrel of rum, and a night with a good woman. Wouldn't you agree, Father?"

He was enjoying the sound of his own amplified voice, and at the mention of rum he felt Terry's presence at his side, smirking at the irreverence.

"In order to be of any use to your future flock, God help them," he continued, vaguely aware now that last night's intoxication had still not worn off, "you have to know something about what they are *up* against. The temp*t*ations. The ways of the *flesh.* What the fuck do *you* know about the Devil?"

The novices stared at him out of thin bony half-human faces, like those of weather-worn sheep, then as though re-activated by a button pressed on a central control panel, they resumed their mopping and dusting.

Chinley turned a corner, and stood alongside an elderly Chinese woman dressed in a dark brown ankle-length overcoat and a furry Russian hat. Her palms were pressed together, pointing at her selected deity, and she was bowing and dipping with the whole of her body. But not even prayer was private in China, and Chinley listened in to her supplication. She was asking for better luck in the New Year with her lottery tickets. Here is somebody who is in touch with the real world, he thought. And Silvia is my lottery. He watched her approach a kind of altar, where she positioned a bundle of incense sticks as large as pokers. He watched her set them aglow, then he asked her where he could find some. She led him to a kiosk in the temple courtyard where they were on sale; he bought half a dozen, then made his way towards the exit.

The man who looked like Grandfather Li was still keeping watch at the temple gates. He stroked his beard as Chinley approached, and told him that he could read faces, and hands.

"How much?" said Chinley.

"Oh, whatever you like. Sixty kwai, for example."

Chinley gave him half the price he was asking, and said: "Just do my face."

He gazed into Chinley's eyes, palmed his forehead, nose, and cheeks, then twisted him sideways by the shoulders in order to examine the profile.

"I heard what you were shouting in there just now," he said. "You're quite right actually. But these monks are young men, and they will improve with age. As we did. Wisdom will come with seniority. What are these for?"

"What?"

"These incense sticks."

"They are for my room at the hotel," said Chinley. "For a bit of atmosphere."

"These are not joss-sticks, you know," said the old man. "They are for ceremonial use. As a holy offering at shrines. For thanksgiving, or for special requests."

"Yes, That's just what I'll be using them for. Like that woman in there. To ask for some special favours."

"What special favours?"

"You're the fortune-teller," said Chinley. "You should be telling *me* what favours I should ask for."

"You are a generous man, sir," said the face-reader, gazing into Chinley's eyes again. "I can see that. And you are not a poor man. So *what,* I wonder, are you asking for, with your incense sticks? Health? Possibly. Peace of mind? Possibly. But it seems to me in this case you're asking for something in a hurry. Yes? Something you want to squeeze in before the end of the year, perhaps?"

Chinley looked at the old man sharply.

"It's odd isn't it?" the fortune-teller continued. "Have you noticed? Getting what you want in life rarely brings peace of mind. But *not* getting what you want sometimes *does*. Those monks in there, they don't understand that yet. They're too young. But *we* understand it, don't we? The blessings of old age."

A silence fell between them.

"Yes?" said Chinley, after a few moments.

"Yes." The fortune-teller looked at his watch.

"No," said Chinley. "I mean, is that *it*? Is that all?"

"Yes."

"I could have told you all that myself."

"Then perhaps there's some truth in it."

The old man closed his eyes, and kept them closed, which Chinley took as a sign that the consultation was definitely over.

He walked on in a wide arc, following the crimson winter sun. Before it set, he estimated, it should bring him back to where he had started from. He needed some time to restore his self-esteem: he was depressed by the thought that he could reach the age he had, yet still half believe in fairies and fortune-tellers. To hand his money over so easily just now. It was understandable, this innate superstition. He and Joe had after all been brought up virtually as Celts, by a half-Irish father and a fully-Irish grandfather. *They* would think twice about sending a fortune-teller packing. And from him and Joe they would expect a human response to the dinginess of the old man's clothes. Especially in a flourishing commercial neighbourhood like this one.

Shops and showrooms were illuminated as darkness fell, and while Chinley was waiting for a gap in the traffic at an intersection he noticed a display of antique weapons: swords, daggers, muskets, and even a range of small canons. A poster in the doorway of the shop showed a scarlet-clad woman, her eyes looking out from either side of a yellow blade held vertically before her. It was like Silvia mocking him and his family. He felt dizzy with anger, and hesitated at the kerbside, but the crowd were building up behind him, pushing into his back, and the traffic lights were changing.

When he arrived back at the Double Rainbow hotel, under a full crystal moon, one of Jane's colleagues told him that Silvia had called in to see him and would return later that evening.

A lascivious-looking porcelain Buddha grinned at him from a shelf in the bric-a-brac shop on the ground floor of the hotel. A flabby naked belly ballooned out of loose-fitting celestial blue robes, and the glee in the holy man's eyes was manic with high expectation.

He bought it. If the woman in the temple could pray out loud for financial gain, he argued, why should he not have an idol in tow at the scene of the planned conjugation? To increase the chances that all would go well? He was buying anything now, which he thought might help his case: flowers, chocolates, wine, after-shave. But his purchases were swift. He should not be out of the room next time she called.

Back in his room he had a shower and put on the boxer's gown. He half-drew the lace curtains, arranged the flowers, sprinkled the after-shave, anchored the Buddha to the bedside table, and experimented with the wall-lighting. He drank a miniature brandy and found the bottle a suitable size and shape to hold a temple incense stick, which leant over slightly from the vertical towards the window, pointing like a rocket at the night sky. There were several such bottles in the mini-bar, and he swallowed their contents mechanically until there was a holder for each of the half-dozen sticks.

He danced up and down the room, barefoot, then ignited the tips of the phallic-red sticks and eyed the slobbering lecherous lips of the pot-bellied Buddha, who now seemed increasingly a kindred spirit. Rooting for him, as it were. The god who puts lead in your pencil. The god of the snake bile, the ginseng wine, and the insect brew. Chinley looked straight into the Buddha's eyes and with his palms held together in supplication, he promised that if everything worked out well tonight then tomorrow he would transform the bedside cabinet into a more presentable place of worship, clearing away the packet of throat lozenges, the shreds of tobacco and the after-shave bottle, for example.

No time for that right now though. He poured out two glasses of dry white wine and opened the box of chocolates; then he flicked the dial on the audio console by the bed and chose some down-tempo sway-dance music, which brought Belinda to mind, breathing odd messages into his ear. He went to prepare a perfumed bath, and as he turned on the taps, he heard a knock at the door: a quiet but persistent Chinese knock. He readjusted the belt on the boxer's gown, reset the light dimmer a notch lower, and relaxed his mouth muscles.

Chapter Twenty-Two

"*Happy Christmas!*" shouted Lisa, as Chinley flung open the door. "Sorry we're a day late! The Chinese knock fool you, did it? I thought it would." With a veil of dark blonde hair screening her face like a beaded curtain, Lisa held out a parcelled box. Reindeer wrapping paper and criss-cross green ribbons tied in a bow. Looking over her shoulder, and peering past Chinley into the room, her nose high in the air, was his wife.

"Good God what a stink," she said, turning away. "We'll come back when you've got rid of the whiff."

"We're just a couple of doors down the corridor," said Lisa. "756, I think." Chinley took the parcel. "And here's something from your pigeonhole."

She handed him a sealed envelope, and followed her mother. Chinley closed the door. He turned up the light-dimmer and sniffed at the envelope. No special fragrance. He ripped it open and slid out the message. It read:

Chinley,
Silvia tells me you are expecting her to visit you tonight. Tough. She will not be coming. I have told her to stay away from you. Touché. So shift your arse to somebody else's camp, not mine. Buy some sandpaper and try the mother hen.
Ward.

Chinley felt his throat contract, and the blood rise in his neck. He crumpled the note and threw it into the waste-paper basket. Then he turned and snarled at the Buddha, and took a swipe at it. It flew off the cabinet, smashed into the wall, and landed on the bedside rug, coming to rest high-bellied on its back.

He bent over it and pressed his knuckles into the mad eyes and the fleshy leering lips. He screwed its neck, tried to pull its head off, and flung it on to the duvet. Then he grabbed one of the two glasses of wine and spattered its contents over the incense sticks. As the sizzling subsided he heard another knock, and a rattling of the doorknob. Before he could reach the door, to lock it, his wife and his daughter had let themselves in.

"We can't stay in there either," said Dorothy. "They've not cleaned it yet. It's all dusty."

She walked through the room, sniffing the air, then she took off her black beret, and loosened the buttons on her fawn overcoat. Chinley kept half an eye on her, fiddled with his pipe, refilled the second glass and took a third one out from the cabinet before they could make any further observations.

She's ridiculously tall after all these Chinese women, he thought. Some of the locals, judging by what he had seen in the windows of department stores, may think of her as a tailor's dummy come to life, with her pale elongated limbs, her perfect wavy light chestnut hair, the straight nose and the rosebud mouth. The eyes hidden by long lashes, and the masculine elegance of her dark grey trouser suit. Like a dominating but for some people attractive headmistress.

She sat down at the desk and faced the bed. Her lashes lifted. She looked around the room and sniffed the air again. "Lovely flowers though," she said. "Courtesy of the hotel? We must have picked the wrong room, Lisa."

"Just something to keep the place fresh," said Chinley.

"They don't mix with the joss sticks," said Lisa. "*Jesus!* You'd suffocate with those things. Look at the size of them. Couldn't you find anything smaller?"

"No."

"Open your present," continued Lisa. "What's that thing doing on the bed?"

"A grinning *ape*," said Chinley, finding a focus for his aggression in the thick lips curling up at him from the duvet.

"Who's it from?"

"From me. I bought it for myself."

"What on earth for?"

"A Christmas present to yourself?" said Dorothy. "Is that the best you can do? How sad. I noticed those things downstairs, actually. Down in the shop. It's just as well you didn't choose the shelf below."

"What?"

"You'll see in a minute," said Lisa, nodding at the parcel. "Open it."

Chinley unwrapped the paper and opened what looked like a hat-box to find a glazed porcelain figure of a Tang Dynasty horse, painted yellow, brown, and green. An exact replica of the other one.

"Perfect," he said, looking from Lisa to Dorothy and back.

"Mum knows all about it," said Lisa. "Ward and all that. And she's seen the man himself. Downstairs in the *bar*. With *Silvia*. What are they up to? She looked straight through me, the little cow. She's just come back with him from the coast, Jane tells me, so maybe she was just tired."

Chinley held the horse loosely by its rump, then placed it on the bedside cabinet where the Buddha had been. He held a glass of wine out to Dorothy. She nodded, then excused herself and went off to the bathroom. He moved close to Lisa and said: "Your idea this?"

"Yes. Well, it seemed silly to be only a couple of hours away, and not get together."

He glanced at the bathroom door and said: "How long...?"

"Mum? I've no idea. I think it's up to you. *I* won't be bothering you though, will I? I've taken up an invitation from Joe to nestle in the haystacks for a while, and sit by the log fire until the winter's gone." She scanned her father's desk. "Chocolates. Not like you."

"Go ahead. You say Jeffrey Ward's downstairs?"

"He is. And his boots. I shouldn't think you'd want to see *him* again though, would you? And Mr Deng was at the reception desk. He said he won't be disturbing you tonight, now that your family's here, but he'd like to see you first thing in the morning.

"Why is it always *first thing*?" said Chinley.

"He seems *very* pleased that we've come. Mum and me." She held up the box of chocolates. "Should I take some of these down to Silvia? Make sure she's not annoyed with us about something? Say they're from you?"

"Don't be silly. Why should *I* be giving her chocolates?"

"Well it's Christmas."

The telephone rang, and Lisa answered it.

"Hello? *Hello!* How are *you?* Yes, it's Lisa. Happy... what? No, I don't think so. Hang on." She placed her hand over the receiver, and said: "It's Mr *Wang* of all people. Phoning from Wuhan. He wants to know if you've seen Belinda."

* * *

Mr Deng stood in the middle of Chinley's hotel room, his eyes downcast. The Buddha and the incense sticks were in the waste bin, and the air was now relatively fresh. With his graveside manner and his dark suit, he could have been watching the lowering of a coffin. He lifted his head and rounded his lips as though to speak, then scratched the back of his neck and held out a forefinger to trace the interwoven lines of the dragon and phoenix on Chinley's duvet. Hilda spoke for him.

"Do you mind if we ask you, Professor Chinley," she said, "how well you know Silvia? Silvia Li?"

"What do you mean?" said Chinley.

"Just, how well do you *know* her? As a person."

"*Silvia?* She became a kind of... adopted daughter. Once."

He looked towards Lisa for confirmation of this but Dorothy, who was unscrewing the cap on her second miniature brandy, reacted first.

"Adopted daughter?" she said, in a loud whisper. "Adopted *bimbo*, more like."

"*Mother!*" said Lisa.

"What's a bimbo?" asked Hilda.

"A bimbo," said Chinley, "is a kind of... vacant..."

"I'll tell you what a bimbo is," said Dorothy. "A bimbo, *this* bimbo, from what I've heard, is a concubine. A *con*cubine!"

She stared at Hilda, then sipped some more of her brandy.

"I'm only a Professor, Dorothy. Not an emperor," said Chinley, with an attempt at a chuckle. " I don't *have* concubines."

"The point is," said Mr Deng, "that Mr Ward wants me to put in a word for Miss Li, to help with processing the paperwork for her visa to the United States."

Chinley and Lisa caught each other looking at the Tang Dynasty horse on the bedside cabinet.

"But you know the Li family yourself," said Chinley.

"Yes," said Mr Deng. "I thought I did. But there are other... considerations. To be quite frank, do you think this young woman will benefit professionally from Mr Ward sponsoring her, or is it just an emotional attachment?"

"Oh yes," said Chinley. "I mean, no."

"You approve of Mr Ward? His character?" said Mr Deng. Chinley hesitated. "I don't mean for China," added Mr Deng, "I mean for outside China."

"Well, yes then," said Chinley. "For outside China."

"Moving on then." Mr Deng shifted the position of his shiny black shoes and looked at Dorothy. "We're all very glad you're here, Mrs Chinley," he said. "*Very* glad. And you'll be staying on of course, with your husband?"

"Staying on?" said Dorothy. "I'd be in his way."

"Oh no," said Mr Deng, his duck lips pouting. "Quite the opposite, I'm sure."

"The truth is," said Chinley, "my wife and I have not finalised our plans yet."

Mr Deng looked at Hilda in the way a prosecuting counsel may look at a jury.

"Professor Chinley," he continued, "how can I put this?" He clasped his hands behind his back and marched up and down the side of the bed. "We all, in Beijing and in Wuhan, appreciate the fine work you're doing in our country. Educating our young people so they have a brighter future. And we all hope you'll be able to carry on with this fine work. But we also think that it would be more suitable for you, now, to be accompanied by your wife."

Dorothy reached down to unlatch the mini-bar. She would be good company for Gladys if it came to the crunch, thought Chinley. *Gladys*. He should return her call. As a diversion. Later. For the moment he was distracted by the net which was being thrown over him. There would be no more Jane, no more Alison, no more Silvia. Not in the same way. No more Molly. Or Mollys. No more Belinda. Why did Wang think Belinda was in Beijing?

"We are prepared to offer you an amended contract," said Mr Deng. "In view of the new circumstances."

"What new circumstances?" said Chinley.

"Your wife being here."

"But I've just told you. She might not stay."

Mr Deng folded his arms, and looked at the ceiling. "In that case, Professor Chinley," he said, "Unfortunately, we would have to offer you the same recommendation we offered to Mr Ward. I believe Hilda may have told you about that recommendation."

"Yes," said Chinley. "Well..."

"Going home for a rest," said Hilda.

"Yes," said Chinley. "Sort of."

"I can tell you now," said Dorothy. She waited until all eyes were on her, then continued. "I will definitely stay. This man needs watching. Look at his veins."

Everyone bowed and smiled, except Chinley.

"Fine," said Hilda. "Are you all free to join us for dinner tonight then? Downstairs in the banqueting suite? Six o'clock?"

"Yes, we're all free," said Dorothy.

"Now we'll leave you alone," said Mr Deng. "It's always a pleasure to see a husband and wife re-united, in harmony. Let's hope your colleague Mr Wang will find *his* wife again soon too."

"Yes," said Lisa. "What's happened?"

"Mrs Wang was last seen on Christmas Day, by Mr Wu and Mr Hu. On her way to Mrs Fox's apartment. But she didn't go home afterwards and she hasn't been seen since. Mr Wang knows she likes her trips to the capital, so he's coming here himself to look for her in case that's where she is. That's all. Nothing to worry about. Well, we'll see you all later then."

Saying she had something to do in her room, Lisa went off with Mr Deng and Hilda, leaving her parents alone together. The telephone rang, and Chinley let it ring. He opened the door to the balcony and stood shoulder to shoulder with Dorothy looking down at the brown smog and the murky concrete pinnacles jutting out of an otherwise blank panorama, laid out below them like a soiled sheet.

"You're very quiet," said Dorothy, startling Chinley by resting an arm on his waist. "What is it? Overwhelmed by the landscape?"

They laughed together, and he kneaded her shoulder for a while then dropped his hand, not fondly to her waist, but to pat his pocket to check that his pipe was still there. Feelings of tenderness had almost resurfaced, but not quite; in time, he imagined, they well might. For the moment Dorothy's firm muscles served only to remind him that if she did come to Wuhan she would prove an effective buffer between himself and Gladys.

* * *

At the banquet table Wang was trying to persuade Dorothy to accept a refill of *baijiu*. "How's Mr Feng?" said Chinley, in an attempt to stop him pestering her. "Has he finished his phrase-book yet?"

"Mr Feng is ill," said Wang. "His bowels, you know. Mrs Fox was feeding him unfamiliar food the other day. With the musicians."

"Nothing to do with the rum then?" said Chinley.

"Yes, that's a possibility," said Wang, his jaws working noisily as though he was chewing on his next words before he spoke. "Dead man's rum."

"And Mr Wu and Mr Hu?" said Lisa. "How are they?"

"They're looking after Mrs Fox. Otherwise they'd be here with us. She's also not feeling too well, after her evening with my wife. Mr Wu and Mr Hu found her asleep in her corridor, next to an empty bottle. She must have been too ill to take herself to bed."

"So where *is* Belinda?" said Lisa. "Any news of her yet?"

Wang shook his head from side to side and roared with laughter. "No," he said. "No news." His face was flushed dark red, and his cheeks were spattered with grains of glutinous rice. Dorothy giggled when he looked at her and she allowed him to fill her glass once more with the spirit he was clutching. Chinley caught a glimpse of Jane beckoning him from beyond the banquet room doorway. He excused himself from the table and followed her to the reception desk.

"It's Mrs Fox again, Mr Chinley," she said. "Sorry to disturb you, but she says it's most important for you to call her back right now. You can use this phone here."

He dialled Gladys's number and heard an awkward clatter as the receiver was picked up.

"Gladys?"

"*Chinley?* Is that you Chinley? Christ, where've you been? Have you seen Belinda?"

"Here?"

"Yes of course there."

"No."

"Are you sure?"

"Of course I'm sure. So she's on her way here then is she? Good. The more the merrier."

"No it's *not* good. Listen. If you see her, stay close to her. Don't let her get out of your sight."

"What? Why, what's the fuss?"

"I was only winding her up. Telling her to go for it."

"Go for what?"

"It was the booze. And when I woke up in the morning it was gone. So was she."

"What was gone? The booze? Gladys? *Gladys!* Shit."

The line was dead. Chinley replaced the receiver. "Cut off," he told Jane. "I'll wait for a bit and see if she phones back."

Jane ushered him to his usual seat on the sofa opposite the piano. Mr Liu would come to play soon, she said. Did he want to use her mobile phone to call Gladys? No, he said, he would wait for her to call back. She gave Chinley a copy of the *China Daily*, then tapped him on the shoulder and pointed to the bar.

Jeffrey Ward was standing there, with his back to them, his reddish-brown hair straggling over the collar of his cream jacket. Jane returned to her colleagues at the desk and Chinley began to read his newspaper. Ward moved away from the bar and was in the process of sitting down when he noticed Chinley. He paused in mid-descent, then continued to lower himself on to the cushion of his armchair. He stared at the carpet separating them, then crossed his boots, raised his beard, and stared over Chinley's head.

Chinley's stomach tightened at the sight of the man, then churned again more violently as a woman, her face hidden in the hood of a purple overcoat, crossed the room and stood behind the oblivious American, a distended soft leather bag the shape of a golf-club carrier slung over her shoulder. She put the bag on the floor and pulled back her hood. Belinda.

She placed her gloved hands lightly over Ward's eyes. His mouth fell open but he didn't move. Chinley heard her say: "Guess who?"

Ward nodded, smiled, and said: "Belinda. What brings *you* here?" She lowered her lips to his ear and whispered something. He nodded again, more vigorously this time, and Chinley watched with a mixture of envy and bewilderment as Belinda shimmied behind the furniture, her hands now moving up and down her legs; then she held up a pale stocking and secured it gently around Ward's head, blindfolding him. At a further whispered instruction, he raised both his hands in the air and rested them just above his ears, palms upwards and curving. Belinda unzipped her bag and took out an elongated inflated green balloon; Ward gripped it obediently as she centred it on his head. His grin widened as she played with the curls of his hair, then she stared straight at Chinley and said: "No melons. Wrong season."

Chinley looked around the room. A scattered audience had formed. Silvia had come into the bar, dressed in a ruby blouse and an ankle-length mother-of-pearl dress. She stood watching, from a distance, oddly duplicating Ward's upward tilt of the chin. Mr Liu, dressed ready to play the piano, was loitering by an imperial crimson pillar; the silently laughing girls at the reception desk were huddled together as though posing for a photograph. The doormen stood stock still and dignified, but allowed themselves a snigger or two. The telephone rang and no-one answered it.

Belinda reached down once more into the bag, and this time Chinley saw the glint of brown metal. He rose to his feet, as she lifted the sword and rested the blunt edge against her nose, then he rushed across the room and threw himself at her. She spun around, crashed into the open keyboard of the piano, then lay flat out on the pink carpet, moaning.

Ward pulled the stocking off his head and held it out like a quoit he was about to throw. Silvia stayed where she was. Five grey figures came flapping towards Chinley like giant hawks, but they were brought to a halt by the booming voice of Mr Deng. The green balloon drifted off towards the reception desk, and the telephone stopped ringing. Ward dropped the stocking and made a move towards Belinda.

"Leave her alone," said Chinley, placing himself between them.

Ward stamped his boot down hard on Chinley's foot, then ran around him and snatched up the sword. Mr Deng and the commissionaires moved closer. Chinley hobbled towards Ward and reached out for him to hand over the weapon.

The two men stared at each other. Silvia kicked off her high heels, lifted her dress, and rushed across the room. Chinley reached out once more for the sword, and Ward swung it blindly backwards, like a golf club, just as Silvia was closing in. She fell in silence to the floor as a kind of second mouth, a wide smudge of ragged lips, opened over her neck. There was a howl and a scurry at the reception desk, and Jane ran over to her sister.

Chinley held Silvia in his arms, gently dabbing her cheek with the sleeve of his shirt. Ward kept his distance, looking on, and Mr Deng raised his palms to the crowd, an orator preparing a speedy reassurance.

Chapter Twenty-Three

Back to the land of Bettys and Arnolds, said Chinley to himself, as he puzzled over the meanders of the River Thames on his descent into Heathrow airport. Dorothy was still asleep. Next to her, in the aisle seat, Belinda kow-towed her long lilac fingernails on the ash-tray lid, and stared at the netting of the magazine pocket in front of her. Six months had gone by since Mr Deng escorted her upstairs to Wang's room at the Double Rainbow hotel. When the ambulance with Silvia and Jane inside left the hotel forecourt, Mr Deng reassured the management that there was no problem which could not be handled: it was just his foreign colleagues, he explained, rehearsing for their cabaret act in Wuhan. Their lack of expertise was to blame for the mishap, he added, and public opinion at least was that Mr Deng always knew best.

Alison's baby boy was now four months old and her father and grandfather were awaiting a similar bonus from Jane, now in her third month of marriage. Silvia was back with her father in Wuhan, and had taken over the bean curd deliveries. Lisa was right about the rash on Mr Li's neck: it was recurring, and it was the bean curd, which caused it. But these days Silvia cared little that she might be affected in the same way. She was content now just to know that her face was healing well, and according to the specialist in Beijing, the wound would in time be virtually invisible. Jeffery Ward paid the full cost of the care, from a distance, having left the country the day after the accident, or incident, his brief and infrequent communication with Silvia becoming ever more brief and infrequent, until it stopped altogether after three months, when she went back to the Dong Hu Campus.

Gladys was now mother-in-law sitting in County Limerick. She and Dorothy had not got on as well as Chinley thought they would. In fact Dorothy stopped drinking once she was settled in Wuhan, and refused to go anywhere near a place with a name like *Madame Klimbams,* but within a few weeks of her moving to the Dong Hu campus the club was anyway closed down, re-opening as a *Happy Burger Palace.*

The only happiness which this place brought to Chinley was the reappearance of Molly, working there as a waitress after a nationwide spree with the missing Dutchman, and now firmly attached to her adopted Irish Christian name. In memory of Terry, she said. When a man no longer appreciates a woman like Molly, Chinley told himself over a burger and a beer at the *Palace*, he should find a pagoda somewhere and jump off the top. He went back to the guest house and flushed away all the camomile pills which his wife had persuaded him to revert to.

Belinda, pirouetting with a wooden sword painted silver, continued to tantalise him from the lawn below the apartment window every so often, the more so when the tower on Pagoda Hill was caged off to public entry, and she would come up to the sitting room now and then for a straight green tea. From Lisa's correspondence with her, Chinley guessed, she had acquired the concept of personal space, but said she could not talk about this with Wang because he had no idea what she meant. He just laughed at her, so she needed time away from him. Time out of the house at least, she said, if she could not get out of the country.

But after her return from Beijing, Wang was advised by Mr Deng and others to keep her *in* the house as far as possible. And whenever Chinley visited Belinda and Wang to convey developments in the long-distance plans which Lisa was laying down with her uncle Joe, Mr Hu and Mr Wu were still always there, downstairs in the bicycle shed, leaning against a concrete post and smoking a cigarette, like a pair of chronic gossipers.

In his hand-luggage Chinley had a gift from them to Lisa: a bottle of spirit for her to take, they said, on her next overland trek as a safeguard against parasites.

Also for Lisa in the hand-luggage was a thinly-bound copy of Feng's *Translated Idioms,* and a message from him written inside the cover ended with the words 'I hope you soon find your husband'. She heard little in return from Silvia, though: a silence which she thought was odd coming, as she put it, from someone who was once just like a sister.

But in her own letters she was as persuasive in print as she was in person: Wang agreed for Belinda to be enrolled in Theatre Studies at a university in the British Midlands, at Joe's expense, in return for keeping house for the gentleman farmer. Chinley explained that in this case 'gentleman' meant 'rich', but it was only when he showed Belinda Joe's official letter of sponsorship that her misgivings were removed.

The only other person who came to Chinley's mind for this *au pair* position was Astrid. He found her name card while clearing his bedroom drawers at the guest house of items which he did not want Dorothy to see; but he decided he could never do his brother such an injustice as to send him the Danish woman, even though she would no doubt be much more at home around the farm than Belinda would. Mr Deng and the British Embassy saw to the rest of the paperwork for Belinda's release.

Chinley and Dorothy waited in the Customs hall for Belinda to emerge from the Immigration channel, then they took her through to the Arrivals lounge to meet Joe. Lisa came first. She and Belinda ran at each other and knotted themselves in a lengthy embrace. Joe stood to attention, his face colouring. Today he looked more like the chairman of a yachting club than a farmer: he was wearing a navy-blue blazer with polished rosewood buttons, and over-pressed light-grey flannel trousers. But his hair was the colour of his haystacks, and he had not succeeded in flattening it down, though Chinley noticed he had managed to camouflage the grey patches in his otherwise dark blonde beard. Belinda kept an arm around Lisa's waist and stared at Joe's heavy-duty black boots.

"Sorry about these," he said, for some reason lifting a foot. Even as a small child he had put Chinley in mind of a carthorse. "I need them for the old bus. I need to give her a bit of stick, you know. *Stick*." The glow on his face deepened. He loosened his tie and suggested they all went off for a drink, but nobody moved.

"Mr Wang telephoned me from Wuhan this afternoon," Lisa told Belinda, still arm in arm. "He's had word from Huban that they might allow him to join you here. In about a year."

She nodded and took a quick look over her shoulder, back at the Immigration Channel. Lisa loosened her grip, pushed Belinda in the direction of Joe, and went off to join her mother, who was in search of an extra luggage trolley.

Chinley reached for the reassurance of the pipe in his jacket pocket, cushioned under Jane's parting gift for him: a sealed brown paper parcel from her uncle. He felt like kicking his brother in the backside. At last Joe reached forward and offered Belinda a huge and hairy fist. Chinley was mouthing the words, go on Belinda, take his hand, he might look rough, but he's as harmless as one of his castrated bullocks. She backed away from Joe, and stared down at the boots and up at the raised beard. Then she moved towards him, her hands pressed together as though in prayer, and she bowed exquisitely. Chinley noticed that nobody in the airport lounge was watching this performance. Or more precisely, he reflected, remembering that he was now back in England, someone certainly would be watching, but pretending not to.